Apple Strudel Alibi

Oxford Tearoom Mysteries
Book Eight

H.Y. HANNA

Copyright © 2018 H.Y. HANNA
All rights reserved.
ISBN-13: 978-0-6481449-5-3

This book is a work of fiction. Names, characters, places and incidents are the product of the author's imagination or are used fictitiously. Any resemblance to actual events, locales, business establishments, persons or animals, living or dead, is entirely coincidental.

This book is licensed for your personal enjoyment only. No part of this publication may be reproduced, stored in a retrieval system or transmitted in any form or by any means, electronic or mechanical, including photocopying, recording or otherwise, without written permission from the author. Thank you for respecting the hard work of this author

CONTENTS

H.Y. HANNA

CHAPTER ONE

Someone once said that the world is a book, and those who do not travel read only one page... And yet it's funny how—no matter where I go—I always seem to end up reading a murder mystery!

Of course, murder wasn't remotely on my mind that Wednesday morning as I stepped back and surveyed the open suitcase on my bed, half-filled with brightly coloured garments which spilled over the edges of the case like a colourful fountain. Pretty sundresses, floaty kaftans, denim shorts, and cute bikinis... I sighed happily as I rummaged through the clothes, picturing the outfits I was going to wear. The island of Malta sat in a prime spot in the Mediterranean Sea, just south of Italy, and boasted sunny skies, turquoise waters, and warm, balmy weather—even at this time of the year.

Which will be a nice change, I thought, glancing out of my bedroom window at the dreary grey sky with ominous banks of clouds that threatened rain soon. Already, it was hard to imagine that only a month ago, we were in the height of the British summer and enjoying balmy days filled with warm sunshine. In the last few weeks, it had turned blustery and wet, with a continuous drizzle becoming almost a daily occurrence and the autumn winds really starting to bite. I smiled at my own thoughts. I had barely been back in England a year, and already I sounded like a typical Brit— completely obsessed with the weather!

"*Meorrw!*" came a voice by my feet. I looked down to see my little tabby cat Muesli staring up at me with her big green eyes and an anxious expression on her whiskered face.

"Don't worry, Muesli. You're not getting left behind. That's why we went to the vet last month— so you could get your rabies vaccination and your very own pet passport. You're going to be sitting with me and Devlin on the beach!" I grinned. "Well, okay, maybe not on the beach... but you'll be with us at the holiday villa we've rented and I'm sure you'll love it. It's got a private garden, a view from the terrace down to the sea, and it even has a cat flap installed. It's just perfect!"

"*Meorrw!*" said Muesli approvingly. She jumped up on the bed and climbed into the suitcase, making herself a little nest in the centre of the pile of clothes.

"Hey... don't do that," I protested. But before I could lift her out, my phone rang. It was my best friend, Cassie.

"Sorry to call you so early, Gemma—did I wake you up?"

"No, I've been up for ages."

"Really?" Cassie said in surprise. "You sound suspiciously chirpy. I wouldn't normally get more than bad-tempered grunts from you at this time of the morning. What's going on? What are you doing?"

I gave a sheepish laugh. "Packing."

"Packing? But you're not leaving until next week."

"Yes, I know, but I woke up this morning thinking about the trip and... I know it's silly, but I'm just so excited about the holiday, I wanted to start getting ready. Just to convince myself that it's really happening."

Cassie's voice was sympathetic. "Yeah, you've been trying to go away with Devlin for a while now, haven't you?"

"Since forever!" I said with some asperity. "Every time we arrange something, it ends up being cancelled or postponed... usually because of a case. Honestly, the CID work him like a slave!"

Cassie chuckled. "Well, who told you to fall in love with a detective? You know they never get any time off."

"It's not just that—I think it's Devlin. He's so bloody conscientious! He never stops. It's like he feels responsible for every crime that happens in Oxford and wants to personally get justice for every victim."

"Ah, but admit it—it's part of why you fell for him! It's his dedication and integrity and passion to help others... although being six feet tall and broodingly handsome doesn't hurt either," added Cassie in a teasing voice. "Anyway, I wouldn't talk if I were you. You should see yourself when you've got your nose in a murder investigation. And you're not even paid to do it!"

"I suppose you're right," I said with a grudging smile. "Anyway, there isn't going to be even a *sniff* of a dead body where we're going—just sun, sand, and gorgeous blue water!"

"I wouldn't speak too soon," warned Cassie. "You know what they say about tempting fate. Anyway, listen—I was ringing to ask if it's all right for me to leave the tearoom early today? I've just had a call from the dance studio: one of their regular teachers has called in sick and they've asked if I can take the class this afternoon. It would be really good temp rates."

"Oh, sure. We'll manage fine. It's not the weekend so it shouldn't get that busy."

"Well, if it does, I'm sure the Old Biddies would be happy to lend a hand."

"They like to lend a hand even when it's not

busy," I said dryly.

But I said it with affection, as I thought of Mabel, Glenda, Florence, and Ethel—the four little old ladies who lived in the village of Meadowford-on-Smythe, where my tearoom was located. Nosy and gossipy, the Old Biddies' love of meddling in other people's business was matched only by their overactive imaginations. As avid readers of Agatha Christie novels, they saw a murder mystery around every corner and a fishy character in every situation—and never passed up any chance to snoop for clues. Okay, I had to admit—they *were* often right in their suspicions, and their enthusiastic "sleuthing" had turned up some useful leads sometimes... if only their meddling didn't also land me in the most embarrassing predicaments!

***

A few hours later, I cycled into the pretty Cotswolds village of Meadowford-on-Smythe and freewheeled down the high street until I came to an old Tudor inn, with the typical half-timber framing and whitewashed walls that adorned so many postcards and chocolate boxes. I smiled as I looked up at the wooden sign above the door, with the name "*Little Stables Tearoom*" painted in beautiful calligraphic letters, and felt a warm rush of pride. It was strange to think that barely a year ago, I had been in this same spot, looking up at that sign and embarking on my dream of running a traditional English tearoom—and now, the Little Stables was a thriving business, with a well-deserved reputation for serving the best scones in Oxfordshire. My smile broadened as I suddenly remembered that today was actually the anniversary of the tearoom's opening, and Devlin and I were going out for dinner to celebrate.

As the bike slowed to a stop, I noticed with surprise that there was a large crowd outside the tearoom. It looked like every senior citizen in Meadowford had decided to gather here! I dismounted hurriedly, but before I could lift Muesli's carrier out of the front basket, I was accosted by a swarm of blue rinses, woolly cardigans, and old rose perfume.

"Gemma! Such *wonderful* news, dear!"

"Marvellous! Just marvellous!"

"Congratulations, my dear!"

"We're so proud of you!"

"Fancy beating all those bigger establishments."

"My dear, you have put Meadowford on the map!"

I stood and looked around in bewilderment as I was surrounded by little old ladies patting my shoulder, clasping my hands fervently, and even giving me kisses on the cheek.

"I... I don't understand," I stammered. "What are you talking about?"

"The award for the contest, dear!" said one pensioner, grabbing my hand and pumping it up and down. "It's the most wonderful news I've heard since the doctor told me my haemorrhoids were gone!"

I gaped at her. "What contest?"

"The Euro-Tearoom Baking Contest," came a booming voice.

I turned to see a formidable-looking lady in her eighties elbowing her way through the crowd. It was Mabel Cooke, the bossiest of the Old Biddies, and she was followed by her cronies: Glenda Bailey, Florence Doyle, and Ethel Webb.

"The Euro-what?" I looked at them blankly.

"It's an annual contest to find the best baking made by tearooms across Europe," Florence explained, her plump face earnest. "Each year, a panel of judges tastes a range of cakes, buns, breads, and scones from different establishments and selects the best to represent each country."

Glenda caught my hands in hers, her wrinkled cheeks pink with excitement. "Oh Gemma! Your scones have been selected to represent England!"

"My scones? But... there must be some mistake," I protested. "I never entered them in the competition."

"No, but we did," said Mabel with a smug smile. "We filled out the form in your name. We knew your scones would be far superior to the others. And we were right—the Little Stables Tearoom has even beaten some posh London bakeries!"

"Oh... wow," I said, slightly exasperated at their meddling behind my back but delighted all the same to have been chosen. "I must tell Dora—after all, she bakes the scones, so she really deserves the credit," I added, starting to head into the tearoom.

Mabel waved a dismissive hand. "We've told her already. But never mind Dora now. The question is when are you leaving for Vienna? The awards ceremony isn't for another two weeks, of course, but I do think it would be nice to get there early to do some sightseeing."

"Yes, yes!" squeaked Ethel. "There are the most marvellous museums and the Hofburg Palace and, oh, the Austrian National Library! I've heard that it's the most beautiful library in the world. When I worked in the village library, all the ladies in the Librarians' Association used to wish they could visit—"

"Wait, wait..." I put a hand up. "I can't go to Vienna. I'm going to Malta, remember? I've got a holiday booked with Devlin."

The Old Biddies stopped in mid-flow, taken aback by my words.

"But Gemma...!" Glenda looked distressed. "You have to go! You're representing England... and Meadowford-on-Smythe! Couldn't you delay your holiday?"

"No," I said firmly. Then, seeing their crestfallen faces, I added more gently, "I'm sorry. I know it's an honour to be chosen and I would have loved to go otherwise... but I'm afraid it can't be helped."

The entire crowd seemed to deflate around me, like a balloon with a leak. The Old Biddies turned away, their shoulders slumping. I felt like a worm. Hurriedly, I held my hands up to get their attention and said with an attempt at a cheerful smile:

"Look, I'm sure one can receive the award *in absentia*... and then we can have our own celebration here in Meadowford afterwards. Tea and scones will be on me!"

Everyone nodded unenthusiastically, and the crowd began to disperse. The Old Biddies shuffled off down the street, looking dejected. I bit my lip, then I shrugged helplessly, hoisted Muesli's carrier out of the bicycle basket, and headed into the tearoom. Inside, I found Dora in the kitchen, busily kneading dough for a fresh batch of scones. She looked up and her usually stern face broke into a wide smile as she saw me.

"Did Mabel tell you the wonderful news?" she asked.

"About the contest? Yes, it's fantastic. And it's really you who deserves the credit," I added warmly. "After all, you're the one who actually bakes the scones. In fact..." I snapped my fingers. "Hey, I've just had an idea! Dora, how would *you* like to go to Vienna?"

She looked astonished. "Me?"

"Yes, you! I can't go because I've already got my

holiday booked, but you can go instead! You can represent the Little Stables at the awards ceremony. I'll fund the whole trip for you. It'll be perfect! I must tell the Old Bid—I mean, I must tell Mabel and the others. They'll be so happy. I felt really bad just now, taking the wind out of their sails like that by saying that I couldn't go, but this is a great compromise. You can fly next week and—"

"Fly? Oh, no, no... I couldn't, Gemma!" said Dora, looking horrified. "I'm not going on an aeroplane!"

I looked at her in surprise. "Why not?"

Dora looked away and said gruffly. "I... I don't like flying. It terrifies me."

"Okay, maybe you can go another way. You could get across the Channel by ferry and then take a train from France to Austria—"

"Don't like ships either," Dora muttered. "I don't like going abroad. I don't know why everyone is always gallivanting off to foreign countries these days—nothing wrong with the English seaside for a holiday, I say."

"Oh." I wasn't sure how to respond. Having made several trips back to England during the eight years I was working in Australia, I had learned to take long flights in my stride. Twenty hours in a plane was never pleasant but I saw it as an irritation more than anything else. It had never occurred to me that there would be people so genuinely scared of flying that they would forego travelling abroad. And knowing my baking chef and how proud she was, I realised that it must have cost Dora a great deal to admit her weakness.

Dora gave me an apologetic look. "Anyway, I'd be no good at a posh awards ceremony." She shuddered. "Wouldn't want to have to stand up in front of a room full of strangers! They'd probably all be gabbling away in German too. No, no... I just like staying in the kitchen here and baking. I'm sorry, Gemma."

I sighed and smiled at her. "It's okay. I guess it's just not meant to be. Oh well, as I told Mabel and the others, we can still have a little celebration here in Meadowford after I get back from holiday. We'll throw a big party in the tearoom, eh?"

CHAPTER TWO

Despite what I'd told Cassie, things at the tearoom were busier than I expected that day and I was kept on my toes serving large tour groups, local residents, students with their parents, and a variety of other visitors. Meadowford's proximity to the famous university city of Oxford meant that there was always a steady influx of tourists at any time of year, and with the new academic term beginning this month, there was even more activity than usual. By now, my tearoom's reputation had spread far and wide, and I was flattered to hear so many customers say that they'd made the trip to the village especially to sample my signature English afternoon tea with freshly baked scones, home-made jam, and clotted cream.

I was just pausing to catch my breath during a

lull in the afternoon when the tearoom door opened and my mother stepped in, accompanied by a chic woman in her sixties.

"Darling!" trilled my mother, leading the lady up to the counter. "You remember my friend, Sofia Fritzl, don't you? She lived in Oxford when you were little—in fact, she helped me teach you how to use the potty!"

I cast an embarrassed glance around, seeing that several customers had overheard my mother's remark and were looking amused. Hastily, I led them to a table in the corner, hopefully out of earshot of the rest of the tearoom.

"Um... I'm afraid I don't really remember—but it's nice to meet you, Mrs Fritzl," I said, giving the woman a polite smile as they sat down.

"Oh, it is Miss Fritzl, actually—I am divorced. But do call me Sofia." She returned my smile, her eyes twinkling. "You were an adorable little girl, Gemma, and it is lovely to see the young lady you have grown into."

She was an extremely elegant woman, with brown hair streaked with grey, caught up in a low chignon, and a slim figure stylishly clad in a cream wool dress, with matching shoes and handbag. Her English was fluent, but with a very slight accent.

"Sofia is originally from Austria, although her family came over to England after the war," my mother explained. "Her father worked in Oxford; they lived just around the corner from us when I was young girl, and Sofia and I used to walk to school together. She is a few years older than me and I think I rather hero-worshipped her!" My mother laughed. "I was very sorry when she returned to Austria after she got married."

Sofia gave her a wry look. "Yes, perhaps I should have married a nice Englishman, Evelyn, and stayed in England... instead of following that scoundrel back to Austria! But in any case, it is done and I am settled now in Vienna. I am happy there."

"I suppose it's always nice to go back to your home country," I said.

"Well, in actual fact, I often think of England as my home country," said Sofia with a laugh. "It is strange, is it not? Perhaps it is because I spent so much of my childhood here. I even find myself speaking in English more often than German— especially if I am in a hurry or upset about something—it seems to be the language I am more comfortable in."

"Yes, I know what you mean," I said. "I spent almost a decade living and working overseas, and I thought I'd become quite cosmopolitan—but since I returned to England, I've discovered that I've remained more British than I realise!"

"Your mother told me all about your decision to give up your executive job in Sydney and return to Oxford to open a tearoom. It sounded like quite an undertaking! I must say, I admire your courage and your spirit in taking on the challenge—and it has obviously paid off." Sofia looked around the tearoom with admiration, taking in the inglenook fireplace, decorative half-timbering, and mullioned windows. "This is a wonderful place, Gemma, and business seems to be going very well." She indicated the tables full of customers around us.

"Thanks! Yes, it's gone far better than I expected. We had a couple of hiccups when the tearoom first opened..." —*like a tourist being murdered by one of the scones*, I thought wryly— "...but things have smoothed out. I was incredibly lucky to find this place; it adds a huge amount to the tearoom's charm, I think, and gives tourists the exact feeling of 'Olde England' that they're looking for. It's an old Tudor inn and all the period features were already here. I just had to restore it to its former glory."

"Well, you have done a fantastic job," said Sofia, looking around the room again. "I have been doing some renovation myself so I understand the work involved and—*OH!*" She reeled back in surprise as a furry bundle jumped up into her lap.

"Muesli!" I cried, mortified as my little tabby cat stretched her nose towards Sofia's face and sniffed curiously. I reached out to push her off but Sofia put up a hand to stop me.

"No, no... it is fine. She startled me, that is all." She laughed and stroked Muesli's soft fur. "She has great personality, this little one. Is she yours?"

I gave a long-suffering sigh. "Yes. Her name is

Muesli. She's very friendly—sometimes too friendly! She comes to work with me every day and she loves going around the tearoom, meeting the customers. Usually she's quite good about not jumping up on the chairs or tables but..." I gestured helplessly. "As you can see, she can be very naughty sometimes."

"Oh, I am sure most of your customers would not mind such an adorable visitor to their table," said Sofia with another laugh as Muesli nestled into her lap and seemed to settle down for a sleep.

"No, you're right—most of them want to know if they can take her home!" I said with a chuckle. "Anyway, you were saying... so are you renovating your home?"

"Well, you could say that... You see, I had a fair amount of money from my divorce and it was always a dream of mine to run my own hotel. A boutique hotel. Small and warm and intimate—like staying in a real Viennese home—but with the highest standards of service, of course. So I bought a property in central Vienna last year and have been slowly converting it. In fact, the work is almost done and the hotel officially opens next week. They are just putting the finishing touches—some last-minute painting and such—and they do not need me, so I thought I would get away for a few days. I know that once the hotel opens, I will not be able to take a break for many months—so this is my last chance for a holiday before the madness begins." She glanced at my mother with an affectionate smile. "And I had not seen my old friend for far too long. It seemed the perfect time to visit England and spend a few days in Oxford."

"And I'm so glad you did!" my mother said, beaming. She turned to me and added, "Your father and I are planning a trip to Vienna next year and we're so looking forward to staying in Sofia's new hotel."

"I hope we will have ironed out all the kinks by then," said Sofia anxiously. "I have tried to anticipate everything and think of all the pitfalls but—oh, I am sure I have missed something! I keep worrying that perhaps I have made a mistake in the design of the hotel or there is something I have not planned properly for or—"

"Now, now, Sofia, I'm sure it will all be fine," my mother said soothingly. "Remember how you used to get so overwrought about your school projects? You once burst into tears just because the teacher said you had two spelling mistakes! But you always received the highest mark in the class anyway. And remember what the teacher said? That you mustn't get too desperate to make sure everything is perfect. It isn't a sign of failure on your part."

"Oh, but the launch *must* be perfect! It must be!" cried Sofia. "I have worked so hard for this; the hotel must be a success! I cannot bear the humiliation if—" She broke off, as if suddenly realising how she sounded, and took a deep breath. She gave me a sheepish smile. "I am sorry; you must think I am being absurd."

"Oh no, not at all," I assured her. "I can totally relate. I felt a bit like you a year ago, when I first opened the tearoom. I think everyone who starts a business feels that way, don't they? They're so anxious for things to succeed. But I'm sure you're worrying for nothing. I'm sure the launch will be a huge success."

Sofia sighed. "I hope you are right. I do have a very good business partner—he is an old friend who has worked for many years in the hospitality industry. He is also quite experienced in PR. I have adopted many of his ideas, such as offering a special discount rate in the first month of opening and inviting some influential members of Viennese society for a complimentary stay. Hopefully they will be impressed during their time with us and will then spread the word about the hotel."

"Wow, you're doing a lot more than I ever did when I opened the tearoom," I said, laughing. "I think all I did was make sure I had enough scones and hang up the 'OPEN' sign!"

"Speaking of scones—I must sample some of yours," said Sofia, eagerly scanning the menu. "We have wonderful cakes and pastries in Austria, of course, but I must confess that I miss the traditional British baking from my childhood. *Ah!* You have Victoria sponge cake... and Chelsea buns! I have not had that in a long time... oh dear, it all looks so delicious, I want to order everything!"

"How about I bring you our set 'Afternoon Tea' menu which has a selection of cakes and buns, finger sandwiches, and of course, freshly baked scones... and this will be on me—I insist," I added with a smile. "And a pot of tea as well? We carry several blends; there's traditional English Breakfast, of course, and Earl Grey—that's my favourite—and we also have Darjeeling and Assam, and several herbal teas."

"Yes, proper loose-leaf tea, served in a teapot with a strainer—not one of those ridiculous little bags," said my mother, pursing her lips.

"Teabags are very convenient sometimes," I protested.

"No, no, I quite agree with your mother," said Sofia. "It may seem 'old-fashioned' but it is nice to be able to do things the 'proper' way. That is one of the things I love about Vienna—there is still much respect for the 'old ways' and a desire to preserve culture and traditions. You can visit many Viennese coffeehouses where things seem to have remained unchanged since the turn of the century and you feel like you are stepping right back in time."

"It sounds wonderful," I said with a wistful sigh. "I hope I'll have the chance to visit someday."

Sofia grasped my hand. "Well, if you do, you *must* come and stay at the hotel, Gemma. The special discount rate will always be there for you. It is the least I can do for the daughter of my oldest friend," she said. Then she looked down at Muesli, still curled up on her lap, and added, "And your little feline friend would be most welcome too! You know, of course, that we Austrians love our pets and they go everywhere with us—in the shops, in the restaurants and cafés, even in the banks and other offices."

"Really? That's amazing. I wish England was as pet-friendly."

"Yes, and this means that many hotels in Vienna welcome four-legged guests. Even the great luxury hotels, like the *Hotel Sacher*, allow dogs to accompany their owners and provide special amenities for their animal guests, such as their own blankets, towels, feeding bowls, and cosy baskets. And my hotel—the *Hotel das Herzchen*—will naturally follow suit." She looked down again at Muesli with a smile. "So we shall look forward to your stay, eh, *Miezekatze*?"

CHAPTER THREE

I had hoped to leave the tearoom early that day so that I could have more time to get ready for dinner, but without Cassie around to help, it was left up to me to check everything after the last customer had gone and to close up the tearoom. In fact, by the time I'd cycled home with Muesli, I barely had time to change my clothes before I had to rush out again. I peered at my reflection as I ran a comb through my pixie crop. Perhaps it was the poor lighting in the bathroom, but I looked tired and drawn, with dark circles under my eyes and a paleness to my cheeks. Hastily, I grabbed a lipstick and dabbed some colour on my lips, then used my fingers to rub some of the light pink colour on my cheeks as well. Hopefully it would be too dark in the restaurant for Devlin to see how haggard I looked.

It's definitely time for a holiday, I thought with a wry smile. *But by this time next week, I'm going to be tanned and relaxed, and the picture of health!*

Devlin had booked a table at Chutneys, a cosy Indian restaurant tucked down a side street in central Oxford, and we'd arranged to meet there, since we were both going straight from work. He was waiting outside the restaurant for me and I paused for a moment at the top of the lane when I saw his tall figure. He was staring into the distance, deep in thought, and looked the perfect fit for Cassie's "broodingly handsome" description, with his dark hair slightly ruffled by the wind and his intense blue eyes narrowed pensively. Then he spotted me and his face brightened; he reached out as I approached and leaned down to give me a swift, hard kiss.

"Have you been waiting long?" I asked breathlessly.

"No, just a few minutes."

He escorted me into the restaurant and we were soon seated at a table by the window, munching on a platter of crispy *poppadoms* accompanied by sweet mango chutney. I chattered away, telling Devlin about my day, and it wasn't until we were halfway through our main courses that I noticed he had been strangely quiet all evening.

"Is something wrong?" I asked.

"No, why do you say that?" he replied quickly.

"It's just that... well, you seem a bit subdued."

He looked away, then cleared his throat and looked back at me. "Er... Gemma... I need to speak to you about something."

"Ooh, this sounds ominous," I said jokingly. Then I sobered as he didn't respond to my grin.

"You remember the big investigation going on in Cowley? The Hayley Smith case?"

I frowned. "Yeah... Some poor woman who was murdered in her own home, wasn't it? They think her boyfriend did it. But you're not on that case, are you?"

Devlin shifted uncomfortably. "Well, no, I wasn't—Shaun Ferguson was handling the investigation. But Ferguson came down with a heavy cold last week, which became a bad chest infection... and now the infection has moved to his lungs. He was hospitalised yesterday for pneumonia."

"Hospitalised!" I stared at Devlin. "But... but I've met Ferguson. He's a big, strapping man!"

Devlin shrugged. "Even healthy people can get ill sometimes. Ferguson's been working very hard lately, putting in crazy hours on the case, and he probably got run down. Anyway, the upshot of it is... there was suddenly no lead investigator on that case."

I had a bad feeling about this. "What are you saying, Devlin?"

He cleared his throat. "They've asked me to take over the investigation. But with the case going to trial, this is a critical time... there are crucial aspects of the investigation that still need to be completed before the trial..." He hesitated, then said, "They can't put the case on hold while the lead investigator goes on holiday."

I gasped. "Are you telling me that we have to cancel our holiday?"

Devlin squirmed. "Gemma, I wouldn't be doing this if it wasn't very important—"

"No!" I cried angrily. "No, not again! You can't!"

"Gemma—"

"No, it's not fair!" I felt angry tears prick my eyes. "Do you know how many times we've had this conversation? How many holidays we've booked which were then cancelled at the last minute, just because you *had* to take over something at work? Why is it always you? Why can't it be someone else?"

"Because they need me. I'm the best person for the job."

"The world won't fall apart if you step out for a moment, Devlin O'Connor!"

"I never said it would," said Devlin, starting to look annoyed. "Can't you try to understand, Gemma? A woman has been murdered and her killer must be brought to justice. This is important!"

"And what about us? Isn't our holiday important too? Why are everyone else's needs always more important?"

"I didn't say they were. But we can always have a

holiday a bit later. It's just a slight delay—"

"That's what you always say, but it never happens. There's always another murder! Another case of assault! Another kidnapping!"

"Gemma..." said Devlin gently. "This is my job."

"No, it's not!" I said furiously. "It's Ferguson's job!"

People at the other tables were starting to stare but I didn't care. Yes, a part of me knew that perhaps I was being unfair: I knew that Devlin wouldn't have done this lightly and that he must have been as disappointed as I was to miss our holiday. But that tiny voice of reason was drowned out by the furious roaring in my ears, and the sense of grievance and indignation which filled me.

I glared at Devlin. "It's not the job—it's *you*! It's because you've got such a high sense of bloody noble ethics or something—you always feel like you're responsible for everyone and everything. You always have to step into the breach, no matter what the cost. No one else would dedicate so much of their lives to the CID!" I shoved my plate away and stood up, trembling with anger and frustration. "I... I'm going home."

Without waiting for him to reply, I grabbed my handbag and stormed out of the restaurant.

***

A shrill ringing woke me the next morning and I struggled out of the depths of sleep as I groped for the phone on my bedside table. I nearly groaned as a familiar voice trilled in my ear.

"Darling! Isn't it the most wonderful news?"

"What news, Mother?" I mumbled, sitting up and rubbing my eyes.

"The Euro-Tearoom Baking Contest! I just ran into Mabel Cooke at the garden centre—by the way, they've got a fabulous deal on succulents, darling; would you like some?"

"No, no! No more house plants, Mother," I said wildly, eyeing the windowsill in my bedroom which was crammed with an assortment of spider plants, trailing ivy, and multiple aloe vera. And this was a small sample compared to the collection in the rest of my cottage. My mother's fervour to "purify my air" meant that she religiously delivered a new houseplant to my doorstep every week. I had ferns in my shower and begonias in my kitchen, and a motley crew of rubber trees, bromeliads and weeping figs taking up half my sitting room.

My mother was still speaking, as if she hadn't heard me: "...so Mabel told me all about the contest. How exciting that your scones have been awarded top place! I simply must tell everyone in the book club. Oh, and that reminds me, darling, would you like to take that novel away with you on holiday? The one I was telling you about? It's got wonderful reviews and even Helen agrees that—"

"I'm not going away, Mother."

"Whatever do you mean, darling?"

All my feelings of hurt and anger from last night came rushing back, and suddenly I felt a childish urge to wail to my mother and have her "make it better", just like when I was a little girl.

I said, in a piteous voice: "Devlin can't go, Mother. He told me last night. He has to work on a stupid case. So we're cancelling our trip to Malta."

"But... that's marvellous, darling!"

What? I lowered the phone and stared at it for a moment, then put it back to my ear. "No, you don't understand, Mother. It's awful—it means I'm not going away on holiday! And I had been so looking forward to it!"

"Nonsense, darling. Why do you need Devlin to have a holiday? One mustn't organise one's life around the menfolk all the time, you know. For example, when your father didn't want to go to Indonesia—Helen Green and I went by ourselves!"

Yes, and left a trail of havoc across Southeast Asia, I thought. But aloud I said, "That was different, Mother. You wanted to try out independent travel. It wasn't as if you had to cancel a holiday you had booked with Dad."

"The particulars might be different but the principle is the same. You must make melons from lemons, as the Americans say."

"Er... I think you mean make lemonade from

lemons, Mother."

"Oh no. Lemonade is full of sugar. It's dreadful for your teeth."

"Huh?" *Why did conversations with my mother always leave me feeling like I was in a parallel universe?* "No, no, the saying is 'when life deals you lemons, make lemona'—oh never mind! Whatever it is, how can you say it's 'marvellous'?" I demanded.

"Well, Mabel was telling me what a shame it was that you can't go to Vienna for the awards ceremony... but now you can!"

"I don't want to go to Vienna," I said sulkily.

"Oh, nonsense, darling—you're just being silly now and feeling sorry for yourself," said my mother, fulfilling my wish and treating me exactly like I was eight years old. "You've always wanted to visit Vienna. This is the perfect opportunity." She gave a squeal. "Oh! And I just had another marvellous idea: you could stay with Sofia in her new hotel! I know she'd love to have you. I'll go and ring her now."

"No, Mother, wait—!"

It was too late. She had hung up. I sighed and flopped back on my pillows. But as I lay there, staring at the ceiling and fuming, my mother's words slowly came back to me. I sat up again. Maybe she was right. Why was I sitting here feeling sorry for myself when I could enjoy a holiday in one of Europe's most beautiful cities?

On an impulse, I rang the customer support for

the travel website where I had booked our tickets to Malta. The girl on the other end of the line was sympathetic when she heard my situation and quickly checked the booking on her computer.

"Hmm... it's too late to get a full refund, I'm afraid..." There was the sound of typing on a keyboard. "But I could issue you with a credit, to be used on flights and accommodation at a future date."

I hesitated, then asked, "How about putting part of it towards a flight to Vienna?"

"Yeah, I could do that," said the girl. "You thinkin' of visiting, then? Lovely city."

"Even at this time of the year?" I asked, thinking regretfully of the sunshine and turquoise water I was giving up in Malta.

"Oh, it might be a bit chilly but that just makes everythin' feel real cosy, don't it?" said the girl cheerfully. "You'll be able to sit in those lovely Viennese coffeehouses, sippin' hot chocolate and tuckin' into apple strudel and stuff..."

The picture she painted was very tempting and my spirits began to lift, in spite of myself. When I'd hung up, I leaned back on my pillows again, this time with a smile on my face.

"*Meorrw?*" said Muesli, getting up from where she had been curled at the foot of my bed and clambering across the blankets to reach my side. She put her front paws on my chest and stretched her face up to mine. "*Meorrw?*"

"Don't worry, Muesli, you're not going to miss out either," I said with sudden decision. I smiled and reached out to pat her head. "You're coming with me to Vienna!"

CHAPTER FOUR

"So... who've we got here then?" The plump, middle-aged woman standing beneath a sign marked "PET RECEPTION CENTRE" smiled at me as she reached out to take the cat carrier.

"This is Muesli," I said, watching nervously as she lifted the cage and placed it on the counter next to her.

"*Meorrw!*" said Muesli, shoving her face against the door of the cage, her green eyes wide and curious.

"Ahhh, what a cutie," the woman chuckled. She stuck a finger between the bars to tickle Muesli under the chin, then she turned back to me and picked up Muesli's pet passport. After a casual glance through the details, she attached a label to the cage and gave me a nod. "All looks good, luv. I'll

31

take her through now. You have a pleasant flight—an' Muesli will see you in Vienna."

"Wait!" I caught her arm as she was about to turn away. "Um... so what happens now? I mean, will Muesli stay here until the flight is ready?"

"Yes, yes—don't you worry, luv. It's all air-conditioned an' ventilated inside, an' we keep it really calm an' peaceful. When it's time to board, we'll get one of our dedicated animal vehicles to drive Muesli to the plane. She'll be the last to board an' the first to get off, so there's no hanging around. An' the captain's always notified if there're furry passengers on board, you know, so they can set a comfortable temperature for the cargo hold."

I looked anxiously at my cat. "So she'll be in the hold by herself... will she be scared by the noise of the engine?"

The woman gave another chuckle. "All our clients ask the same things! Honestly, luv, the owners get more stressed than the pets. Most of 'em just sleep right through the whole flight." She patted my arm. "You'll see. You'll pick her up in Vienna and she'll be happy as Larry."

Reluctantly, I stepped back and watched as the woman picked up the cat carrier and disappeared through the double doors. However, as I made my way across the airport to the departure terminal and joined the queue at the check-in counter to get my own boarding pass, I felt my worry fading and a pleasant sense of anticipation fill me instead. *I'm going on holiday!* I thought, smiling broadly as I watched my case being tagged and shunted onto the conveyor belt, ready to be delivered to the plane.

Then my smile faltered as I heard a familiar booming voice next to me:

"We would like to have seats next to that young lady, there."

I whipped around in disbelief to find the Old Biddies standing at the counter next to me.

"Mabel... Glenda... Florence... Ethel... What are you doing here?" I gaped at them.

"We're coming to Vienna with you, dear," said Mabel, heaving an ancient lavender suitcase onto the scales.

"*What?*"

Mabel frowned at me. "You really shouldn't say 'what', dear—it's very uncouth. You should say 'pardon'. I'm sure your mother has taught you better."

I ignored her words and demanded, "What do you mean you're coming to Vienna with me?"

"Well, when your mother told us that you had changed your travel plans, we decided that we were long overdue a holiday too," said Mabel.

"And wasn't it lucky that her friend, Sofia Fritzl, had rooms for all of us?" twittered Glenda.

Florence rubbed her hands eagerly. "Ohhh, I simply can't wait to sample all the delicious Viennese pastries."

"Yes, I found a lovely cookbook in an Oxford

bookshop about Viennese cuisine, with names of all the cakes and pastries," said Ethel, pulling an enormous tome out of her handbag. She licked a finger and began flicking through the pages. "There's the *Gugelhupf*—that's a Bundt cake—and *Kaiserschmarren*, a fluffy, shredded pancake with plum sauce... oh, and the curd cheese dumplings—"

"Are you ladies checking in or what?" came an irate voice behind us. A businessman in a dark suit flicked his wrist to check the time on his watch, then gave the Old Biddies an impatient look. "I haven't got all day."

Mabel turned back to the woman behind the counter, shoved four passports at her, and said, pointing to me, "Make sure you give us seats next to this young lady."

The woman pursed her lips. "Madam, I'm afraid I can't—"

I looked at the Old Biddies, then at the businessman and the growing queue behind him, and gave a resigned sigh. "It's all right," I said to the woman. I gave her my seat number. "We're... um... travelling together."

Two hours later, as I buckled my seatbelt and prepared for take-off, I told myself that perhaps it wouldn't be as bad as I'd thought. Aside from searching Duty Free for a perfume that had been discontinued in 1977 and asking the Immigration officer if he had a girlfriend, the Old Biddies had been remarkably well-behaved so far. I glanced over my shoulder and smiled to myself as I saw Mabel and Ethel sitting in the seats next to me, arguing over the best way to buckle their seatbelts, and Glenda and Florence in seats across the aisle, arguing over something in the Viennese cookbook. Whenever I'd looked forward to this day, I'd always envisaged Devlin by my side as we headed to a beach holiday—I never thought I'd be heading to Vienna with four little old ladies for company! And yet, now that they were here, I found that I was enjoying their company.

I leaned towards the window and watched the landscape skim past, then recede into the distance as the plane roared down the runway and lifted off into the sky. Despite having taken off in planes many times before, I still felt a familiar thrill in the pit of my stomach. Then my thoughts were interrupted by a finger jabbing my shoulder. I turned around to find Glenda leaning across the aisle, waving something at me.

"Gemma! Gemma! Put these on!" she said urgently.

She thrust two long pieces of nylon in a hideous shade of mustard yellow at me. I held them up gingerly with a thumb and a forefinger.

"Er... what are they?"

"Compression stockings, my dear!" Glenda beamed at me from across the aisle. "They're the very latest style. I ordered them especially from

Seniors Accessories Direct. A hundred percent nylon! It was their 'Seasonal Special' in their latest mail order catalogue. I hope I got your size right. I couldn't remember if you had fat calves, but I took a guess."

"Uh... right... thanks," I said, not sure if I should have felt insulted or touched.

"You must put them on right away," said Glenda earnestly. "They say that wearing compression stockings reduces the risk of blood clots in the legs by more than twelve times!"

There was no way I was wearing those hideous things, but I didn't want to hurt Glenda's feelings. "Um... I'll put them on a bit later, okay? Thanks for thinking of me. That was really sweet of you."

Mabel tapped me on the shoulder. "I brought something for you too," she said with great importance.

I was almost afraid to ask. And a moment later, my worst fears were confirmed. The flight attendants were just coming around serving a light snack of cheese and crackers, and as they set my tray down, Mabel eagerly extracted a plastic bag from her huge leather handbag. She opened it to reveal several large slimy black blobs nestling inside.

"Ugh! What's that?" I said, recoiling.

"Stewed prunes, dear. I made them yesterday."

"Oh... er... no thanks," I said.

"Flying gives you *dreadful* constipation, you

know," said Mabel, wagging a finger in my face. "It's crucial to have additional fibre to keep you 'regular' and prunes do a marvellous job. I always have some stewed prunes with my breakfast and my GP tells me that I have the most impressive bowel movements he's ever—"

"Okay, okay, I'll have some," I cut in hastily, squirming as I imagined Mabel's booming voice carrying through the whole cabin.

"Gemma! Gemma!" Glenda was beckoning to me frantically from across the aisle again. She held up another two limp pieces of nylon. "I just remembered—I also bought a pair in grey with yellow stripes! Do you like this colour better?"

I sighed. It might have only been listed as two hours, but I had a feeling that this was going to be a *long* flight...

CHAPTER FIVE

Sofia's hotel—the *Hotel das Herzchen*—was set in the heart of the Innere Stadt, a district that covered the Old Town of Vienna and which was encircled by the famous *Ringstrasse*—the Ring Road—a grand boulevard that followed the old city walls. It was an area steeped in history and crammed with most of Vienna's famous sights, from the Hofburg Imperial Palace with its magnificent Baroque architecture to the opulent State Opera House, and of course, Vienna's most famous landmark: the huge Gothic tower of *Stephansdom*—St Stephen's Cathedral.

It was in a side street, in the shadow of the great cathedral, that Sofia's hotel was located. The taxi negotiated the Innere Stadt's narrow one-way streets with expert skill and deposited us as close to the hotel entrance as possible. I helped the Old

Biddies with their cases as we mounted the front steps of the classic turn-of-the-century building. The ground floor had been retained for offices, so the official hotel lobby was actually on the second floor, accessed via a wide sweeping staircase that led up from the building foyer. We paused in wonder as we reached the top of the stairs and entered the main lobby. It was not a big place but what it lacked in size, it more than made up for in historic grace and charm, with high ceilings, rich stucco details, and soft cream walls adorned with elegant wainscoting. A smooth expanse of wood parquet flooring in a fishbone design stretched in front of us, leading the way to a polished mahogany reception desk.

"Gemma, *willkommen*—welcome!" cried Sofia Fritzl, stepping out from behind the desk and hurrying forwards to greet us.

She looked very different to the way I'd remembered seeing her back in England. She was dressed in something that resembled a pretty peasant outfit—though no peasant outfit could have ever boasted such stylish tailoring and luxurious fabrics. She wore a bodice dress in a shade of silky rose pink, with a gathered waist, a full skirt, a matching apron of embroidered lavender, and a puff-sleeved white blouse. It reminded me of the dresses worn by Maria and the Von Trapp children in *The Sound of Music*.

Sofia saw me looking and smiled. "You like my

dress? It is a *dirndl*—the traditional costume for women in Austria."

"It's gorgeous!" I said. "I didn't realise that women still wore traditional outfits."

"They do not, normally. The *dirndl* is usually only worn at formal occasions, such as at weddings, and in traditional events and festivals. However, those of us who work in the tourism-related businesses often wear them for the pleasure of the tourists." Sofia fingered the soft, silky fabric of her apron and laughed. "It is a nice change from a sombre suit or other business attire." She put a hand on my shoulder. "Anyway, come, you must be tired after your journey and wish to see your room... Ah, I see you have brought Muesli!" She bent down to look through the door of the cat carrier I was holding.

"Yes, I was worried about how she'd cope with flying, but she seems to be taking everything in her stride."

"*Meorrw!*" said Muesli, peeking out at Sofia. She put a little white paw through the bars of the cage and patted Sofia's hand playfully.

"I have prepared a blanket and some bowls for her, and a tray with some litter in your bathroom. But please let me know if you need anything else."

"Oh, that's really kind of you—I wasn't expecting you to provide anything for her," I said in surprise.

Sofia smiled. "Ah, at the *Hotel das Herzchen*, we aim to make you feel like home." She turned to the Old Biddies. "And you must be Evelyn's friends?"

"Oh, yes—sorry, how rude of me!" I said and hastily made introductions.

Then we waited as Sofia turned to the wall behind the reception desk. This was fitted with rows upon rows of wooden cubbyholes that reminded me of the "pigeon holes" in an Oxford college Porter's Lodge, and from the topmost row, she pulled out an old-fashioned key attached to a heavy medallion keychain.

"Here you are," she said, handing it to me. "The key to your suite. You can leave it at Reception when you go out."

I curled my fingers around the heavy weight in my palm and smiled to myself. I couldn't remember the last time I had been given a real key to a hotel room and not an electronic swipe card.

As we turned away from the reception desk, a thin man with greying hair and a trim moustache came out of the lift beside the staircase. Sofia's face brightened as she saw him and she gestured, saying:

"Ah... may I introduce the hotel concierge—and my business partner—Stefan Dreschner."

"Delighted to meet you... Ah, had I known that you were arriving, I could have come down to assist you," said Stefan smoothly, taking the cases from us. Like Sofia, he spoke English fluently but with a stronger Austrian accent, and he had the knowledgeable air and smooth confidence of a good concierge.

"Stefan has been a great help to me," said Sofia, looking at him with such warmth that I wondered if he might soon be a partner in more than a business sense. "He has had many years' experience working in various hotels in Vienna and he has so many contacts in the industry! In fact, many of the regular guests that he met during his time at other hotels have become like old friends, and he was able to invite some of them for a complimentary stay during our opening month."

"Oh yes, I remember you mentioning that the day you came to my tearoom," I said. I turned to Stefan. "I think it's a brilliant idea."

The concierge inclined his head. "Thank you. Yes, it is hoped that they will enjoy their time here and tell their friends and acquaintances—perhaps even publish some reviews online."

"Oh... reviews!" Sofia made a face. "I cannot believe how we in the hospitality industry are now completely at the mercy of online reviews and blogs and social media! People treat them as gospel for making their decisions and an establishment's reputation can be made or broken by a few words on the internet. It is so wrong!"

"*Ah*, Sofia... that is the way the world is going now and one must work with it, not fight against it," said Stefan. "In any case, it is a fair process, to allow guests to share their feedback with others."

"But that feedback may be prejudiced!" cried Sofia. "And after all, it is only one opinion, one experience. Besides, there are some who have far more influence than they should—"

"I'm sure you'll get wonderful reviews," I said soothingly. "I'll be sure to leave a positive review myself as soon as I get back."

Sofia calmed down slightly. "Thank you, Gemma—that is very kind, although I would only want you to be honest, of course."

I laughed. "I *will* be honest and I'm sure it'll still be a fantastic review. I love this place already," I said, looking around again.

"Oh, let me show you around," said Sofia quickly. "We have just served 'afternoon tea', which guests can enjoy in the dining room or the lounge. The Austrians favour coffee over tea, of course, and it is taken any time rather than as a specific afternoon ritual... but I confess, tea is one aspect of my English childhood that I have clung to," she said with a laugh. "Come, I will show you... oh, do not worry about your bags. Stefan can take them up to your suite."

"I think we will go with him, dear," said Florence. She shifted her weight and placed a hand against her back, grimacing. "It'll be nice to sit down and have a cuppa..."

I realised suddenly that the Old Biddies had been very subdued since the taxi had dropped us off; even Mabel was not her usual domineering self, and now she made no protest to Florence's suggestion. I looked at their tired old faces and felt a pang of guilt. It was hard to remember it sometimes, given how active they were, but the Old Biddies *were* in their eighties and travelling was exhausting even for those half their age. It was amazing that they were doing as well as they were. I felt bad for not being more considerate.

"Of course," I said quickly. I held up the cat carrier. "Would you mind taking Muesli with you? I'm sure she'd like to stretch her legs and have a little explore around our room."

As the Old Biddies followed Stefan to the lift, Sofia led me through a set of double doors into a wide hallway beyond. Several large rooms opened off from the hallway, each elegantly furnished and decorated in a classic style. The first room was a guest lounge, with a small "library" tucked into an alcove at the other end of the room. The place had the feel of an antiquated gentleman's club, decorated in shades of beige and forest green, with old leather sofas, dark wood panelling, and even a stag head or two mounted on the walls.

A Chinese couple with a little girl sat in the main lounge area, examining some tourist brochures, and at first I thought they were the only guests in the room. But as I followed Sofia across to see the "library" in the alcove around the corner, I realised with surprise that there was a man sitting in the wingback armchair by one of the bookcases. He had been hidden from view by the tall back of the chair, which was set partially behind the corner of the wall. He jumped guiltily as we stopped beside him and I saw that he was balancing a plate of apple strudel on his knee and had an open book in one hand.

"Herr Müller... you know guests are not allowed to bring food into the library," said Sofia in a gently scolding tone, although her indulgent smile belied her words.

The man hurriedly put his plate on the side table and stood up. He smiled at us, his eyes twinkling. "My apologies, I could not resist a second slice of apple strudel. As I was keen to return to my book, it seemed ideal to combine the two pleasures. I had forgotten the house rules."

He was a small man, with a balding head and pale brown eyes in a narrow, clever face. His suit was conservative but well made, and he wore a maroon bow-tie in a way that managed to look dignified instead of comical. He reminded me of the dons back at Oxford and I wondered if he was an academic.

Sofia introduced us and added, "Herr Johann Müller is the owner and curator of a wonderful private museum. You must make time to visit it!"

Müller coughed modestly. "It is but a small museum. It does not compare with the great institutions that most tourists come to Vienna to see."

"Ah, but it has a very fine collection of paintings, particularly from the Art Nouveau and Vienna

Secession periods—there is even an original chair designed by Koloman Moser! And a painting by Klimt that is believed to be one of the portraits originally seized by the Nazis for Hitler's private museum." Sofia smiled. "It is such a romantic story how Herr Müller spotted the painting in a deceased estate sale; you must ask him to tell you sometime."

Müller gave that modest cough again. "I was extremely lucky, that is all. And I was not even sure if my hunch—that is what Americans call it, is it not?—if my hunch was correct. I did not dare celebrate until several experts had examined the painting and declared it genuine."

"Yes, and how exciting it was when it was authenticated! I remember the day when it was first placed on public exhibit." Sofia turned to me. "Many tourist sites for Vienna now list Herr Müller's museum as a must-visit attraction for art lovers."

"What's the painting of?"

"It is the portrait of a lady, holding her Siamese cat in her arms. Klimt was a great lover of cats, did you know that?"

"No, I didn't—I thought he was a great lover of women," I laughed.

"Well... he was that too," agreed Sofia, her eyes twinkling. "But it is true. Klimt loved cats and always had many around his studio. There is a well-known photograph of him holding his favourite cat, in his infamous artist's smock which he always wore when he was painting—and underneath which, apparently, he wore nothing at all!"

"Sounds like a typical eccentric artist," I said, rolling my eyes. "But I do like his work, especially *The Kiss*. I remember first seeing a reproduction of that when I was a little girl. I can't wait to go and see the original at the Belvedere Palace." I glanced at Müller. "But I'll be sure to visit your collection too, Herr Müller."

He made a slight bow. "I should be delighted to take you around personally."

"Oh, no, there's no need—"

"It would be my pleasure to take a lovely young lady such as yourself around my museum," he said with old-fashioned gallantry. "I consider it a bonus of my stay at *Hotel das Herzchen*."

"We were so happy that you accepted Stefan's invitation," gushed Sofia. "As a respected member of the Viennese arts community, your patronage of the hotel is a great compliment."

Müller made that quaint bow again. "Not at all, it is I who am delighted and honoured to be one of the first guests here. It has been most comfortable so far and in particular—" he gestured to the plate, "— your apple strudel is magnificent. One of the best I have tasted! Do you make it yourself? I would return to stay at the hotel for the apple strudel alone."

Sofia laughed. "Yes, it is an old recipe of my grandmother's. And since I know how much you love your apple strudel, I will take that as an even greater compliment. Thank you."

We left Müller to his book and his favourite treat, and Sofia showed me the rest of the rooms on the ground floor: a large dining room across the hall from the lounge and, beyond the bend of the L-shaped hallway, a large room which contained an old grand piano and two overstuffed armchairs next to a large fireplace. It had a strong smell of cigarettes and the air was hazy, despite the partially opened French windows which led out onto a wide balcony.

"This was once the music room—but some guests have been using it as the smoking room," said Sofia with a grimace. She saw my look of surprise and added, "Yes, you will find that many places in Austria still allow smoking indoors—particularly in restaurants and cafés. I know it seems unbelievable in this day and age—and indeed, the government has talked of plans for a total smoking ban—but smoking is part of the café culture in Austria. It was always what was done in a typical Vienna *Kaffeehaus*: you took your coffee and your cigarette." She shrugged. "So while other countries banned smoking in bars and cafés, in Austria they simply decided to adopt separate smoking and non-smoking areas."

She led me to the French windows and we stepped out onto the wide balcony. It was lined with a variety of potted plants and flowers—a couple of tired-looking geraniums, a selection of herbs, and a potted climbing rose which was still holding on to a few faded blooms. I walked to the edge of the balcony and looked out. Below me was a small private courtyard garden, and beyond that, a view of the street behind the hotel which led to a small park in the distance.

"I thought if I could create an attractive outdoor area, it might encourage guests to go outside to smoke," Sofia explained, gesturing to the potted plants with a sigh. "But it is quite late in the season now and things are becoming brown and dry—oh, careful…" She reached out and helped me disentangle myself from the climbing rose, which had snagged my sweater with its thorny canes as I turned away from the railing. "Sorry, I have been meaning to give that a prune—it has just been growing so fast!—but I have been too busy with the opening of the hotel…" She looked around at the pots again with a fretful sigh. "Everything needs a bit of tidying up, really. It is all looking so messy—"

"It looks fine," I said soothingly. "Honestly, I don't think most people will notice. And when the weather warms up again, you can put a couple of chairs out here—there's a lovely view and I'm sure guests will enjoy sitting out here, even if they're not getting their nicotine fix."

We finished our tour and Sofia took me up to our suite. It was a lovely airy set of rooms: a main living area, a shared bathroom, and two adjoining bedrooms. Like the rest of the hotel, it had been decorated in a simple but elegant style, with blue patterned wallpaper and oil paintings depicting pastoral scenes on the walls.

"I am afraid each of the bedrooms only holds two beds," said Sofia apologetically. "So I have put in an extra bed in this alcove here—I hope you do not mind, Gemma."

She showed me the far corner of the living area, which curved around the side of the building and led into a large alcove tucked around the corner. I realised that it was a mirror image of the library alcove downstairs—in fact, our suite was set right above the guest lounge and library. By an odd quirk, the original building had been designed with a corner jutting out on one side—almost a sort of turret—which meant that many rooms in the interior did not follow conventional proportions. Nothing was perfectly symmetrical, and it was probably a hassle when it came to furnishing the rooms, but somehow it added to the charm of the whole place.

I scanned the alcove: a folding bed had been set up, together with a makeshift bedside table and a small chest of drawers beside the window. A blanket for Muesli had been laid at the foot of the bed and my case had been neatly placed on a luggage rack in the corner.

"Oh, this is great," I assured Sofia with a smile. "I've got a fantastic view too," I added, walking over to the windows.

"*Meorrw?*" said Muesli, jumping up on the windowsill and looking out with me. I stroked her absent-mindedly as I looked out. Straight in front, I could see a slightly surreal view of the rooftops of Vienna, whilst down below, to my left, I could see the music room balcony where we had been standing a few minutes ago.

"And now, I will leave you to unpack—then perhaps you'd like to come downstairs for refreshments?" Sofia said as we walked back into the main living area together. "There is still tea and coffee and a selection of traditional Viennese cakes and pastries at the buffet in the dining room."

I glanced towards the two bedrooms. I was pleased to see that the Old Biddies seemed to have recovered their equilibrium; they were busily unpacking and Mabel was even consulting a guidebook and bossily telling the others about tomorrow's itinerary. She looked up as she heard Sofia's comment and said:

"Speaking of traditional cakes—it says here that when you visit Vienna, you must sample a *Sacher-Torte*."

Sofia laughed. "Oh yes, I definitely recommend that. The *Sacher-Torte* is supposed to be the most famous chocolate cake in the world."

"What's in it?" I asked.

Sofia shrugged. "No one knows exactly—the original recipe is kept a secret. But it is basically a very rich, bittersweet chocolate cake, with layers of apricot preserve applied by hand."

"Ooh, you had me at 'rich, bittersweet chocolate'," I said jokingly.

Sofia laughed. "Well, why don't you go and taste it for yourselves? The *Hotel Sacher* is only a short walk from here. And while you are there, you must sample some of the traditional Viennese coffees too, such as the *Einspänner*—this is a shot of espresso, topped with whipped cream, that is served in a glass. In olden times, it was the favourite drink of the carriage drivers, and it is said that the whipped cream helped to insulate the coffee and keep it warm."

"What a wonderful story," squealed Ethel. "I'm going to order that and imagine myself driving a carriage."

I gave her a funny look. *Oh-kay.*

"You can eat an early dinner there too, if you like," Sofia continued. "The café serves simple meals, like soups and sandwiches."

"It sounds like we've got our evening sorted," I said, chuckling. "*Sacher-Torte*, here we come!"

CHAPTER SIX

The *Hotel Sacher* was a Vienna institution and certainly seemed to live up to its famous reputation. Built in the late 1800s as a "grand salon for the cultural life of Vienna", it had been the favourite haunt of members of royalty, powerful politicians, and famous celebrities—and was still one of the most luxurious hotels in the world. The sumptuous interiors were filled with Persian carpets, priceless antiques, and Baroque and Rococo furnishings, and everything exuded an aura of imperial elegance.

I felt in slight awe as I stood in the opulent foyer, staring around at the glamorous surroundings. It was the kind of place where you expected a Hollywood movie star or European princess to come swanning out at any moment, flashbulbs popping and paparazzi following, and I was slightly disappointed when the guests exiting from the beautiful vintage lifts turned out to be nothing more than a group of jovial American tourists.

We were directed by the friendly doorman, clad in a top hat and crimson coat with tails, to the Café Sacher, which had its own entrance at the side of the hotel. The café was no less opulent than the main hotel, with upholstered red velvet seats, shimmering chandeliers, and marble-topped tables. A waitress in a traditional black-and-white maid's costume (yes, including the frilly white cap!) settled us in a cosy nook and left us to peruse the menu.

Our attention, though, was soon distracted by a couple sitting next to us. The salon was not a large space and tables were placed close together, making it hard to ignore those around you—especially when they were enthusiastically kissing each other, the plate of cake on their table forgotten.

"Tsk! Tsk! Young people nowadays…" said Mabel, giving them a disapproving look. "No sense of shame at all!"

"I think it's rather romantic," said Glenda, looking at them wistfully. "To be so in love that you don't care who sees you…" She sighed dreamily. "I can remember being in love like that once!"

"Once?" snorted Mabel. "I would say you're in love at least once a week, Glenda!"

Ethel and Florence tittered.

"I might have had the odd gentleman friend on occasion," said Glenda with great dignity.

"Odd is the word for it," said Mabel. "Really, Glenda, that fellow you were chatting to at bingo last week—he didn't even have his own teeth!"

Glenda glared at her. "Well, *some* of us aren't too old and shrivelled up to appreciate romance…!"

"Er… so have you decided what you're ordering?" I asked, hastily changing the subject.

"Ooh, yes, *I'm* looking forward to having a romance with a slice of *Sacher-Torte*," said Florence, chuckling.

When the waitress returned to take our orders, the Old Biddies demurely ordered a slice of *Sacher-Torte* each, but I—motivated by the recent walk through the chilly autumn evening (and okay, perhaps a bit of greed too)—decided to opt for the "Sweet Sacher Tower": a four-tiered cake stand featuring generous slices of *Sacher-Torte* accompanied by fresh whipped cream, a rich chocolate mousse with juicy strawberries and tangy sorbet, a soft, fluffy pancake filled with berry compote and dusted with icing sugar, and a plate of chocolate bonbons to finish.

It was a magnificent sight when it arrived, although I did feel slightly daunted as I picked up my fork. Thank goodness that Florence—who loved her food—needed no second urging to join me, but even with her help, I felt quite ill by the time we had made our way through the four tiers. As I leaned back from the table, trying not to groan in an unladylike manner, I caught the eye of a gentleman seated at the next table, who was watching me with amusement. He was a handsome, suave-looking man in his fifties, very well dressed in a dark suit and grey silk tie that enhanced the silver hair at his temples. I noticed that he only had a small tray with a black coffee and a glass of water on his table.

"I'm beginning to wish I had your restraint," I said ruefully.

He laughed. "It is something those of us who live in Vienna quickly learn, if we are to keep our sanity amidst all the delectable cakes and treats on offer. Although... it seems like this lovely lady has had no trouble," he added with a smile to Glenda.

She simpered. "That is very kind of you to say, but really, at my age, you know, one has to watch one's figure."

The gentleman did an exaggerated double-take. "*At your age?* But I cannot believe that you are much more than my fifty-five years."

I wanted to roll my eyes, but Glenda giggled and flushed with pleasure. Soon she and the gentleman were engrossed in conversation, whilst the other Old Biddies and I looked on, slightly bemused. When it finally came time to pay the bill and leave, we had to drag a reluctant Glenda from the table.

"It has been so lovely chatting with you, Herr Wagner. I do wish we could talk for longer..." said Glenda wistfully, as the gentleman rose politely as well.

"Please, call me Moritz," he said smoothly. "And

the centre of Vienna is not a large area—perhaps we might come across each other again. May I ask if your hotel is nearby?"

I hesitated, unsure about telling a complete stranger where we were staying, but Glenda immediately said, "Oh yes, we're staying at the *Hotel das Herzchen* just around the corner."

His eyebrows shot up. "The *Hotel das Herzchen*? What a coincidence! I am staying there myself."

"But... I thought you said you lived in Vienna," I said.

He inclined his head. "I do. However, a friend of mine was offered a complimentary stay at the newly opened hotel, and he suggested that I come as well. I am an art critic," he explained. "I have a large following on social media, as well as a popular column in a national newspaper, and I am often invited to review new establishments in the city."

"Oh, that's wonderful!" Glenda squealed. "So perhaps we'll see you at breakfast tomorrow morning?"

He made a slight face. "If I can bear to suffer another meal in that dining room. The place is a disgrace, particularly the service—"

"Perhaps it's just teething troubles," I suggested, feeling an urge to defend Sofia Fritzl. "I'm sure all new places have some hiccups—it's only to be expected."

He sniffed. "On the contrary, an establishment of a truly high standard cannot afford to make mistakes and I shall not hesitate to say so in my review. There is far too much acceptance of and excuses made for low quality these days. If those with authority—such as myself—did not point it out, how can there be any hope of improvement?"

"Um... I suppose you're right," I murmured, feeling a flicker of dislike for the man and his pompous, uncharitable attitude.

I kept my thoughts to myself, however, particularly as Glenda seemed completely besotted with him and spent most of the walk back to the hotel gushing about his many charms. Muesli was waiting eagerly for us when we returned to our hotel room and, after I fed her, I decided to take her outside to get some fresh air. Leaving the Old Biddies taking turns to have their baths, I clipped the harness onto my little tabby cat, then picked her up and carried her downstairs. The guest lounge and lobby seemed deserted, and I let Muesli wander around for a bit, keeping an eye out to make sure she didn't scratch the furniture, before leading her down the main staircase and out onto the street.

It was dark now and there was a definite nip in the air. I turned the collar of my coat up around my neck, then gently guided Muesli around the corner into the lane which bordered the side of the hotel. I'd only planned a quick walk up and down the lane, but Muesli slowed down and stopped beside a patch of grass growing alongside the hotel building.

"Come on, Muesli," I said impatiently, tugging gently on the leash.

She ignored me, her head down, and I realised that she was eating grass. Back in Oxford, I kept a little pot of cat grass growing on the windowsill and grazing on it was one of Muesli's favourite things to do. She'd obviously been missing her usual green treat because she was chomping eagerly away now, ripping the blades up and chewing slowly. I sighed and stopped to wait for her to finish. As I stood there, however, I became conscious of the sound of familiar voices. They seemed to be coming from above me. I glanced up at the brightly lit window a few feet above my head. From my memory of the hotel layout, I guessed that this was the side with the private wing, where Sofia and Stefan lived. It sounded like they were having a heated argument. Sofia's voice, shrill and angry, rang out in the night air.

"...do not care what he says, it was an honest mistake and there was no need for him to be so rude about it!"

Stefan's voice was placating. He said something in German and when she did not reply, he added in English, "Moritz Wagner is a particular type of customer; it is well known in hotel circles—they are difficult and demanding and completely unreasonable. But unfortunately, they are a fact of life in the hospitality business. You must not let him affect you so."

"I cannot help it! You know he is writing a review of the hotel—"

"And there is nothing we can do to influence that. We simply have to serve him the best we can and hope that he gives us a fair review."

"But it will *not* be a fair review!" said Sofia bitterly. "You know Wagner takes pleasure in tearing down others in that column of his. He says it is for the education and entertainment of his readers, but I think he simply enjoys the feeling of power and superiority over others. Did you read his review of that new Hungarian restaurant last month? It was horrible!" She made a moaning sound. "I cannot bear it if he wrote something similar about us—he could ruin the whole launch!"

"Sofia..." Stefan sounded like he was losing patience. "You could be worrying for nothing. Wagner may not give us a poor review. And besides..."

His voice grew louder as he approached the window and I stepped back hastily, worried about being seen. The long grass tangled beneath my feet and I stumbled, feeling my right foot step on something soft. The next moment, there was a high-pitched yowl. I gasped as I realised that I had trodden on Muesli's tail.

"*Was zur Hölle!* What is that?"

I froze as the window was suddenly flung open and I found Stefan and Sofia staring down at me.

"Oh! Er... Hi..." I said, plastering a bright smile

to my face.

"Gemma!" Sofia looked at me in astonishment. "What are you doing out there in the dark?"

I gestured to Muesli, who was grooming her tail and looking at me reproachfully. "I... um... brought my cat out for some fresh air."

"Well, do not stay out long," said Sofia, looking disapproving. "It is chilly outside. What will your mother say if you catch your death of cold?"

"I'm just heading back in now," I assured her. I saw Stefan looking at me thoughtfully and hoped that he wouldn't realise that I had overheard their conversation. Before he or Sofia could say anything else, I scooped Muesli up, bade them both a hasty good night, and hurried back into the hotel.

CHAPTER SEVEN

Breakfast the next morning was a merry affair, with all the guests in the hotel congregating in the dining room and mingling as they helped themselves from the buffet. I had come down first—the Old Biddies still busy taking out their rollers and sprinkling talcum powder in their shoes—and I decided to make a start on the extensive Continental breakfast selection laid out on the sideboard. There were freshly baked bread rolls, pastries and croissants, platters of gourmet hams and cheeses, home-made jam, cereals and muesli, and fresh fruit salad. I wasn't normally a fan of Continental breakfasts; I liked a hearty cooked meal in the mornings—preferably with eggs and lots of bacon!—but everything looked so fresh and delicious that I found myself piling my plate high. Then, balancing my overflowing plate, I looked around the room for somewhere to sit. There were several smaller tables scattered around the outer edges of the room but most people seemed to opt for the long, communal table in the centre.

I paused in surprise as I saw Moritz Wagner. After his scathing comments last night, I hadn't expected him to be here. He was sitting at one of the individual tables, with Johann Müller opposite and a strange woman next to him. She was very glamorous, with dark, arched eyebrows and deep red lipstick. Her hair was swept back from her head in a bouffant style and gold sparkled at her ears and neck. I also saw with a slight shock that she was wearing a fur stole draped around her shoulders, and from the rich colour and sheen of the fur, it was very obviously not fake. With the politically correct environment these days, it was rare to see someone flaunt a fur garment so blatantly—at least back in England.

The most striking thing about the woman, though, was the expression on her face. It was like thunder. She was saying something angrily to Wagner but he was barely paying her any attention, talking and laughing with Müller instead. I saw her put a hand on his arm but he shrugged it off coolly and said something in a dismissive manner which brought another angry rush of colour to her face. Standing up suddenly, she stormed out of the dining room, rushing past me in a wave of cloying perfume.

"Oh my goodness, do you think they've had a row? She looks a right miserable cow, dontcha think? I wouldn't have thought you could be so sour married to a handsome fella like him—though I wouldn't know, I suppose, seeing as I've never been married myself... Not that I'm sure they're married, you know... but I did see them check in together... but then they could just be boyfriend and girlfriend—seems a bit strange calling them that when they're so old, dontcha think? Not really *old*, of course, just sort of... mature-like, you know... like that George Clooney chap, the type that gets dishier as they get older... what do they call them? Silver wolf—no, silver fox..."

I turned in surprise at this extraordinary flood of conversation and found myself looking at a tall, skinny woman in her late forties, with a plain, good-natured face and dark-rimmed glasses that gave her the look of a friendly owl. She was obviously English, both from her dress and her accent, but she certainly didn't fit the stereotype of laconic British reserve. She beamed at me and chattered on, barely pausing for a breath between sentences.

"...seeing as I always wanted to visit Vienna, I thought: why not? You only live once, that's what they say, isn't it? And there was such a great deal at this hotel—opening month discount, it said on the website... Although I did wonder if I should have gone to Venice instead. That's another place I've always wanted to visit... Get them mixed up in my head, sometimes, you know, because they sound the same—not that they're similar, of course—one's in Italy and one's here in Austria, and the language is different... I quite fancied learning Italian, you know... sounds a lot nicer than German, dontcha think? You speak any German? I was thinking of learning before we came—there's a local college that does night classes round the corner from where I live—but then Claire—that's my best friend—told me to just use this app you get on your phone... Hmm... I'm not sure about all these apps... Mum says I should have bought an old-fashioned phrase book and maybe she's right—oh, have you met my mum?" The woman paused for a split second to draw a breath and indicate an elderly lady standing behind her. "This is my mum—and I'm Jane—Jane Hillingdon." She thrust a hand at me.

"Er... nice to meet you. I'm Gemma Rose," I said, shaking her hand.

"You're English, aren't you? Whereabouts are you from?"

"Oxfor—"

"Oh, I love Oxford! Used to work near there. Well, in Reading, actually, which isn't *that* close but you can hop on the train and get there in like half an hour... You here on holiday? So nice to meet someone *English*, you know! Not that the other guests aren't really friendly—there's a Chinese family with the sweetest little girl and that quiet chap who's sitting there now with Mr George

Clooney—something to do with museums, isn't he?—oh, and this American fella who arrived yesterday—that's him now, by the buffet—quite dishy too, isn't he? ...and of course, Mrs Fritzl is a lovely lady and she grew up in England herself... but it's not the same, dontcha think? I was just telling Mum yesterday that there's something about sitting down with a nice cuppa and someone from your own country... We were in the lounge yesterday morning and *that* woman was in there and she didn't say a word to us once! Did she talk to you, Mum?"

Old Mrs Hillingdon opened her mouth to answer but didn't get a word in before Jane chattered on:

"You know, now that I think about it, they're probably not married because I heard her give her name—it's Ana Bauer—and I don't think Bauer was his last name... I heard the concierge call him yesterday but I can't remember now what it was... can you, Mum?"

Again Mrs Hillingdon opened her mouth and again Jane cut her off.

"Some kind of German name... Walter? No... Wenger? No... oh, I remember now—Wagner! Of course, they say it 'Vag-ner', you know—they say the 'w' as 'v' here... funny sort of language, German, isn't it? You speak it at all?"

"Er... no, I'm afraid not, although I can understand a few words... Um... I'm just going to find a place to sit down," I said and beat a hasty retreat before Jane Hillingdon could open her mouth again.

Whew, I thought, sitting down at random at the big table. *That woman could probably talk her way out of Alcatraz!* I didn't think I'd ever met anyone so loquacious. I glanced around and realised that I had sat down next to the Chinese family. The couple gave me polite smiles but didn't seem inclined to engage in conversation; the little girl, however, caught my eye and smiled at me shyly, revealing a gap in her front teeth.

"Hi... I'm Gemma," I gave her a friendly smile. "What's your name?"

"Mei-Mei," she said in a soft voice.

"Are you in Vienna on holiday?"

She nodded, giving me another shy smile.

"What's the favourite thing you've seen so far?"

She hesitated, then pulled something from her lap beneath the table. I saw that it was a sketchpad. She flipped through a few pages, then turned it around and showed it shyly to me. It was a drawing, beautifully done in coloured pencil, of a pair of white horses pulling a gleaming black carriage. It was obviously one of the many horse-drawn carriages that took tourists on tours around Vienna.

"Wow, did you draw that yourself? You're very good! Yes, the horse carriages are so romantic, aren't they? Have you been on one?"

A shadow crossed the girl's face and she stole a

glance at her parents, then turned back to me and said in a low voice, "No, Ma-Ma say not allowed."

"Wasting money," the Chinese woman suddenly spoke up. "No use—going around. Learn nothing. Only look at horse."

"Oh... er... well, I suppose you're right. It *is* a bit of a tourist gimmick..." I said, although as I looked down at the little girl's dejected face, I couldn't help thinking that sometimes it might be worth doing something "useless" just to enjoy the beauty and romance of the moment.

"You are from England?" The Chinese woman looked at me curiously.

"Yes, I live in Oxford," I said.

Her stern face relaxed and she smiled approvingly. "Ah! Oxford. Very top university." As if I was now considered worthy of acquaintance, she inclined her head and said, "I am Mrs Chow. This my husband... and this my daughter, Mei-Mei." She frowned as her eyes fell on her daughter's drawing of the carriage and horses and she sighed irritably. "Mei-Mei always want drawing animal... you see animal anywhere! Come to Vienna... must see museum, study history and Europe government, learn famous composer and classical music—"

"Aww, but you can't come to Vienna and not see the Lipizzaner stallions!" came a drawling voice across the table. It was the handsome young American that Jane Hillingdon had pointed out to me earlier. He was leaning forwards, his blue eyes earnest and an almost comical expression of dismay on his square-jawed face.

The Chinese couple looked at him blankly.

"You don't know about the Spanish Riding School?" asked the American, staring at them in disbelief.

"I know!" cried the little girl. "It's where beautiful white horses do dancing!"

The American gave her a wide smile. "Yeah, that's right. It's more than four hundred and fifty years old, and it's the only place where they still teach classical dressage in its original form... And the Winter Riding School—man, you gotta see that place! It's like this giant ballroom with chandeliers and pillars and ornate ceilings... it's just awesome! When the stallions come out with their riders, it's like they're dancing ballet... seriously, you gotta try and catch a performance in there!"

The little girl was staring at him starry-eyed. She turned hopefully towards her parents and said: "Ma-Ma, we can go? Please?"

Her mother ignored her. Instead, she said to the American, "We go see Imperial Apartment Museum in Hofbug Palace today—"

"Well, that's perfect!" he said, beaming. "The Spanish Riding School is housed in the palace complex. In fact, you pass the courtyard of the Imperial Stables on your way to Michaelerplatz, where the entrance to the palace museum is. You can just stop and ask in the ticket office—"

"Thank you for suggest but no time see dancing horse," said Mrs Chow curtly. "We want Mei-Mei learn important Europe history and culture. She become top lawyer one day," she added proudly. "Will be very high education."

"But—" the American started to say, but he was interrupted by a very loud and plaintive "*Meorrw?*"

"Oh! That's Muesli!" I cried, looking around.

A furry shape appeared in the doorway of the dining room.

"*Meorrw? Meorrw?*" said Muesli mournfully.

"Muesli! What are you doing down here?" I said, getting up from my chair.

The little cat gave a delighted chirrup as she saw me and bounded over, her tail vibrating. She twined around my legs, meowing loudly and rubbing her chin against my jeans. Then she turned to the chair next to mine, where Mei-Mei was watching her, fascinated.

"*Meorrw?*" she said, reaching up to sniff the little girl.

Mei-Mei's face broke into a delighted smile and she stretched out a tentative hand towards Muesli, but before she could touch the cat, Mrs Chow gave a horrified cry and yanked her daughter's hand away.

"*Ayah!* No! No touch—dirty animal!" she said. Scrambling to her feet, she backed away, regarding Muesli with disgust. She gestured at her daughter. "Come, Mei-Mei! We go now."

She turned and stalked out of the room with her husband meekly following. Mei-Mei hesitated, looking wistfully at Muesli, and for a moment I thought she might try to pat her again, but then her mother called her sharply from the dining room doorway and she scurried off.

CHAPTER EIGHT

"Man, it's a real shame the way they're controlling that kid like that," complained the American as soon as they were out of earshot.

Privately I agreed with him but—unlike Jane Hillingdon—I found that I was more of a slave to my British middle-class upbringing than I realised, and I couldn't bring myself to publicly talk about the Chows behind their backs. Instead, I changed the subject and asked him what he was doing in Vienna.

"Oh, I'm here 'cos of the Lipizzaners," he said, grinning as he bent down to scratch Muesli under the chin. Like many Americans, he had a relaxed, outgoing manner which made him very easy to talk to. "My name's Randy, by the way. Randy McGrath. And you're Gemma, right? I heard you telling the little girl. I saw you yesterday, actually—I checked in right before you, I think. You were with a couple of lil ol' ladies, right? You guys here on vacation?"

"Yes, and *I'm* definitely going to see the Spanish Riding School," I said with a smile. "I was interested anyway, but after your big talk-up, I wouldn't miss it for anything now."

"You're not gonna regret it. Best show in town! 'Course, I might be a bit biased," he admitted, chuckling. "I think anything with horses is awesome."

"Oh—are you a horse trainer or something?"

"Sort of. I own a ranch back in Florida and I breed Lipizzaners. I've produced some of the best Lipizzaner foals in the States," he said proudly. "I train 'em in the dressage moves too—just the stallions, of course, not the mares and geldings— and we put on a regular show at the ranch every weekend. We tour around the country too."

"Wow, sounds like you keep really busy."

"Yeah, running a ranch ain't for the faint-hearted, that's for sure," he said with a grimace. "It's twenty-four hours, seven days a week—you're either out there mucking out the stables or feeding the horses or exercising 'em... but I love it. I've been around horses all my life—wouldn't wanna do anything else."

"So... are you in Vienna to pick up more breeding stock or...? I'm sorry, I don't know how horse breeding works," I said.

He hesitated for a fraction of a second, then he gave me that easy smile and said, "Nah—this trip's just for pleasure, actually. I got the opportunity to come and I thought: I'm not gonna pass up the chance to see the Lipizzaners in their own home! I mean, I've visited before, of course, but it's still awesome every time." He drained his coffee and glanced at his watch. "Anyway, I'd better make tracks—I wanna get to the Morning Exercise at the Riding School. Nice talking to you."

After he left, I turned back to my own breakfast and hurriedly finished it, keeping an eye on Jane Hillingdon at the other end of the table and hoping that she wouldn't decide to come and join me, now that the seats next to me were empty. Muesli jumped up on the chair that Randy had vacated and started to make herself comfortable. I glanced at her worriedly, wondering if she should be allowed to do that—and as if in answer to my thoughts, Sofia hurried over.

"Gemma..." She looked at me apologetically. "I'm really sorry—pets are welcome in most of the places in the hotel but just not in the dining room."

"Oh, of course," I said, standing up quickly. "I completely understand. I'm sorry—I think Muesli was feeling a bit lonely in our suite and she must have slipped out and come down looking for me. I'll take her back up."

"Why don't you take her to the music room?" Sofia suggested. "It's usually fairly empty and she'd be very welcome to play in there any time. You can leave her there for now, with the door shut, if you like, while you finish breakfast."

"Thanks, that sounds great."

Muesli looked excitedly around as I set her down in the music room a few minutes later and immediately trotted off to explore the room. I made a quick inspection myself, wanting to make sure that there wasn't anything dangerous or fragile lying around. I was a bit nervous leaving my mischievous little cat unsupervised, but the room seemed safe enough and there were even two comfy armchairs for her if she wanted to have a nap. So with a stern "Be good!", I left her to it and returned to the dining room and my half-finished breakfast.

As I sat down again, I wondered where the Old Biddies were. Surely they couldn't still be applying cold cream or whatever else they did in their morning regime? Then I spied them sitting at the table in the corner with Moritz Wagner and Johann Müller. They must have come down while I was in the music room with Muesli. Hurriedly finishing my breakfast, I got up and went over to join them. I found them deep in a heated discussion with the two Austrian men about an item of national pride: the apple strudel.

"...always thought strudel was a German dessert," Glenda was saying.

"Certainly not!" said Müller, bristling. "The oldest surviving recipe is in the Vienna City Library!"

Wagner chuckled and patted the older man on the arm. "You can see that my friend Johann is sensitive about his favourite treat. In fact, this has always been a sore point between the Germans and the Austrians: both countries claim to be the creator of the strudel. The truth is... there are variations found throughout Central and Eastern Europe—the Hungarians, the Slovenians, the Czechs, the Poles all have a variation of the strudel and they are all nice in their own way."

"There is nothing like a Viennese strudel," insisted Müller. "The thin, crispy layered pastry—so light and soft—and the sweet, juicy fruit inside... Of course, a home-made apple strudel is very different to the monstrosity one gets in the supermarkets these days. And a true apple strudel should always be made of dessert apples, mixed with raisins and some breadcrumbs to soak up the juices as it bakes."

"I always think the breadcrumbs make it stodgy," Wagner protested. Then he laughed and said to the Old Biddies, "But we will not bore you now with our age-old argument. Johann and I have been known to debate the merits of strudel fillings until the early hours of the morning."

He paused and looked up, an expression of displeasure crossing his face. I turned and saw that Ana Bauer had returned. She was standing beside the table, her scowling gaze taking in the Old Biddies and me. She seemed to be waiting for an invitation to join us, but Wagner made no move to invite her. After an awkward pause, Müller sprang up and hurried to bring another chair for her.

"Here you are, Ana." He ushered her to the seat, making sure that she was placed next to Wagner.

His solicitousness seemed to mollify her slightly and she settled herself with an exaggerated sigh, looking at Wagner expectantly. He made no move to introduce her to us and the silence stretched awkwardly again.

Once again, Müller hurried to step into the breach. "This is Ana Bauer, a close friend of mine and Moritz's. Ana is an art dealer and she owns an art gallery nearby."

Ana gave us a wintry smile, her eyes barely flicking over us before returning to Wagner. He continued to ignore her and said to us:

"Where are you ladies planning to visit today?"

Mabel sat up importantly. "Well, we have a few days free before the awards ceremony—"

"Awards ceremony?" Wagner raised his eyebrows.

"Yes, Gemma is the winner for the whole of England!" said Glenda proudly, putting a hand on my shoulder.

"It's just a little baking contest," I said quickly, embarrassed as I saw Wagner, Müller, and Ana all looking at me. "I... um... run a tearoom and our scones have been selected. Anyway, what does your guidebook recommend, Mabel?" I asked, hastily changing the subject.

"Oh, they recommend that we just walk around the Innere Stadt on the first day and get our bearings," Mabel said. "And then we shall probably visit several of the museums in the next few days."

"Ah, you will be spoilt for choice," said Wagner with a complacent smile. "They call Vienna the 'City of Music' but it could just as easily have been called the 'City of Museums'! There is the magnificent *Kunsthistorisches*—the Art History Museum, which you must not miss. And then there is the Albertina Museum, the Sisi Museum and Imperial Apartments, the Belvedere Palace with its wonderful collection of Klimt paintings... and of course there are the smaller, specialist museums such as the Sigmund Freud Museum and the Mozarthaus. There are even some museums that are not on the usual tourist routes that are perhaps even more interesting—such as the Museum of Art Fakes."

"The Museum of Art Fakes?" I said, intrigued.

"Yes, it is a museum devoted to art forgeries," said Wagner, grinning. "It is filled with fake paintings of the masters, done by some of the world's most famous forgers—"

"It is ridiculous to encourage visitors to Vienna to waste time looking at fake art," snapped Ana Bauer suddenly. "There are many much more worthwhile museums to visit."

Müller put a placating hand on her arm. "Ana... Moritz is only teasing. You know how he is."

"There is nothing amusing about art forgery!" Ana said.

Wagner leaned back and looked at her properly for the first time. "Why so touchy, Ana?" he asked with a smirk. "Surely you are not worried that any pieces in *your* gallery might be fake, are you?"

Ana gave a gasp of outrage and stood up. She hissed something in German to Wagner which made Müller look slightly shocked, but Wagner just laughed. Then she turned and stalked out of the dining room. Müller hesitated, then mumbled an excuse and hurried out after her. He'd barely left when Sofia hurried over to the table carrying a cup of coffee which she set down in front of Wagner.

"About time," he growled. "I ordered the coffee nearly half an hour ago!"

Sofia compressed her lips. "Actually, it was not even ten minutes ago—I took the order myself. But I apologise for the wait, Herr Wagner. Our coffee machine had a slight problem."

"Well, I hope it is not boiling this time," said Wagner, looking down at his cup with disdain. "Coffee should be served at between seventy and eighty degrees Celsius, no more, no less. In fact, it should really be served at an even lower temperature than that if one is to taste all the subtle flavours of the beans."

Sofia flushed. "I am sorry, Herr Wagner—you did not mention any problems when I brought your coffee earlier. I would have been happy to bring you a fresh cup."

"Coffee should be served right the first time, especially in a hotel of this calibre," snapped Wagner. "You are not a country inn. And while I am on the subject, does no one check the amenities here? The remote control in my room has weak batteries. It is a disgrace!"

Sofia's face was bright red now and she looked as if she was going to burst into tears. She bit her lip, mumbled something about asking Stefan to attend to it, then hurried away. I watched her go, feeling sorry for her. I was also taken aback by the change in Wagner's manner. Gone was the charming, genial man from a few minutes ago—now that he was talking to "staff", he was arrogant, demanding, and downright rude. The little scene with Sofia left us sitting in an awkward silence, this time without Müller to smooth things over, and the Old Biddies and I soon got up and excused ourselves.

However, as we trooped out of the dining room, Glenda lingered behind, still talking and laughing with Wagner. She was so long that I collected Muesli from the music room and we went up to our suite first without her. When she finally joined us, she looked very much like the cat who'd got the freshly whipped, full-fat, organic cream. Mabel had been thumbing through her trusty guidebook, looking for recommendations for dinner, but now, as we started discussing the options, Glenda fluffed her white hair and said casually:

"I won't be joining you tonight."

We all stopped and looked at her in surprise.

"Why not?" Mabel demanded.

"Well..." Glenda gave a coy smile. "Moritz Wagner has invited me to dinner."

"Glenda!" gasped Ethel, shocked. "Why... he's young enough to be your son!"

Glenda tossed her head. "Age is just a number."

"Except when the number is twenty-five years," said Mabel tartly.

"Whoever said he has romantic intentions?" said Glenda. "We are simply having dinner together, as friends."

"Oh, Glenda—you know men like Wagner always have intentions," said Florence, her plump face worried. "He seems like a terrible ladies' man— remember the way he was talking to the waitress at the Sacher Café? And what about that lady who was at breakfast with him?"

"Oh, Moritz told me about Ana," said Glenda airily. "They had been together for a while but it wasn't anything serious. In any case, they're no longer together."

"Then how come she's here at the hotel with him then?" I asked.

Glenda wrinkled her nose. "That is just Ana being a nuisance, dear! Moritz told me he had made it clear to her that they were no longer a couple, but Ana just would not accept it. She insisted on coming to the hotel with him. Perhaps she thought she could change his mind. It was really very silly of her." Glenda looked at us and added huffily, "Anyway, I know what I'm doing and I can look after myself."

The other Old Biddies and I exchanged looks but we didn't say anything more. It was true—at the end of the day, it was Glenda's personal affair. Besides, she wasn't an inexperienced teenager—she was a mature lady of eighty who'd had far more life experiences than me! It seemed silly and ironic for me to be worried about her "getting involved with the wrong kind of man".

Pushing my concerns out of my mind, I followed the Old Biddies out of the suite and we set off for a day of sightseeing.

CHAPTER NINE

I grew up in Oxford, one of the most beautiful cities in the world, so I should have been used to grand historic buildings and spectacular architecture. And yet as I walked around the streets of Old Vienna, I was still stunned by the beauty of my surroundings. It really was like stepping into a real-life fairy tale with the Gothic towers, majestic arches and ornately carved Baroque façades, the winding cobbled lanes and pretty arcades housing antique shops and quaint cafés, the street musicians filling the air with lilting classical music, and the timeless romance of the beautiful horse-drawn carriages sailing past.

As we walked towards Michaelerplatz—St Michael Square—and the entrance to the Hofburg Palace, I noticed a crowd of people hovering outside a set of large double doors embedded in the walls of the palace complex. Mabel marched briskly past, with the other Old Biddies toddling behind her, but I paused, curious as to what the crowd was looking at.

The double doors—roped off by a chain to prevent the general public entering—led into a huge arcaded courtyard with rows of stable doors arranged on three sides. *This must be the Imperial Stables*, I realised, and even as I had the thought, my heart gave a little leap of delight as an equine head appeared suddenly in one of the open stable half-doors. It was a Lipizzaner stallion, with a snowy white mane, soft velvety muzzle, and liquid dark eyes that regarded us curiously from across the courtyard. Even just relaxing in its stall, it was one of the most beautiful, majestic creatures I'd ever seen.

The crowd shifted and I pushed my way to the front for a closer look. I leaned over the chain, peering eagerly around the courtyard, hoping to catch a glimpse of another stallion, and was rewarded a moment later by a second head appearing in the stall next to the first. This one was more of a pale dappled grey but just as beautiful. The two horses stretched their noses towards each other until their muzzles were almost touching, then they snorted and turned away, like two friends who had had a little spat. I heard a giggle next to me and looked down to see a familiar head of shining black hair. It was Mei-Mei, the little Chinese girl from the hotel, with her eyes bright and laughing as she watched the horses.

"Hello, Mei-Mei! How nice to see you here," I said, crouching down next to her.

She jumped, then relaxed as she recognised me. "Hello," she said shyly.

I looked around for her parents but couldn't see them. "Did you convince your mother to come and see the Lipizzaners after all?"

She shook her head and said, "Ma-Ma and Ba-Ba are buying tickets for Imperial Apartment Museum. It is long queue."

"Do they know you're here?" I asked. "They might be worried if they can't find you."

She gave me a slightly guilty look. "Ma-Ma think I go look at National Library... there!" She turned and pointed to the imposing building across the road from the Imperial Stables.

"Ah... right..." I gave her a conspiratorial smile. "Well, I won't tell anyone."

She grinned, showing me that adorable gap in her front teeth again. Then she lifted the sketch pad she was holding and held it bashfully up to me. I looked down and my eyes widened. She had drawn one of the Lipizzaner stallions looking out of his stall and, despite the childish hand, the sketch seemed to sing with life. In fact, somehow, with a few simple strokes, she had captured all the horse's beauty and majesty on paper, so that he seemed almost to be looking out at me from the sketchpad. I regarded Mei-Mei with new eyes. This little eight-year-old had incredible talent.

"That's amazing!" I said. "Have you always been so good at drawing?"

She gave an embarrassed shrug. "I love drawing." She looked up across the courtyard at the horses and said wistfully, "I wish I can draw animals all my life—I want to become famous animal artist!" Then she looked slightly shame-faced and added quickly, "But this is just wishing. Ma-Ma say I become lawyer. It's good job—never worry about money. I can have big house and nice car..."

"Um... yes, I suppose she's right," I said reluctantly, thinking of my best friend, Cassie, who also possessed a wonderful artistic talent and yet struggled to make a living from her art. She worked at my tearoom and part-time at the dance studio, just so she could support herself while she focused on her paintings and built up her portfolio.

Then I thought of myself and how I had turned my back on a lucrative, prestigious career to follow my dream... and I had never been happier since.

Impulsively, I said: "You know, it *is* possible to have a career in Art—for example, my best friend did a Fine Art degree at Oxford and it's got a broad curriculum that allows you to experiment with working in different mediums..." I trailed off as I saw Mei-Mei frowning, not really taking in my words. I tried again, more simply: "You can study Art at university—and maybe become an artist."

Her eyes sparkled. "Really?"

"Yes, but..." I shifted uncomfortably. "But your mother's right. You wouldn't have the same job security. It's really hard to make a living—to earn money—as an artist. Studying law and becoming a lawyer is a lot safer."

Mei-Mei turned back to look at the Lipizzaners and I wondered if she had heard me. Her face was dreamy as she watched the horses. I felt a twinge of unease again. I hoped I hadn't opened a can of worms...

She looked up at me suddenly and asked: "Are you going to watch horses dancing?"

"Um... well, I'm going to try. I was just on my way to the Spanish Riding School ticket office, actually, to see if there are any seats available in the upcoming performances." I hesitated, then added, "I don't know if I'm allowed to take photos but I'll try and get some to show you."

She gave me that sweet, gap-toothed smile again. Then she looked at her watch, gasped and said: "*Ayah!* I must go back!"

Giving me a hasty wave, she clutched her sketchpad to her chest, pushed her way through the crowd and ran down the street towards the Hofburg Palace museum entrance. I followed at a slower pace and arrived several minutes later at the great copper dome which stood over the gate on the north-eastern side of the palace, and which housed the entrance to the Imperial Apartments on one side and the entrance to the Spanish Riding School on the other. I found the Old Biddies standing just outside the latter, arguing over a map of Vienna.

"Gemma! We were just beginning to wonder where you had gone, dear," said Florence as I joined them.

"Sorry, I got side-tracked looking at the Imperial Stables. Listen, I'm just going to pop into the Spanish Riding School and see if we can get tickets to a performance. I won't be a moment."

When I stepped into the main foyer, however, my heart sank as I saw the long queue that snaked around the room and the looks of desperation of many people's faces.

"Are you here to buy tickets?" I asked the two girls at the end of the queue.

"Oh no, we got ours online months ago," one girl said. "We're just picking them up."

"You're trying to buy tickets now? Good luck," said the other sarcastically. "I think they're all sold out until next year."

When I finally arrived at the counter, I was dismayed to discover that she was right. The woman behind the counter gave me an apologetic smile and informed me that the first available seats would be for a performance in January, three months from now. Then, seeing my crestfallen face, she added:

"But there are still tickets available for the Morning Exercise the day after tomorrow. It is not the same as the full performance, of course, but it is a chance for you to see the stallions in the ballroom of the Winter Riding School and watch the riders take them through their dressage moves."

"Okay," I said, my spirits lifting. "That sounds like a good compromise."

"So... five tickets for the Morning Exercise?" She looked at me, her fingers poised over her keyboard.

I started to nod, then paused as the image of a wistful little face suddenly came to my mind. "No," I said impulsively. "Make that six."

***

I was still wondering if I'd done the right thing when we finally returned to the hotel late that afternoon. A part of me knew that I really should have just minded my own business... but another part desperately wanted to give a little girl a rare treat. As I followed the Old Biddies up to our rooms, I mused on how to approach Mei-Mei's parents... perhaps over breakfast tomorrow? And was there a way I could present the Lipizzaner stallions in an educational light that Mrs Chow would consider worthy?

I flopped onto the sofa as soon as we reached our

suite, grateful to rest my aching feet, whilst the Old Biddies hurried to make themselves a restorative cup of tea. Well, all except for Glenda, who promptly disappeared into the bathroom and did not reappear for nearly an hour. When she finally joined us again, her white hair was beautifully fluffed out, her eyelids heavy with blue eyeshadow, and her wrinkled old cheeks bright pink from liberal use of rouge.

"Wow, you look... er... beautiful," I said.

"Thank you, dear," she beamed, smoothing down her mauve dress with the matching jacket and pearl brooch on her lapel.

I had never seen Glenda so dressed up before. She was even wearing a pair of kitten heels, instead of the sensible arch-support lace-ups that she normally wore. Despite my misgivings, I found it quite sweet to see someone in their eighties get so excited about a date.

"I hope you have a great time," I said, giving her an impulsive hug.

After she'd left, the other Old Biddies took turns freshening up in the bathroom while I went to check on Muesli. I found my little cat fast asleep on my bed in the alcove. It seemed like her adventures at breakfast that morning had worn her out and she had spent a lazy day dozing on my bed. Now she arched her back in a perfect cat stretch and gave a little chirrup of greeting as she saw me.

"Hello, you... have you been good?" I asked,

scratching her under her chin.

Quickly, I changed into a warmer top and picked up an extra sweater to take out to dinner with me. Then I filled Muesli's bowl with fresh food and left her munching happily away as I went back out to the living area. The Old Biddies were still getting ready and, after pacing restlessly around the room a few times, I decided to head downstairs first. I remembered seeing a metal rack next to the lift, filled with brochures and leaflets, and thought I might look through those for sightseeing recommendations.

When I got downstairs, I found that a few of the other guests seemed to have also had the same idea. Jane Hillingdon was standing next to the rack of brochures and with her was Randy McGrath. Judging from the pained expression on the young American's face and the way he kept shifting his feet, as if trying to edge away, I guessed that the poor man had been walking past and probably politely stopped to answer a question, then had been unable to extricate himself from Jane's talkative clutches.

Glancing the other way, I was surprised to see Glenda standing forlornly by the main staircase leading down to the ground floor. It had been at least twenty minutes since she had come down and I had expected her to be long gone.

"Glenda! What are you doing here?" I asked, hurrying up to her.

She turned a worried face towards me. "Moritz hasn't come."

"Oh. Do you think... maybe he changed his mind?" I asked hesitantly.

Glenda bristled. "Moritz is a gentleman—he would never stand me up without any reason."

"Well... do you want to go up to his room and knock on his door?"

"I can't go to his room!" said Glenda, looking slightly scandalised.

"Okay... it's probably not a good idea anyway," I said, suddenly remembering Ana Bauer and wondering how she would have taken the news of Wagner's date with another woman—even if the woman was old enough to be his mother. Perhaps it was worse that the other woman *was* old enough to be his mother!

"Listen, why don't we go and ask Reception to call Wagner's room," I suggested, putting a hand on Glenda's shoulder. "Come on."

We found Stefan behind the reception desk, busily typing on his laptop. He was so engrossed in what he was doing that he didn't even notice us as we walked up and I had to clear my throat loudly to get his attention.

He frowned. "Herr Wagner? But I saw him about twenty minutes ago. He was on his way to the music room to have a smoke... I am sure he is still there."

"Perhaps he fell asleep in one of those comfy

armchairs in there," I joked to Glenda.

She pursed her lips, not looking very amused, and thanked Stefan, then hurried down the hallway towards the music room. She had barely been gone a few minutes, however, when the air was suddenly split by a terrified scream. I took off at a run down the hall, nearly colliding with the Chinese family who rushed out of the dining room, and Johann Müller and old Mrs Hillingdon, who came hurrying out of the guest lounge, their faces filled with alarm.

"Oh my goodness, what happened?"

"Who scream? Who scream?"

"*Was ist passiert?*"

I darted around them and continued down the hall towards the music room, crashing into someone who came running out just as I was about to enter.

It was Glenda. I caught her by the arms as she teetered backwards and I saw that she was as white as a sheet, the pink blush on her cheeks standing out in stark contrast. Her eyes were wide and staring, and she was trembling.

"Glenda? Glenda, what's wrong?"

She pointed to shaking finger back towards the music room door. "It's Moritz... He's... he's dead!"

CHAPTER TEN

There were several gasps and a commotion behind us.

"Dead?" Sofia Fritzl rushed over, her face pale. "What did you say? Who is dead?"

Without waiting for an answer, she pushed past us and hurried into the music room with the other guests following at her heels. I wanted to follow too but Glenda swayed suddenly; I cried out in alarm and Stefan, who had been hurrying after the others, caught and steadied her.

"I'm... I'm all right, dear..." said Glenda breathlessly. "It's a bit upsetting, that's all."

Despite the gravity of the situation, I found myself wanting to laugh at her British talent for understatement. "*A bit upsetting*"? Glenda had almost fainted. I would hate to see what would make her really distraught!

"Perhaps you had better sit down," said Stefan distractedly as he looked towards the music room doorway. He was obviously torn between feeling obliged to stay with Glenda and wanting to follow the others to see what had happened.

As it was, the other guests didn't stay in the room long. I heard a muffled scream, followed by a commotion, then the Chows came out again, their faces grim as they hustled Mei-Mei past us. I could hear the little girl asking: "What happened, Ma-Ma? I did not see!" and her mother retorting sharply in Chinese. They were followed by Randy McGrath, his face so ashen beneath his tan that, for a moment, I wondered if he was going to faint too. A few minutes later, Johann Müller and the Hillingdons came out, escorted by Sofia, who shut the door to the music room firmly behind her. They all looked very dazed—even Jane Hillingdon was unusually subdued, saying nothing more than: "Oh my goodness... oh my goodness..." as she followed her mother out of the room. Sofia hurried over to Stefan and said something urgent in his ear. He looked stunned.

"I'll... I'll call the police," he mumbled. "And the ambulance—"

"It is too late for that, Stefan," said Sofia grimly. "You can go down to check the body if you like, but the way his neck..." She looked queasy. "He is dead."

"Glenda? Gemma? What on earth has happened?"

I felt a rush of relief at the sound of the familiar booming voice and turned to see Mabel, Florence, and Ethel emerging from the lift. Ana Bauer was with them.

"Oh Mabel..." Glenda cried in a quavering voice as she rushed towards her friend. "It's so dreadful! Moritz is dead!"

"*Grosser Gott*! Moritz dead? No! Noooo!" Ana shrieked. "*Wo ist er*? Where is he? Where is he?" she asked wildly. Then her eyes fell on the circle of people standing around the closed music room door and she rushed towards it.

"Let me see him! My beloved Moritz—I must see him!"

Sofia tried to put a placating hand on her arm. "No, Frau Bauer... I do not think it is a good idea—"

Ana shook Sofia's hand off and flung herself at the music room door again. Randy rushed forwards to intervene. The distraught woman gave a wild cry, struggling against him as he caught her arm and pulled her away from the door.

"No! No, let me see him! I do not believe you!" sobbed Ana Bauer. "He is not dead. Why will you not let me see him?"

"Because... because you don't wanna see the state he's in, okay?" cried Randy in desperation as he wrestled with her.

All of a sudden—like a balloon that had been

pricked by a pin—Ana collapsed sobbing against the American's shoulder. Randy patted her arm awkwardly and looked helplessly at Sofia but she seemed to have become paralysed, her face scared and blank. The other guests all began talking at once and agitated voices filled the hallway.

"...Did anyone call the police?"

"...I was only talking to him earlier this afternoon!"

"...Oh my God, what do you think happened..."

"...get her some brandy!"

"...am going to have nightmares—"

"...Moritz... Moritz... no, nooo..."

"A NICE CUP OF TEA—THAT'S WHAT WE ALL NEED!" Mabel declared suddenly in her booming voice.

There was a moment of stunned silence as we all gaped at her. Then, to my disbelief, everyone began to calm down. Even Ana Bauer subsided into gulping hiccups. Ridiculous as it seemed, people seemed to take strange comfort in the quintessential English suggestion that a cup of tea would be the solution to everything. Now they followed meekly as Mabel led the way back to the dining room and sat down at the long table.

Sofia disappeared and returned a few minutes later with a tray laden with a huge steaming teapot and several mugs, but she stepped back as Mabel took over to make sure that the tea was brewed to her "British standards". I winced slightly as I watched her pour out the tea at last—so dark and strong and thick with tannins that I could practically feel my tongue furring over—further fortified with a generous dollop of milk and a heaped spoonful of sugar. But to my surprise, when I finally received my cup and took a sip, I found that the sweet milky drink somehow did soothe my nerves and make me feel better. And it seemed that everyone else felt the same. As Sofia passed around a plate of vanilla *Kipferl* cookies, I saw colour begin to slowly return to people's cheeks and the hum of quiet conversation gradually fill the room.

I glanced at Glenda, who was sitting at the very end of the table with the other Old Biddies. Her mauve dress was rumpled now, her white hair limp against her head, and her lipstick smeared. I remembered how smart she had looked and how excited she had been when she had left our suite not even an hour ago, and my heart constricted. I went over and sat down near her, putting a hand on hers.

"Glenda... are you all right?"

She nodded. "I just... I keep seeing his... his body..."

"What happened?" asked Florence in bewilderment. "We heard that Herr Wagner is dead."

"Did he have an accident?" Ethel looked at me.

I shrugged. "I don't know—I didn't get a chance to go into the music room." I turned back to Glenda and said gently, "Can you tell us what happened? Did Wagner have a heart attack or something?"

Glenda shook her head. She took a deep breath and said in a rush, "Moritz wasn't in the music room when I went in... but the doors to the balcony were open... so I... I went out... and then I saw him... in the garden below..." She swallowed convulsively. "His body was twisted in a horrible fashion and his neck..." She shuddered. "He must have fallen off the balcony."

"Or he was pushed," said Mabel suddenly.

I laughed at the ludicrous suggestion. "*What?* Why would anyone push him off the balcony?"

Before Mabel could reply, Stefan returned and announced:

"The police will be here soon. We are all to remain here until they arrive."

"Ah!" Sofia sprang up "I... I must go and tidy the music room before they come."

Stefan looked at her in surprise. "Sofia, I do not think the police will be concerned about the tidiness of the room."

"Nevertheless! I do not want their first impression of the hotel to be... to be negative."

She slipped out. Glenda shifted restlessly in her chair.

"I... I wish we could go back to our room," she said. Then she looked down and gave a little gasp. "Oh! Where's my handbag?"

"Maybe you dropped it in the hallway just now.

I'll go and look," I offered, rising.

"It might be on the balcony," said Glenda. She swallowed. "I think I dropped it when I saw the bo—when I saw him."

There was no sign of the handbag in the hallway so I headed towards the music room. The door was slightly ajar and when I pushed it open and stepped in, I found Sofia crouched in front of the fireplace. She was leaning into the inner hearth, groping around with her hands, and she jumped up as she heard me come in, smacking her head on the underside of the mantlepiece in the process.

"Oh my goodness—are you all right?" I hurried over to her, wincing in sympathy.

"Yes, fine... fine..." said Sofia, sounding annoyed. She rubbed her head as she hastily moved away from the fireplace. "It was my own clumsiness."

"I'm sorry—I didn't mean to startle you."

"Oh no... no, no..." said Sofia with a nervous laugh. "You did not startle me. I was just... ah... wondering if I should start a fire... You know, the weather is turning chilly now. I am sure the police officers would appreciate a warm room when they come in." She looked at me questioningly. "Can I help you?"

"I'm looking for Glenda's handbag. She thinks she might have dropped it in here..."

I turned and scanned the room. It looked just like yesterday when I had first seen it, with the old grand piano in the far corner and two plush armchairs by the fireplace. The only sign that anyone had been in here recently was the half-drunk cup of coffee, a pen, a scrap of paper, and a hardback book lying on the side table next to one of the armchairs.

I walked across to the French doors and stepped out onto the balcony. Instantly, I spotted the bright mauve handbag against the cast-iron balustrade. I picked it up, then paused. Bracing myself, I leaned over the railing and looked down. Despite the fact that it was past twilight now, the lights from the city meant that the sky was still lit with a faint glow and the area below was further lit by powerful spotlights attached to the hotel walls.

My heart gave a jolt as I saw the body of a man. It was Wagner. He had fallen smack onto the hard stone slabs of the courtyard below. His body was twisted, as if he had been flailing his arms, and his head was tilted at a sickening angle. I looked away, feeling queasy.

It was not actually a long distance—we were only one storey up, and I wondered if he might have survived if there had been some shrubbery to break his fall—but with the hard surface of the courtyard, there was no doubt that he had broken his neck. *At least death would have come quickly*, I thought with a shiver. I hadn't really liked Wagner but this was a horrible way to die.

CHAPTER ELEVEN

I heard someone clearing their throat and glanced back to see a police officer standing in the balcony doorway, frowning at me.

"Please—can you go to the dining room and stay there, *Meine Dame*?" he said curtly.

When I returned to the dining room, I saw another officer in the uniform of the Austrian Federal Police standing by the door, and somehow the presence of an official authority suddenly made everything feel more real and grim. As I sat down next to the Old Biddies, I glanced around the room. Ana Bauer was huddled by herself at one end of the table, with her tea untouched in front of her. Jane Hillingdon and her mother sat beside Ana, with Jane trying several times to speak to the Austrian woman, but she was completely ignored. Randy

McGrath sat a little bit farther up the table; he was jiggling his leg up and down nervously and kept looking at the door, like someone wanting to bolt. Opposite him sat Johann Müller with a large glass of brandy in front of him that was definitely not "un-touched"—in fact, I suspected that it had been refilled several times already. The Austrian museum owner looked shocked and bewildered, and I remembered suddenly that Wagner had been a personal friend. Beyond him, the Chows sat in a stoic silence, and for once Mrs Chow didn't seem inclined to chastise her daughter as Mei-Mei quietly drew in her sketchpad.

The atmosphere in the room was thick with tension and it was a relief when Stefan, Sofia, and the senior police officer joined us. The latter conferred for a moment with his younger colleague by the door, then came forwards to address the guests.

"My name is Herr Inspektor Patrik Gruber," he said in heavily accented English. "I think you all know that there has been an unfortunate accident. One of the guests, Herr Moritz Wagner, is dead." He looked around the room. "I would like to ask who saw him this afternoon?"

"Well, several of us saw him..." said Sofia. "He came into the dining room with everyone else when we laid out the buffet for afternoon tea."

Johann Müller nodded. "Yes, Moritz was with me. We arrived in the dining room together."

"But he did not stay with you?"

Müller shook his head. "He told me that he wanted some peace and quiet—he said he would take his coffee to the music room. No one usually sits there."

"And did you see him again?"

"No, I decided to go to the library, in the guest lounge. That is where I usually like to sit—there is a very comfortable chair there. I took my apple strudel and my book, and I sat there... until I heard the scream."

"Yes, my mum was in there with Mr Müller— weren't you, Mum?" Jane Hillingdon piped up. "She was in the lounge, getting on with her knitting, when she heard the awful screaming... Gave her a real fright, it did! So she came rushing out to the hallway—well, not 'rush' exactly, because you can't do much 'rushing' when you're eighty-three, you know, but she got off the sofa as quick as she could—with Mr Müller's help, of course—and came out to see what all the commotion was about—"

Old Mrs Hillingdon opened her mouth to say something but Jane rambled on:

"—which was just as well because I heard the awful screaming too and thought something must have happened to Mum... I had these visions of her falling down the stairs, like you see in the movies in these grand old houses with the sweeping staircases—women are always tumbling down and breaking their necks, aren't they? ...except it wasn't

Mum who had broken her neck but that Mr Wagner—can you believe it? I must say, I didn't until I saw it for myself... oh my goodness, I'm going to be having nightmares about that for *weeks*, I can tell you... I'm terribly sensitive, you know—when my best friend Claire had her wisdom teeth out, her mouth swelled up something awful... just terrible to look at... and I had nightmares about that for days... so I hustled Mum out of the room as soon as I could because you just don't know what seeing a dead body might do to someone her age..."

Jane Hillingdon finally ran out of steam and had to stop to take a breath. Inspektor Gruber, looking slightly shell-shocked, said hastily:

"Er... yes, thank you." He cleared his throat and looked around the room. "And did anyone else speak to Herr Wagner? You, *mein Herr?*" He looked at Randy McGrath.

The American jumped. "Me? Oh no... no, no, I had nothing to do with Mr Wagner."

"You have never spoken to him?"

"No!" said Randy quickly—perhaps a shade too quickly, but the inspector didn't seem to notice. Instead, he turned his attention to the Chows and asked if they'd spoken to Wagner. As they shook their heads, Sofia glanced at Ana Bauer, who had remained silent the whole time, and said, indicating the woman:

"Er... Herr Inspektor... This is Frau Ana Bauer. She came to the hotel with Herr Wagner. They were staying together in a room."

But when Inspektor Gruber tried to speak to Ana, she simply stared at him dumbly, her eyes blank. The poor woman seemed to have gone into a catatonic state. The inspector beckoned to his younger colleague and said something low; I heard the words "*herr doktor*" and, a few minutes later, Sofia gently escorted Ana out of the room. The inspector sighed, then looked around the room. His eyes alighted on Glenda.

"*Meine Dame*, you are the person who found Herr Wagner's body? Can you tell me how it happened?"

Glenda swallowed and then, in a trembling voice, recounted what had happened. The inspector nodded and made notes in a writing pad but did not say anything. When Glenda had finished, he looked at her speculatively and said:

"So you were having dinner with Herr Wagner?"

"Y-yes," said Glenda, her cheeks reddening slightly as she glanced around the room at the other guests.

I saw Müller look startled and Jane Hillingdon give a scandalised gasp, but the inspector made no reaction. Instead, he addressed the whole room again and said, in an apologetic tone, that they would need to get individual statements from each person. My heart sank; I had been in a similar situation before when police had to question a large group of people following a sudden death and I had a bad feeling that it was going to be a long night.

"You can use the manager's office, if you like, Herr Inspektor," said Stefan. "It is behind the reception and quite secluded."

The inspector nodded and left the room. As the ambulance arrived to remove Wagner's body, we were all asked to wait in the dining room until we were called. By the time the police were satisfied and we were released to return to our rooms, it was too late to even consider going out for dinner. In any case, no one had any appetite. The Old Biddies announced that they were retiring to bed and I was left alone in the living room. I glanced at Muesli, who was pacing restlessly around the living area. I felt a bit bad that she had been cooped up in the suite most of the day and decided that I would take her out for an evening stroll before going to bed. However, a glance outside the window put paid to my plans: it was spitting with rain, and looked cold, wet, and miserable. Then I remembered Sofia's offer of the music room. It would be convenient, warm, and dry—and Muesli wouldn't even have to wear her leash and harness.

"Come on," I said to Muesli, scooping her up and letting myself out of the suite.

The police hadn't left yet; I glanced at the open door of the manager's office as we walked past and saw Inspektor Gruber at the desk going over some papers with Sofia, whilst behind the reception counter, Stefan and the younger officer talked quietly. They barely paid me any attention as I walked past, carrying Muesli in my arms, and I hurried down the hallway and around the L-bend to the music room. It was only as I was stepping in that I suddenly thought of Wagner and hesitated on the threshold. But they had removed the body now from the courtyard below and the police hadn't locked this room, so I assumed that it wasn't off limits.

In any case, I only intended to stay a few minutes. I set Muesli down and watched her scamper about. She seemed to have got a sudden burst of mad energy and was zooming around, jumping on the armchairs and bouncing off again, darting between the legs of the grand piano, scooting along the walls, scrabbling around in the fireplace...

"Hey! Don't play in there!" I said, waving my arm. "Muesli, get out of the fireplace!"

The little cat jumped out of the hearth and pounced on something I couldn't see, then did a loop of the armchair, her tail bristling with excitement. I had only intended to stay a few minutes but she was having such a great game with her invisible prey, like she sometimes did at home, that I felt bad ruining her fun. So I sat down on one of the armchairs and just let her get on with it. Finally, after several more loops of the room, Muesli calmed down at last and padded over to join me on the armchair. She jumped up and made herself comfortable on my lap, then settled down to wash. I watched her idly for a few moments, but when it looked like she was curling up for a long sleep, I got up and carried her back to the suite.

When I let myself in, I found the living area in darkness, with the lights off in both bedrooms—it looked like the Old Biddies were asleep. I tiptoed back into my alcove and glanced at my phone, which I'd left on my bedside table. There were two missed calls. They were both from Devlin. I hesitated, wondering if I should ring him back. I was still furious with him—but I was also keen to tell him what had happened to Wagner. And to be perfectly honest, I missed him and wanted to hear his voice. Still, the Old Biddies had already gone to bed and I didn't want to disturb them, if they had fallen asleep—especially poor Glenda, who really deserved a decent night's rest. *I'll call him tomorrow*, I decided.

Switching off my bedside lamp, I climbed into bed and tucked the blanket under my chin. Muesli jumped up and curled up next to me. The rhythmic sound of her purring was very soothing—and yet I found myself unable to sleep. Instead, I lay there, staring into the darkness while I thought of Wagner's untimely death. Something about the whole incident bothered me. *Well, who wouldn't be bothered if a fellow hotel guest died suddenly?* Turning over, I pushed thoughts of Wagner from my mind and drifted off to sleep.

CHAPTER TWELVE

It was strange walking into the dining room the next morning to see that it looked exactly the way it had the previous day—almost as if nothing had happened. The atmosphere, however, was very different. People talked in hushed tones as they walked around the buffet and nobody seemed to have very much appetite, despite Sofia doing her best to keep up a cheerful flow of conversation while serving tea and coffee.

As I joined the queue by the buffet, I saw Mei-Mei standing farther up the line with her parents. I caught the little girl's eye and gave her a wave. She flushed with pleasure and smiled shyly back. I glanced at her parents, wondering if this would be a good time to approach them about taking Mei-Mei to see the Lipizzaner stallions, but I still hadn't figured out a good way to broach the subject and I didn't want to blow my chance.

As I was debating what to do, I glanced across the room and caught sight of someone sitting by herself at one of the side tables. It was Ana Bauer. I was surprised; after the state she had been in yesterday, I hadn't expected her to leave her room today. She was a shadow of her former glamorous self. Her hair was tied back in a messy bun, her skin sallow, and there were dark circles under her eyes. She looked like she hadn't had any sleep, even though I knew a doctor had come last night and had probably given her some heavy sedation.

The sound of raised voices made me turn in surprise. It sounded like the Old Biddies. Abandoning my place in the line, I hurried out of the dining room and followed the source of the sound to the manager's office. There, I found Mabel, Glenda, Florence, and Ethel standing with their arms akimbo as they faced Inspektor Gruber, with Stefan and the younger police officer hovering around them.

"...assure you there is nothing suspicious about Herr Wagner's death," the inspector was saying. "It is clear that the gentleman was in a distressed state of mind and decided to take his own life."

"Suicide?" Glenda spluttered. "That's... that's ridiculous! Moritz wouldn't take his own life!"

The inspector gave her an impatient look. "There was a note on the table beside his chair, clearly stating his intentions."

A note? I cast my mind back to the music room yesterday, trying to remember if I'd seen a note on the table next to the chair. Yes, now that I thought about it, I might have seen a scrap of paper tucked under one corner of the hardback book...

"Where is this note?" Mabel asked. "Can we see it?"

The inspector stiffened at her peremptory tone. "It is police property, *Meine Dame*, and not for public viewing."

"Are you sure he wrote it?" Mabel demanded.

Inspektor Gruber looked affronted. "Yes, I am sure," he said curtly. "Rest assured, Frau Cooke, it is his handwriting. We have checked that. And the paper matches a notepad in his room. Furthermore, we have spoken to Herr Wagner's good friend, Herr Müller, and he has told us that Herr Wagner had been down in spirits lately. It may be that he was suffering from 'depression'."

"Oh nonsense!" cried Glenda. "Moritz was not depressed! Mr Müller must be wrong!"

Inspektor Gruber raised his eyebrows. "Johann Müller has been a friend of Herr Wagner for many decades. Have you known Moritz Wagner for long?"

Glenda flushed. "Well, n-no... I only met him the day before yesterday," she admitted. "But... but we spent a lot of time talking together... and I feel like I got to know him very well... He was a charming man—clever and cultured and—oh, such a flirt! He was so keen to show me around Vienna... I'm telling you, he wasn't depressed!"

"It is not always easy to see the symptoms of depression," said the inspector. "Those suffering from mental illness often hide their suffering, even from their close friends and loved ones."

He was right, and even to my ears, Glenda's protests sounded weak and silly, especially considering her brief acquaintance with the dead man.

"And now, you will please excuse me..." said the inspector. He turned to Stefan and indicated his junior officer, adding, "I must go now, Herr Dreschner, but my officer will finish organising the statements here in your office, if you will permit. I have another case that requires my attention on the other side of Vienna."

We were hustled out of the room and the door shut firmly behind us. Stefan and the inspector shook hands, then—with a slight bow to us—the inspector made his farewells and left. Glenda watched him leave and sighed loudly in frustration, but Mabel patted her hand and said:

"Never mind, dear. There are other ways to bake an apple strudel."

I looked at the Old Biddies suspiciously. "What do you mean?"

Mabel shot a wary glance at Stefan, then hustled us farther down the hallway until we were out of earshot.

"Now we can discuss the investigation," she said.

"What investigation?" I asked.

"The investigation into Wagner's murder, of course!"

I groaned. "You just heard Inspektor Gruber: it's not a suspicious death. Wagner left a suicide note. He committed suicide."

Glenda shook her head vehemently. "That can't be true, dear. Nobody loved life as much as Moritz! He was telling me of his travel plans for later in the year and the concerts and operas he was hoping to go to... He just didn't sound like someone who was planning to kill himself. Somebody murdered him!"

"Glenda..." I said gently. "I know you liked Wagner but you can't let your emotions—"

"I'm not being emotional," Glenda insisted. "It just doesn't make sense."

Florence and Ethel nodded. "Glenda is right, dear—we don't believe Herr Wagner committed suicide either."

"People don't decide to kill themselves just before they're going on a dinner date," declared Mabel.

"How do you know?" I argued. "People who are feeling suicidal don't necessarily think in a logical way. Maybe Wagner felt so depressed, he just got up and... er... decided to jump off the balcony..." I trailed off. I hated to admit it, but the Old Biddies were right: it did sound a bit ridiculous. Still, I soldiered on. "And besides... who would want to murder Wagner anyway?"

"That woman who came to the hotel with him," said Glenda instantly. "Ana Bauer."

"Ana?" I shook my head. "No, I can't believe it. She was distraught yesterday when she heard the news. You saw her—she was practically hysterical with grief!"

Mabel sniffed. "I thought her reaction was excessive, myself. There is nothing like dramatic hysterics to cover up your real feelings. No one would suspect you of being the murderer if they thought you were terribly distressed."

"I don't know... I thought she seemed genuinely upset," I said. "And anyway, even if it's true that she was exaggerating her feelings, why would she want to kill Wagner?"

"Ah... 'Hell hath no fury like a woman scorned'," Glenda quoted. "Moritz said she caused a terrible scene when he told her that their affair was over. In fact, he didn't even want her coming to the hotel with him, but she insisted. Perhaps she thought that they could have a reconciliation... and she was terribly angry when Moritz paid her no attention."

I thought back to the angry scenes I had witnessed at breakfast the day before, with Ana's sullen rage and Wagner's cold apathy towards her. It did fit what Glenda said. But still, I was sceptical of the motive. A crime of passion? Did those kinds of things really happen in real life?

Then I thought of something else. "Wait—you're forgetting about alibis," I pointed out. "Ana couldn't have killed Wagner because she was upstairs. I saw her arrive after the body had been discovered—she got out of the lift with you."

"Ah, but can we prove that she was upstairs the whole time? Is there anyone to confirm that? What if she had pushed Wagner off the balcony, slipped out of the music room, and somehow made it upstairs without being seen? Then she could simply come down in the lift and 'pretend' to hear about the death for the first time. That would explain her exaggerated reaction," said Mabel triumphantly.

"I don't know..." I frowned. "Her reaction seemed genuine to me... Did she say anything to you in the lift?"

"No..." Mabel started to say but Glenda interrupted her:

"Oh, Ana did say one thing; she was picking some crumbs off her clothes and when she saw me looking, she gave me a rueful smile and said 'apfelstrudel'—"

"That means 'apple strudel' in German," said Ethel proudly. "I read that in the Viennese cookbook I bought."

"So she was eating apple strudel in her room and dropped some crumbs on herself," I said with a shrug. "I don't think that means anything."

"What about that young American chap?" asked Florence suddenly.

"Randy?" I looked at her in surprise.

Florence nodded. "He seemed awfully nervous

yesterday after the police came. I noticed because he kept jiggling his leg and I do so hate it when people fidget."

"Yeah, I noticed that too," I admitted. "But maybe he was just shaken up. I mean, some people get like that when they encounter death."

"He does not have a motive that we know of," said Mabel thoughtfully. "Hmm... it would be worth finding out more about Mr McGrath... Perhaps we could sneak into his room—"

"What? No, no sneaking anywhere!" I said. "This a respectable hotel. We can't just go breaking into people's—"

"Of course, what we really need—" Mabel continued, completely ignoring me, "—is someone with a strong motive for wanting to get rid of Wagner. Maybe someone who was frightened of him or what he could do to them..."

I turned slightly away from the Old Biddies as an uncomfortable thought struck me. *Sofia Fritzl.* I thought of the strange way my mother's old friend had behaved in the music room yesterday. Why had she really rushed back in there? Just to light a fire for the police? And what about that conversation that I'd overheard the night I had taken Muesli out for the stroll down the side lane? It had been obvious from her bitter complaints that Sofia resented Wagner and his rude, demanding manner. But could you really kill someone just because you didn't like them criticising your hotel?

"Gemma, dear—are you all right?"

I started and came back to the present to see the Old Biddies looking at me worriedly. I realised that I had been staring into space for several minutes.

"Uh... yeah... fine. Sorry, my mind wandered for a moment." I gave them a distracted smile. "Anyway, shall we go and get some breakfast? I might have the—"

"Oh no!" cried Glenda. "I must have a look at that note first."

"The suicide note? But you heard Inspektor Gruber: it's police property now and they've probably taken it back to the station—"

"No, they haven't, dear," said Ethel. She pointed to the closed door of the manager's office. "I saw it in there just now. At least, I think I did... I didn't have my glasses, of course, but my long sight *is* very good... I saw a scrap of paper that was in a clear plastic wallet. It had handwriting on it."

"Where was it?" asked Mabel eagerly.

Ethel frowned in an effort to remember. "It was on top of the pile of guest statements... on the desk by the window."

"By the window, eh?" Mabel said, rubbing her hands. "Hmm... I wonder if one could get a view of the note looking in from outside..."

"Wait on a minute—what are you suggesting?" I asked in alarm.

Mabel looked at me innocently. "Well, dear... haven't you noticed? They are doing some repair work to the exterior of the building and there is temporary scaffolding erected alongside the wall of the hotel. I noticed it yesterday when I looked out of the guest lounge windows. In fact, there is a plank of wood which runs from outside the guest lounge window to the manager's office window. One could easily climb across—"

"That's a crazy idea!" I burst out. "You can't just climb out on scaffolding! You need to be trained, and probably wear some kind of protective harness—"

"Oh, tosh," said Mabel, waving a hand. "We're not that high up. And people have been using scaffolding for centuries before Occupational Health and Safety was invented. I'm sure a nimble young person could easily climb across." She looked at me expectantly.

"*Me?* Oh no! No way," I said firmly. "I'm not going to climb around the hotel like a monkey! What if I fall?"

"Oh, there are some nice big bushes underneath to break your fall if you do happen to lose your grip, dear. It's not as if you'd fall on hard stone like Wagner did and break your neck."

Oh. Thanks. I feel so reassured now.

"And what if the officer looked up and saw me peering in through the window?" Then I realised what I was saying and gave my head an impatient shake. "Argh! That's a moot point—I'm not climbing over there in the first place!"

Mabel acted like she hadn't heard me. Instead, she turned to Ethel and said, "Do you think you could do your fainting act again? The one that got us out of that art gallery in Oxford?"

"Oooh yes," said Ethel excitedly. "That was ever so much fun! And I think I've perfected my faint now. I might even give a little twirl as I fall down—it will look so much more graceful."

"Good, good... you can do it here, just up the hallway a bit... and then Florence, Glenda, and I will call the officer for help. That will distract him and get him out of the office. Glenda, make sure you scream nice and loud, dear. You have the shrillest voice."

Glenda nodded importantly and cleared her throat in an experimental manner.

"Now, Florence—when the officer comes out, I want you to keep a lookout and make sure that no one else goes into the office while Gemma climbs over and looks in the window—"

"*GAH!* I've *told* you—I'm *not* climbing over! I'm not doing it!" I said.

The Old Biddies looked at each other. Then Mabel gave a theatrical sigh. "Really! Young people these days have no sense of adventure. Well... Ethel, you're the smallest and lightest—you could probably—"

"*What?* No!" I said, looking with horror at Ethel's frail frame. "You can't be serious! She'd fall... no, absolutely not!" I put on a stern face and glared at the Old Biddies. "Nobody is climbing around and looking in windows—and that's final!"

CHAPTER THIRTEEN

Twenty minutes later, I found myself heaving open the sash window in the guest lounge and climbing out, grumbling under my breath. I couldn't believe I was doing this. But there was something about the Old Biddies when they got their (false) teeth into a murder investigation. It was like fighting a giant tsunami and it was almost impossible not to be swept along in their wake.

I shot a furtive glance over my shoulder to check that no one had come into the guest lounge, but all the other guests were still busy having breakfast in the dining room. Besides, I knew that the Old Biddies were hovering in the hallway outside, ready to intercept anyone who did come out of the dining room and try to get into the guest lounge.

I turned my attention back to the window. It was relatively easy to climb out and I soon found myself standing on the narrow wooden plank which ran alongside the wall of the building. I glanced down, wondering what to say if anyone saw me, but thankfully this was a quiet side street with very little traffic from people or cars. There was also a row of maple trees growing along the side of the pavement, their dense foliage effectively shielding the side of the building from the casual onlooker. In fact, a few branches were growing so close to the building that they thrust into the scaffolding and I would have to duck underneath them to walk across.

I shifted my weight on the wooden plank and swallowed nervously as I felt it move under my feet. It didn't feel particularly stable. I leaned sideways and peered down again. Mabel had been right: there was a mound of dense shrubbery growing against the side of the building, just underneath the scaffolding. It was tall, thick, and bushy, and would cushion my fall, so that I doubted I would have any injury worse than a couple of scratches or bruises. Still... I swallowed again. Falling from a second storey was not something I fancied adding to my list of life experiences.

Taking a deep breath, I began shuffling forwards along the wooden plank, keeping my feet aligned one behind the other, so that they stayed at the centre of the narrow surface. After a few moments, I had to stop and rest, panting slightly. The concentration required and the slow controlled movements were much more tiring than I'd expected. I tilted my head to see how much farther I had to go and my heart sank. The other window looked so far away! I closed my eyes for a moment, gathering my strength, then opened them and took a deep breath. But just as I was about to start moving again, I heard a familiar voice:

"*Meorrw?*"

I jerked my head up to see Muesli's little head peering out of a window above. *That must be the window in my bedroom alcove*, I realised. Muesli had taken to sitting on the windowsill so she could watch the street below. I had left the window slightly open earlier to air the room and I'd thought that the gap was narrow enough that my little cat couldn't squeeze through.

Well, it looked like I was wrong.

As I watched in horror, Muesli wriggled through the opening until she was on the outside of the window, perched precariously on the ledge.

"Muesli! What are you doing?" I gasped. "Get back in the room!"

"*Meorrw!*" said Muesli. She tilted her head and eyed me speculatively from her higher position, then she crouched slightly, as if preparing to jump.

"No!" I cried, horrified. "No, don't jump, Muesli! You'll hurt yourself! Get back in the room! Get back in the room!"

The little tabby leapt from the window ledge—straight for the maple tree towering up next to the window.

"Ohhh!" I cried, my heart pounding with a mixture of fear and relief as I saw her land safely on a thick branch.

With surprising nimbleness, Muesli climbed down the tree until she was level with me. Then she walked out along the tree branch which jutted out between the two windows and stopped just before the end, looking at me curiously.

"*Meorrw?*"

"You little minx! I thought you were going to break your neck!"

"*Meorrw!*" said Muesli, eyeing the wooden plank I was standing on.

"No, no, don't even think—" I started to say but it was too late.

With another skilful leap, Muesli jumped from the branch and landed next to me.

"*Meorrw! Meeeeorrrw!*" she said happily, butting her head against my ankles.

I wobbled and had to throw my arms out to regain my balance. "Hey, don't do that! You're pushing me off! Go away, Muesli... get back on the tree!"

She took no notice, purring loudly as she rubbed herself against my legs.

I sighed. I couldn't believe this. It was like something out of a farce. Then I glanced towards the office window and remembered that I had limited time. The Old Biddies would only be able to keep the police officer distracted for so long. Gritting my teeth, I started shuffling forwards along the plank again, trying to ignore the little cat who was tangling around my ankles. Finally, after what seemed like a hundred years, I made it to the other end with a huge sigh of relief. I peered slowly around the side of the window frame, wanting to check if the room was empty. Muesli trotted up to the window and peered in.

"*Meorrw?*"

"Shh!" I hissed, making frantic hand motions. "Muesli! Get away from there!"

She ignored me and I darted a fearful look into the window. My heart gave a jerk as I saw the police officer through the glass. He was sitting at the desk by the window, but thankfully he was facing into the room, with his back to us. He had his head down, busily typing into a laptop, and on the desk next to him were a pile of papers. On the very top of the pile was a clear plastic wallet, just as Ethel had described, with a scrap of paper inside. That had to be the suicide note. But—my heart sank—there was no way I could read the badly scrawled handwriting from this distance. Even if I pressed my nose against the glass, I still wouldn't be close enough.

Then my spirits lifted as I looked at the window again. It was an old-fashioned sash window and the bottom section was slightly raised so that there was a gap of around two inches—probably to let some fresh air into the otherwise small, stuffy office. I could easily hoist the window up farther, so that there would be a gap wide enough for me to climb into the room and get a closer look at the note, if the officer could just go out for a moment...

Even as I had the thought, there came an ear-piercing scream from deeper within the building and the young police officer sprang up from his chair. I heard a muffled exclamation in German, then he rushed from the room, leaving the door slightly ajar. I smiled to myself. It looked like the Old Biddies had done their part.

Quickly, I gripped the window frame and heaved, trying to raise it. The wood was old and stiff and refused to budge. I cursed under my breath and tried again, yanking upwards as hard as I could. It shot up suddenly several inches with an awful screech that made Muesli jump and hiss. I froze, looking fearfully towards the door of the office, but no one came rushing back in. In fact, I could hear the faint sounds of a commotion outside, farther down the hallway. It sounded like the Old Biddies were doing a good job of keeping everyone distracted.

Relaxing slightly, I started climbing through the gap. It wasn't the easiest thing, since I had to go head and shoulders first, and then wriggle the rest of the way through. As I was hanging half in, half out of the window, I suddenly felt a furry body squirming next to me and, the next moment, Muesli pushed through the gap and landed inside the office.

"Muesli!" I hissed, horrified. "What are you doing? Come back here!"

"*Meorrw,*" she said, with a defiant twitch of her whiskers. She looked inquisitively around the room, then jumped up onto the desk.

"Muesli!" I cried, infuriated. "Get off the desk!"

She ignored me, stepping daintily over various papers, pens, and other stationery until she reached the other side of the laptop. There was a small silver tray placed on the desk there, holding the usual trio of coffee, teaspoon, and glass of water. The coffee was a *Melange*—a Viennese speciality made of espresso mixed with steamed milk and topped off with milk froth. Muesli bent her head towards the milk froth and began licking it enthusiastically.

"Aarrghh! Muesli, don't do that!" I groaned.

I scrambled through the gap and landed on the floor with a thump. Hastily, I stood up and brushed myself off, then turned towards my cat. But she had jumped off the desk and was now strolling around the room. I made a move to chase her, then stopped, reminding myself that I didn't have time to play games. I had to see the note before the officer returned.

Turning back to the desk, I grabbed the plastic wallet. I was surprised to see how small the scrap of paper was—no more than a torn corner, really—and there were only a few words scrawled across it:

I couldn't take it anymore. I had suffered enough and I had to leave. I might be forgiven for

I frowned. Admittedly, I had never seen a suicide note in my life—except for those in books and movies—but there seemed to be something strange about the note. Well, there wasn't time to ponder it now. I whipped my phone out of my pocket and hurriedly snapped a picture of the note, before replacing it on the desk. Then I turned back to look for Muesli. The little minx had jumped up onto one of the filing cabinets in the far corner of the room and had made herself comfortable on a pile of old newspapers stacked there.

"Come on, Muesli—time to go," I whispered, starting across the room towards her.

But I was barely halfway across when I heard the sound of footsteps approaching the door. *Cripes!* Was it the officer coming back?

I looked wildly around. There was no time to get to the window and wriggle out through the gap. The only option was to hide. But where? The room was organised with typical German efficiency and there was nothing large I could hide behind. Then I spotted it: an old-fashioned wooden hat stand in the corner of the room, bulging with coats, hats, bags, raincoats, scarves, umbrellas... It would never pass muster if anyone was really scanning the room, but if they were just walking past without really looking...

I darted across and shoved myself into the corner, into the gap between the hat stand and the wall, and pulled the voluminous coats and scarves in front and around me. Then I held my breath, listening.

The footsteps had slowed and paused outside the door. Puzzled, I leaned slowly sideways so that I could peek around the sleeve of a large wool overcoat. To my surprise, it was not the young police officer that I saw—it was Randy McGrath!

What was *he* doing here? As I watched, he hesitated on the threshold, throwing a glance over his shoulder, as if checking that no one was watching. Then he slipped into the room and hurried across to the desk. There, he began rifling through the papers, muttering under his breath. He was obviously searching for something—and equally obviously, it seemed that he couldn't find it, as he swore several times in frustration.

Then I heard the sound of footsteps again. This time they were brisk and purposeful—the sound of someone who had business in the room. The officer was coming back.

Randy swore again and ran back towards the door, getting there just as the officer stepped in.

"*He!*" the Austrian cried in surprise. He frowned. "*Was machen sie hier?* What are you doing here?"

"Oh... er... I was just looking for you... I... uh... I wanna make sure you got my name spelled right on my statement," Randy said, plastering a smile on his face. "It's a small 'c', you know, after the 'M' in 'McGrath'."

"Your name is correct in the reports," said the officer stiffly.

"Oh, cool... Well, you have a nice day!" Randy gave him another breezy smile and quickly slipped out the door.

The officer watched him go in puzzlement, then turned back to the room. His gaze fell on the desk, with the disturbed piles of paper, then to the half-open window, and his eyes narrowed. He frowned, turning to scan the room. I stiffened as his gaze travelled towards the corner where the hat stand stood. Would he see me? My heart was pounding and I could hear the blood rushing in my ears.

The officer took a step towards me—

"*MEEEEORRW!*"

He jumped and cried out in surprise as a bundle of grey tabby fur sprang off the top of the filing cabinet and landed on the floor next to his feet.

"*Heilige Scheisse! Es ist eine Katze!*" he said, clutching his chest. He waved his hand and made a shooing noise at Muesli. "Shh-shh-t! Go! Go!"

"*Meorrw?*" said Muesli, looking up at him innocently with her big green eyes.

The officer looked befuddled. He hesitated, then bent down and gingerly picked up the little cat.

"*Meorrw...*" said Muesli, nuzzling against him in a coquettish manner. I swear, she almost batted her eyelashes at him.

The officer stared at her in bewilderment, then looked around helplessly. Finally he turned and left the room, carrying Muesli in his arms. As soon as he was out the door, I pushed my way out from behind the heavy coats and scarves, panting with relief. Glancing towards the window, I hesitated: I had to get out before he returned—I didn't think saying that *I* had also come to check the spelling of *my* name would go down very well— but the last thing I felt like doing was climbing back out onto that scaffolding again.

I hurried to the door and peered out into the hallway. There was still a small group of people— the Chows, Johann Müller, and Stefan Dreschner— gathered at the far end, talking amongst themselves. The Old Biddies, though, were nowhere in sight. The officer was wandering along the corridor, looking slightly at a loss, with Muesli cradled in his arms like a baby. The little cat had a smug expression on her face and was obviously enjoying the ride. I had to stifle a laugh. I might have been mad at Muesli earlier for her mischievous antics, but I had to concede that she had just saved my skin. If it hadn't been for her timely interruption, the officer would definitely have found me.

I slipped out of the office and turned in the opposite direction—and collided with the Old Biddies.

"Ahh!" I yelped, clutching my chest like the officer had done.

"Well? Did you see it?" Mabel demanded.

I drew a breath. "Yes... I saw the note."

"What did it say?"

For an answer, I pulled my phone out of my pocket and showed them the picture I'd taken. The Old Biddies crowded around me to peer at the screen. I saw Glenda's face fall in disappointment.

"It does seem like Wagner wasn't in a good frame of mind," I said gently to Glenda. "You know, maybe he really did take his own life."

Glenda shook her head vehemently. "No! I don't care what this note says. I just don't believe Moritz could have committed suicide. He was murdered!"

"Well, I think you're reading too much into things and letting your imagination run away with you," I said irritably.

I was starting to lose patience. I had missed my breakfast and had just spent the last hour alternately being terrified that I was going to fall and break my neck or terrified I was going to be arrested by the police. I was hungry, tired, and thoroughly fed up—and in no mood for more of the Old Biddies' wild theories.

"Look, Wagner's death has been investigated by the Austrian police and they're satisfied that it's suicide. So you have to accept that, okay?" I took a deep breath. "Come on, let's go and do some sightseeing."

CHAPTER FOURTEEN

By the time I rescued the young police officer from Muesli's clutches, returned her to our room (now with the window safely locked), grabbed some breakfast and then finally hustled the Old Biddies out of the hotel, it was late morning and I was worn out. Still, I grabbed a tourist map of Vienna and marched determinedly to the nearest bus stop with Mabel and the others in tow. I could see that the Old Biddies would really rather have stayed at the hotel (and done some more snooping!) but I hoped that a day of sightseeing would distract them from thinking about Wagner's death.

We took the bus to the Belvedere Palace, once the summer residence of Prince Eugene of Savoy and now a world-famous museum housing the greatest collection of Austrian art, including works from perhaps the most famous Viennese painter of all: Gustav Klimt. I was a fan of Klimt, especially the paintings from his "Golden Phase" when he made liberal use of gold leaf in his paintings, and I was looking forward to seeing *The Kiss* at last. The Old Biddies, however, didn't seem to share my enthusiasm and they soon lagged behind, leaving me to wander through the galleries alone.

As I was climbing up the grand central staircase to the upper galleries, I heard a voice behind me call out my name. I nearly groaned out loud as I turned around to see Jane Hillingdon and her mother.

"Gemma! Fancy meeting you here!" said Jane, beaming. "You know, I said to Mum: 'I wonder if we'll meet anyone from the hotel', but I wasn't expecting to, really... Not that Vienna is *that* big and all the tourists *do* go to the same sights, of course... although it's not a small city either and some of these museums are so big that you could get lost in them for *days!* But I just had to get out of the hotel, you know—oh, I'm sure I had nightmares all night, thinking about that poor man... Suicide! Can you believe it?"

I sighed. So much for trying to forget about Wagner's death.

Jane rambled on: "And what a horrible way to kill yourself—jumping off a balcony like that... it's not even very high—I mean, what if you didn't die and were left paralysed or something? If I was going to do it, I'd go for something more... well, more 'guaranteed', dontcha think?" She looked at me expectantly.

"Er... yes, well, I suppose people who are feeling suicidal aren't in a very logical frame of mind," I said lamely. I felt like I was repeating this excuse over and over.

"I wouldn't have thought he was the suicidal type at all! No, you could have knocked me over with a feather when the police said suicide... I tell you, I would have been less surprised if they'd said he was murdered... A real Casanova type, that Mr Wagner was—I bet he's always having lots of affairs and things—and there'd be some jealous husband wanting to do him in... like that creepy pharmacist, you know, in *Desperate Housewives*, who tried to kill Bree's husband after he had an affair with her—well, that's the reverse, actually, but you know what I mean... and I would have thought there'd be loads of jealous husbands wanting to push Mr Wagner off the balcony... That's what I told Mum—didn't I, Mum?"

Old Mrs Hillingdon opened her mouth but never got a chance to say anything before Jane rushed on.

"But I just don't know how anyone could have done it! How would they have got into that music room without anyone seeing them? I was standing in the lobby by the brochures and I'm sure I would have seen someone go in—"

"Were you watching the hallway the whole time, though?" I asked, intrigued in spite of myself.

I remembered that the hallway bent in an L-shape, with the lobby at the top of the "L", followed by the guest lounge and the dining room on either side of the main "trunk" and then finally the music room situated around the bend of the "L". So if Jane Hillingdon had been standing in the lobby, she would have been able to see down the hallway as far as the bend, but not the actual doorway of the music room. Still, since the music room was the only room beyond the bend, anyone turning that corner had to have been going there.

"Well, no, I was looking at the brochures," Jane admitted. "And then that American chap came out of the lift and I asked him to tell me which museums he thought were the best to visit—seeing as he's been to Vienna before, you know, and they say there's nothing like asking a local... not that he's a local, of course, but then maybe that's just as well because then he'd know better what a tourist might like... and he's so easy to talk to, dontcha think? I'm surprised he's here alone—you would've thought a good-looking fella like him would have a girl... maybe he's got a girlfriend back in the States—though he never mentioned anyone, just kept talking about his horses... He seems kind of lonely, if you ask me... he's an only child, you know, and both his parents are dead now, isn't that tragic? And his mum not that long ago too—poor woman had breast cancer, he said—not that I was prying, of course—but you know, when you get chatting, it's nice to get to know the other person... and he's so easy to talk to, *such* a nice smile—don't Americans always have great teeth?"

She finally paused to draw breath and I jumped in quickly.

"So Randy was with you the whole time?"

"Let me see now... I helped Mum get some tea and cake from the dining room—well, actually she had a slice of apple strudel; it did look delicious and that nice Mr Müller recommended it to us—and then I took Mum to the lounge and left her knitting there because I wanted to go and see the brochures myself and anyway Mr Müller was having his strudel in the lounge too, so she wasn't alone—not that Mum minds being alone for a bit, do you, Mum? But I do worry, you know, at her age, and I don't like to leave her alone for too long—"

I glanced at old Mrs Hillingdon, who looked like she would have loved to have been left alone for several days, especially by her garrulous daughter.

"—and so I nipped out into the lobby really quick to have a look at those brochures and I was just wondering whether to do the 'Vienna All-In-One' tour or the 'Best of Vienna' tour when Randy came out of the lift... So I wasn't standing there all that long before he arrived... must have been... let me see... around five minutes? Maybe seven minutes? Not that I was really watching the time, of course—"

"And did you see Ana Bauer anywhere?"

"No, didn't see her at all, not even in the dining

room for tea... not that she ever says much—bit of a snob, dontcha think? And I told Mum—"

"And what about..." I hesitated, then said, "What about Sofia?"

"Sofia?" Jane looked at me blankly for a moment. "Oh—Sofia who runs the hotel! No, I didn't see her—wait, actually, I did see her earlier—she was laying out things on the sideboard for the afternoon tea buffet, and she asked how my day went and I started to tell her, but then she suddenly had to hurry away—something about forgetting the apple strudel in the kitchen, I think—and I didn't see her again after that." She peered at me curiously. "Why are you asking about *her*?"

"No reason," I said. Hurriedly I changed the subject. "Um... so have you seen *The Kiss* yet?"

"Oh no, we were just on our way up to the Klimt gallery. Shall we go together?" asked Jane happily.

"Er..." The last thing I wanted was to tour the Belvedere with Jane Hillingdon as a companion, but I couldn't think of any way to extricate myself now without coming across as rude. "Um... sure."

We climbed the rest of the steps up the staircase and wandered into the gallery hosting Klimt's paintings. As the highlight of the collection, *The Kiss* had a wall to itself and I joined the crowd of people gathered beneath the large square canvas. Unlike the *Mona Lisa,* which tended to be a bit of an anti-climax when viewed in real life, Gustav Klimt's most famous work was just as impressive when viewed in person. The canvas depicted a couple embracing in the centre, with billowing colourful robes surrounding them. Their faces and arms were painted in a delicate, realistic style but their robes and the rest of the painting dissolved into a shimmering mosaic pattern, filled with geometric and floral shapes, and exotic colours, all overlaid with layers of gold leaf. The mix of realism and surrealism was fascinating, and the painting had an opulent and sensuous feel that added to its appeal.

"You know people used to accuse Klimt of pornography—that's what it says in my guidebook," said Jane, coming to stand next to me and looking up at the painting. She tilted her head. "Don't know why, really, seeing as the couple aren't up to any hanky-panky... not as compared to some of the things you see on the telly these days! He looks like he's just kissing her, doesn't he? Shame he's dead— Klimt, I mean, not the man—would've been nice for him to see how famous his painting's become... And he'd be a rich man too if he still owned it—it must be worth millions, dontcha think? I read that one of his other paintings sold for four-hundred and thirty-five million dollars."

I turned to gape at Jane. "Four-hundred and thirty-five million dollars? How can something ever be worth that much?"

Jane giggled. "Wish I could paint something worth four-hundred and thirty-five million dollars... not that I'd have much chance of that—can't even draw stick men, me... but some people are just born with the talent, aren't they? Like that little girl at the hotel—have you seen her drawings? They're terrific, dontcha think? My best friend Claire told me that some people are so good, they can even copy one of the masters and you can't tell the difference... she showed me this article in the papers which said fifty percent of artwork sold on the market could be fake!"

Jane nodded emphatically as she saw my sceptical look. "Oh yes, fifty percent, it said. That's like half of the stuff selling in art galleries could be forgeries—can you believe it?"

"But... how can people not realise?" I asked. "Surely they must have experts who can spot a forgery—"

"Ah, but these forgers are ever so clever—they know all the tricks, that's what this article said... like painting over a genuine old painting that they find in a car boot sale, so that the canvas would look old from the back—"

"Provenance," said old Mrs Hillingdon suddenly.

I was so shocked to hear her speak that I turned to stare at her for a full minute. Her voice was hoarse and croaky, as if it hadn't been used for a long time.

"Oh yes, that's right—'provenance'—that's the most important thing," said Jane. "That's like the painting's record. If you have good provenance, nobody will ask any questions because they'll think it's all been checked by art experts already. Even big auction houses like Sotheby's can be totally fooled and some art galleries are just selling fake—"

"SHHH!" The couple next to us suddenly turned around and scowled at Jane.

"Can you shut up?" the wife snapped. "Some of us are trying to enjoy the paintings here!"

Jane flushed bright red and spluttered incoherently. I felt a bit sorry for her, although I did think she deserved the reprimand. I also realised that the interruption gave me an opening that was too good to miss. Quickly, I excused myself, saying that I needed to go and look for the Old Biddies. With a last regretful look at the Klimt painting, I made my escape.

CHAPTER FIFTEEN

I found the Old Biddies sitting together on a long bench in the main hall of the Belvedere, next to one of the Atlas pillars that supported the vaulted ceiling. They were busily comparing their purchases of art postcards, fridge magnets, and coasters, and I wondered if they'd spent most of their visit in the museum shop!

We took a bus back to the Innere Stadt and picked up a late lunch from a *Würstelstand* kiosk— a traditional Viennese hotdog stand offering a bewildering variety of sausages, each about a foot long and served in a soft baguette, accompanied by lashings of mustard, ketchup, and tangy gherkins. By the time we walked back to Sofia's hotel, we had just managed to finish eating the enormous hotdogs and were still licking ketchup from our fingers as we walked into the foyer.

I was surprised to find the lobby a hive of activity, with several strange men milling about, carrying video cameras and sound equipment. Curious, I wandered over to the reception desk while the Old Biddies went up to our suite. I found Stefan behind the desk, looking a bit flustered. When I asked what was happening, he explained that with Moritz Wagner being a bit of a local celebrity, several media networks had sent reporters to the hotel to get the scoop on his sudden death.

"Sofia is with a journalist now, actually," he said.

As if on cue, the door to the manager's office opened and Sofia stepped out, looking more glamorous than I'd ever seen her. Although she was wearing a sombre black dress, her hair was beautifully coiffed and her make-up gleaming. She was followed by a thin man with a wispy beard who was carrying a laptop and wearing a lanyard with ID around his neck. He paused to shake her hand and said with an American accent:

"Thanks for speaking to me, Ms Fritzl."

"Not at all," said Sofia, her smile just the right mixture of fortitude and sorrow. "It is such a tragic thing to happen—I had no idea that Herr Wagner was so disturbed in his mind... especially as he seemed to be enjoying his stay at the hotel so much."

I blinked at the blatant lie, but Sofia continued smoothly:

"In fact, he was just telling me yesterday morning that he would be recommending my hotel highly in his column. Since he is no longer able to fulfil his intentions, I hope you might be able to carry out his wishes in your article..." she said with a meaningful look.

"Oh sure—I'll definitely give it a mention."

Sofia gave him a gracious smile. "Thank you." Then she turned to another man standing nearby and said, "I am sorry to keep you waiting! Please, come in..." —and disappeared back into the office with another journalist.

I watched the door close behind them with troubled eyes. Wagner's death certainly seemed to be benefiting the owner of *Hotel das Herzchen*: not only was she no longer worried about a negative review from an influential public figure, but she seemed to be gaining some free publicity into the bargain! And she was obviously not abashed about taking advantage of the situation.

The question was: was she *just* taking advantage of a serendipitous situation? Or could she have played an active part in "creating" the situation?

I shied away from the thought. The idea that my mother's old school friend could be a murderer was horrifying and I was ashamed to have even considered it. Quickly, I headed for the lift and went upstairs. As I came out of the lift, I nearly collided with a small figure darting across the landing. It was Mei-Mei. The little girl was giggling, sounding happier and more carefree than I'd ever heard her, as she chased a bundle of grey tabby fur around the landing. Muesli had obviously slipped out of our suite when the Old Biddies had returned and was now having a great game of chase with her new friend.

"*Meorrw!*" said Muesli cheekily, pausing just long enough to let the little girl almost reach her, then scampering off again.

Mei-Mei gave a wild squeal of laughter and darted after my cat. At the same moment, the door to the suite opposite ours flew open and Mrs Chow appeared on the threshold.

"Mei-Mei!" she cried. "What you doing?"

"Oh! Ma-Ma..." The little girl faltered to a stop.

Mrs Chow's gaze fell on Muesli and she cried in alarm, "*Ayah!* Dirty cat again! You touch? You touch?"

"N-no..." said her daughter, thrusting her hands guiltily behind her back.

"*Meorrw?*" said Muesli, trotting up to the Chinese woman.

"Aaahhh! Go! Go away!" screeched Mrs Chow, flapping her hand at Muesli.

The little tabby looked at her quizzically and went closer, arching her back as she rubbed herself against the woman's ankles.

"AAAHHH! NO! NO!" the woman screamed, hopping around on one foot and flailing her arms in a panic. It would have been almost comical if it hadn't been obvious that she was really terrified.

I hurried to intervene, bending down to scoop up my cat and stepping away from the Chinese woman.

"It's all right," I said. "She won't bite."

Mrs Chow calmed down slightly. Then she gave Muesli a worried look. "All animal very dirty... Bacteria... Disease!"

"No, no, Muesli is very clean," I protested. "She's vaccinated and she doesn't have any worms or fleas. I bathe and groom her regularly—honestly, she doesn't carry any disease."

The woman didn't look convinced. Instead, she edged a bit farther away from me and Muesli, and reached out to grab her daughter's arm, pulling the little girl back towards their suite door. She fussed over the girl, checking her over as if to reassure herself that Mei-Mei hadn't been infected with some deadly parasite.

"They were just playing," I ventured.

Mrs Chow sniffed. "Mei-Mei is good girl; need to study."

"She can study and still enjoy time with a pet," I tried to explain. "In fact, research shows that children with pets develop better communication skills and have higher self-esteem and get sick less often—"

"Mei-Mei no need pet," said Mrs Chow coldly. "No waste time with animals. She not going to be farmer! She going to be lawyer, work in high-class office." She turned to her daughter and said something in Chinese which sent the little girl scurrying inside. Then the Chinese woman gave me a polite nod and retreated into her suite.

I stared at the closed door in frustration, unable to believe the woman's attitude and feeling sorry for her daughter. Then I reminded myself that it was really none of my business and, with a sigh, I returned to my own suite.

CHAPTER SIXTEEN

I found the Old Biddies in the living room, their feet propped up on various cushions and ottomans, as they enjoyed their obligatory cup of "afternoon tea". Putting Muesli down next to them, I wandered into my alcove to take off my own shoes. My phone rang. I glanced at the screen: it was Devlin. I remembered belatedly that I had been planning to call him today. We hadn't really spoken properly since our fight that night in the restaurant, although I'd sent him a couple of curt texts to inform him of my travel plans, and now I answered the call with a cool hello that would have unnerved a lesser man.

"Still mad at me?" Devlin asked with a laugh in his voice.

"Yes," I said shortly. "I don't think I'll ever forgive

you."

"Aww, come on, Gemma... I don't know how else to say I'm sorry. I'll do anything to make it up to you."

I was struck by an idea. "Anything?" I asked.

"Well, within reason," said Devlin, suddenly wary. "I'm not watching a rom com or doing anything that involves going to a garden centre with your mother."

"Oh no, this will be easy: all I want is information."

"Information? About what?"

I told Devlin everything that had happened since we arrived in Vienna. Well, everything except the Old Biddies' crazy plan and my little jaunt on the scaffolding. Somehow, I didn't think Devlin would appreciate the importance of risking a broken neck to peek at the suicide note in the police files. And I was right to be cautious—he was disapproving enough already when he heard about our interest in the case.

"Gemma..." he said in a warning voice. "You're not letting the Old Biddies drag you into meddling in a police investigation again?"

"But you have to admit, they have a point," I said. "There are lots of things that don't add up about Wagner's death. I mean, people commit suicide in the privacy of their bedrooms, not in a public hotel lounge—and not just before they're due to meet someone for dinner! Plus, Jane Hillingdon might talk a lot of nonsense but she's right about one thing: it does seem like a strange suicide method to choose. Most people take pills or something, but if they decide to jump, they tend to pick the top of a tall building or a bridge. The second storey of this hotel isn't that high—you could be really unlucky and end up with broken limbs or half-paralysed instead. If he really wanted to commit suicide, why didn't Wagner go to the top of the hotel and jump from there?"

"Gemma—"

"And there's more: the police are not treating the death as suspicious because Wagner left a suicide note on the table next to where he was sitting. But the thing is, we... er... managed to see the suicide note and there's something odd about the words—"

"How did you 'manage' to see the note?" asked Devlin suspiciously.

Bugger. I should have known that Devlin would be too sharp.

"Oh, it was just... er... lying around in the manager's office and I happened to see it," I said casually. Then, before he could ask for more details, I rushed on, "Anyway, the point is, the message sounded so strange. I mean, it *could* be a suicide note, I guess, but it just sounded a bit... I don't know... odd..."

"What did it say?"

"Um... something like: he couldn't take it anymore... he had suffered enough and he had to leave. Then he ended with 'I might be forgiven for', which seems like a weird sign-off." I paused, then added thoughtfully, "I've been thinking about it and I realised one reason why it's been bothering me. It's in the past tense... but most suicide notes are in the present tense."

"Hmm..." Devlin didn't sound impressed. "It *is* a bit unusual... but it could just be a personal writing style. You say he was Austrian? Perhaps with English not being his first language—"

"Oh no, Wagner's English was completely fluent. As good as you or me. He wrote columns for international newspapers and websites."

"It's still too weak a reason to suspect foul play. Did the police check the handwriting?"

"Yes, it's Wagner's writing."

"Then it sounds like the Austrian police are doing what's necessary. I would stop interfering and just let them get on with their job—"

"But they're *not* getting on with it. I mean, they've pretty much closed the case! The inspector seems to have accepted the suicide verdict and is moving on."

"Well, perhaps you should move on too—"

"I just want to make absolutely sure, Devlin," I pleaded. "You realise that if Wagner was murdered, that means the killer is likely to be a guest at the hotel? There was no opportunity for anyone to come from outside—there were too many people about; any stranger in the hotel would have been noticed.

So that means there's potentially a murderer here, loose, amongst us. And there's a family with a little girl staying in the hotel. What if the killer were to strike again? When we could have done something?"

"The thing to do is to go to the Austrian police with your suspicions."

"But they'd be more likely to listen to me if I had more to show them! Please, Devlin—I just want to find out a bit more about a couple of the other guests."

There was a pause, then Devlin said, "Even if I were to agree—which I'm not saying I would—unless these other guests are British nationals, I wouldn't be able to get very much information about them."

"I thought you had a great friend at Interpol," I said. "I'm sure they could get some background information for you if you asked. Isn't that what you did in the past when you had suspects who weren't British?"

Devlin sighed. "Who are the people you want to check out?"

"There's an Austrian woman called Ana Bauer. I don't know much about her, other than the fact that she's Wagner's mistress. Ex-mistress, actually, since apparently he broke up with her just before they came to stay at the hotel. She insisted on coming with him anyway—I think she was hoping for a reconciliation—and I saw them having a row the morning of the day he was killed. He was quite nasty to her and she was clearly furious."

"Where was she when Wagner's body was discovered?"

"She was upstairs—she didn't join us until after the body was discovered. She was really distraught, actually, when she heard. Broke down in hysterics and had to be physically restrained."

"If she was so upset about Wagner's death, why do you think she murdered him?"

"Well, I suppose it could be a 'crime of passion' kind of thing. You know, because he'd just dumped her and she was bitter about it... and Mabel thinks that her reaction was so extreme, it might have been an act."

"Hmm... Mabel Cooke thinks a lot of things," said Devlin dryly.

I ignored that and hurried on. "The other person is an American called Randy McGrath. He's a guest here. He's involved in horses—like, he breeds them and trains them. He told me he has a ranch back in the U.S. He's obsessed with the Lipizzaner stallions—he seems to know everything there is to know about them."

"What's his connection with Wagner?"

"None. At least, so he says. He told the police that he had never even spoken to Wagner. But I think he's hiding something. He was acting really twitchy when the police were here and then I saw him—" I broke off.

I was about to tell Devlin about Randy's furtive search in the manager's office but I realised that there was no way I could do that without also implicating myself and admitting that I had been illicitly snooping in there too.

"Yes?"

"Er... I saw him... um... jiggling his leg a lot," I stammered.

"That's hardly a sign of guilt," said Devlin impatiently.

"Yes, but... there *is* something a bit fishy about him. I just would like to find out a bit more about his background. Please?"

"All right," Devlin said with a sigh. "I'll see what I can do. But that means I want you and the Old Biddies to stop doing any more 'investigating' of your own, do you understand? Remember, you're not in England now and this isn't Oxford CID; if you get in trouble with the Austrian authorities, I can't help you."

"Okay," I said meekly. "And thank you *so* much, Devlin!"

"I'm not promising anything," he warned me. "But I'll do my best." He paused, then added in a different voice, "It's quite lonely in Oxford without you."

I smiled in spite of myself and said nonchalantly, "Yeah... I might have missed you a bit too."

A few minutes later, I hung up with a silly grin on my face and decided that maybe I could forgive

Devlin after all. I was about to toss the phone on my bedside table when it startled me by issuing a high-pitched beeping noise. I looked down and did a double take as I realised that it was a FaceTime call... from my *mother.*

As far as I knew, my mother had barely mastered the art of dialling a "Contact" on her phone (as opposed to laboriously tapping in a number from her ancient phonebook which she still carried everywhere in her handbag) so I couldn't quite believe that she had graduated to video communications. Still, I hurried to answer the call... and found myself looking at the ceiling of my parent's sitting room.

"Darling!" my mother's voice came out of the phone, echoing strangely. "Isn't this marvellous? Helen Green has just shown me how to use FaceCall on the iPad and now we can see each other when we're talking!"

"Er... yes, except I can't see you, Mother—all I can see is your ceiling. You need to hold the iPad up."

"Darling, can you hear me?"

"Yes, Mother, I can hear you fine but I can't see you—"

"Hello? Can you hear me? *Oh, sugar! Helen, I don't think this is working...*"

"Mother! I can hear you fine!" I shouted. "You just need to lift the iPad up so I can see you as well!"

"Oh! She's come back, Helen—I wonder if it wasn't working the first time..." My mother cleared her throat and said brightly, "Hello, darling! Isn't this marvellous? Helen Green has just shown me how to use FaceCall on the iPad and now we can see each other when we're talking!"

I sighed. "Yes, Mother—I heard you the first time. We're still on the call. And it's not called 'FaceCall'—it's called 'FaceTime'. But listen, you need to hold the iPad up—hold it vertically and raise it up, to the level of your face."

"Ah!" The screen went blurry for a moment as the sound of fumbling came over the speaker, then a hugely magnified image of my mother's ear came on the screen. "Is that better, darling? Can you see me now?"

"No, no, Mother—don't hold it to your ear like a phone. Hold it up in front of your face—like a mirror."

More fumbling and the screen tilted crazily, almost giving me vertigo, then suddenly I was staring at a view of my mother's forehead, plus a large portion of the sitting room wall.

"Can you see me now, darling?"

"Um... yes, sort of, but can you just lower the— oh, never mind. Yes, you look great, Mother," I lied.

"Oh, it's this lovely new silk blouse I bought from M&S yesterday. I was worried that coral might be a bit bright but it is such a nice shade... shall I get one for you too, darling?"

"No, thanks, Mother," I said hastily.

"Well, it's not coral exactly—more of a bright orange, really..."

Ugh. This blouse was sounding worse by the minute. "I really don't need a blouse, Mother, in any colour, but thanks for asking. So, um... how're things back in Oxford?"

"Oh, yes—that's the reason I was ringing. I found an Elizabeth Arden compact in the guest bedroom which Sofia must have left behind when she came to stay. Will you ask her if she'd like me to post it to her?"

"Um... sure." I hesitated, then said, "Actually, Mother...speaking of Sofia... I was wondering if she ever got in trouble when you were at school together?"

"In trouble?" My mother sounded confused. "What do you mean?" Then she gasped and said in a scandalised tone, "Gemma Rose! I cannot believe you asked that question! A girl from a 'good family' like Sofia would never engage in pre-marital relations and fall pregnant—"

"No, no, that's not what I meant. I mean—did she ever do anything 'wrong', you know, like break school rules or something like that?"

"Oh no, Sofia was one of the most disciplined, well-behaved, and hard-working girls at school. In fact, she was so concerned with being the 'perfect pupil' that she would work herself into quite a state, poor thing, if she didn't always come top of the class."

"And if anyone prevented her from coming top, would she... um... you know, would she ever do something to them?"

"Whatever do you mean, darling? Why would anyone prevent Sofia from coming top of the class?"

"Just suppose, Mother," I said impatiently. "Would Sofia ever do something to someone who was standing in the way of her achieving what she wanted?"

"I don't understand—what would she do?"

"Well, like... bully them...? Or be nasty to them...?" *Or murder them*—I bit my tongue on the words.

"Certainly not!" said my mother. "Darling, why are you asking this?"

"Oh... er... no particular reason. Just curious."

"Well! I do think it's very ungracious of you to be wondering such things about your hostess," said my mother severely. "I hope you haven't been asking Sofia any questions like this."

"No, no, of course not," I said, her reprimand making me feel slightly ashamed. It was true—it did seem wrong to think of Sofia this way when she had been so generous and welcoming.

My mother's forehead disappeared from the screen and I heard the murmur of conversation, then it reappeared again and my mother said:

"Oh, darling! Helen just told me that they do the blouse in turquoise too. Such a *lovely* colour. I'll get that for you, shall I? And it will go beautifully with the beige culottes I bought for you from Jaeger."

"No, Mother, I don't want it in turquoi—what culottes?" I demanded. "I'm not wearing any culottes!"

"Now, don't be silly, darling—the lady in the store said they're the height of fashion. Anyway, I must dash. Helen is driving us to the Philips Pasta Maker demonstration at Debenhams. It sounds simply *marvellous*! Seven pasta shapes and automatic extrusion. Shall I get you one too?"

"NO!" I shouted. I took a deep breath. "No, no, thanks, Mother. I think the... er... turquoise blouse and culottes are quite enough for now."

CHAPTER SEVENTEEN

As none of us felt like going out again, we decided to stay in and have a lazy evening in the suite. The Old Biddies had letters and postcards to write—yes, the old-fashioned kind with real pens, on real paper—and I was quite happy to lounge around on the sofa with Muesli, flipping through various magazines while channel-surfing Austrian TV. The hotel didn't serve evening meals in the dining room but they did provide platters of cheese and crackers for the room, together with a selection of cured meats, pickles, dried fruit, nuts, and condiments. Since we all felt like we were still digesting those huge *wiener* hotdogs from earlier, this suited us fine for dinner.

Late that evening, as the Old Biddies were taking turns having their baths, I clipped Muesli's harness on and led the little cat down out of the room to get some fresh air in the street outside. Rather than take the lift, I decided to walk down the stairs. For one thing, Muesli seemed a bit spooked in the lift, and for another, it was good exercise. As I pushed open the emergency exit at the end of the landing and stepped into the stairwell, however, I was surprised to hear the sound of crying. I peered around, my eyes growing accustomed to the dim light, and I saw a small shape huddled on one of the steps. It was the little Chinese girl.

"Mei-Mei! What's wrong?" I cried, crouching down next to her.

She sniffed and gulped, turning slightly away from me and rubbing her eyes. "N-nothing."

"Come on... something has obviously upset you," I said, looking at her red eyes. I fished in my pocket and pulled out a tissue, which I handed to her. "Here..."

She hesitated a second, then took the tissue and dabbed her eyes. I reached out and gently rubbed her back as her sobs subsided into hiccups.

"What's wrong?" I asked again. Then I remembered the little scene on the landing earlier. "Oh God—I didn't get you in trouble with your mother, did I?"

She shook her head. Then she said in a small voice: "Ma-Ma see me drawing picture of Muesli. She... she get very angry. She take my sketchbook away... She say no more drawing."

"Oh." I didn't know what to say.

I was furious with Mrs Chow's lack of compassion, as well as her lack of appreciation for her daughter's talent, but I didn't want to badmouth the girl's mother to her.

Muesli came up and nuzzled against the girl and Mei-Mei brightened slightly. She noticed the harness and leash, and asked in a quavering voice:

"W-where are you going?"

"I'm just taking Muesli out for a bit of fresh air."

"Oh… I can come?"

I hesitated, not sure I should be taking her without asking her mother's permission. On the other hand, we were only going out the hotel's front door and walking for five minutes on the street… Mei-Mei's tear-stained face wrenched at my heart and I desperately wanted to cheer her up.

"Okay. Here… would you like to hold Muesli?" I offered the end of the leash to her. "She doesn't really walk like a dog—she sort of stops and starts. But if you just keep giving her gentle tugs, you can guide her in the right direction."

Mei-Mei nodded again, her eyes shining as she took the leash in her hands. Gripping it tightly, she went ahead of me down the stairs, with Muesli trotting next to her. The back stairs didn't go all the way down to the street—they ended on the lobby level, coming out through an emergency exit at the end of the hallway. We hurried past the music room, dining room, and guest lounge, through the lobby and finally down the sweeping staircase to the main entrance, stepping out into the chilly autumn night.

Too late, I realised that Mei-Mei didn't have a coat. She was just wearing a flannel long-sleeved top and matching bottoms, which I suspected were her pyjamas. Quickly, I shrugged off my own coat and wrapped it around her. The last thing I needed was for the child to catch a bad cold when she was sneaking out of the hotel with me! She seemed oblivious to the cold, though. Her face was glowing and her almond eyes sparkled with delight as she led Muesli down the side lane. I could hear her busily chattering away, breaking into happy giggles every so often and sounding so different from her usual subdued self. I sighed, wishing that there was some way Mei-Mei could have a pet in her life.

As if reading my mind, Mei-Mei said softly: "I wish I can have pet."

"Have you asked your parents—?"

She nodded sadly. "Ma-Ma say no. Too much work. Ma-Ma and Ba-Ba say animals very dirty, always have disease..." She gave me a wistful look. "Do you see dancing horses?"

"Oh... no, not yet. I couldn't get tickets for the proper performance. But I'm going to see them at their daily training session tomorrow morning."

She gave a small sigh, then said, "After you go... can you... can you tell me how they look like?"

My heart went out to her and impulsively I said,

"Listen, Mei-Mei... are you doing anything tomorrow morning?"

The little girl shook her head. "Ba-Ba is busy at conference."

"Okay, well, I... I have a surprise for you. I got you a ticket to go with me to see the Lipizzaner stallions at their morning training."

She stared at me in wonder. "Me? Go see dancing horses?" Then a shadow crossed her face. "But Ma-Ma—"

"Oh, don't worry—I'll sort it with her. It'll be no problem," I said blithely.

She gave me a brilliant smile and grabbed my hand impulsively. "Thank you! Thank you, Gemma!"

I shivered and rubbed my arms. "Come on—we'd better keep moving."

We continued down the side lane and, as we paused by the same patch of grass again to let Muesli have her little snack, a group of teenage boys came walking down the pavement from the opposite direction. They had obviously been out partying and were loud and raucous, calling each other names and shoving each other playfully. As they approached us, one of them lunged towards Mei-Mei with his hands thrust out menacingly and yelled:

"BOO!"

The little girl screamed. The next moment, there was a loud hiss and a yowl, and a bundle of grey fur hurled itself at the teenage boy.

"*Scheisse!*" the boy yelped, reeling backwards. He flailed his arms, trying to fend off his feline attacker. "Aaagghh!"

"Muesli!" I cried, mortified. "Muesli, stop—what are you doing?" I jumped to grab my cat, pulling her off the boy. Holding her squirming body in my arms, I looked at him in concern. "I'm so sorry! Did she hurt you?"

The boy looked down. His hands had been scratched in a couple of places but otherwise he seemed unhurt—although he was badly shaken up. "*Nein...* is okay," he said, stumbling backwards to join his friends, who all backed away, eyeing Muesli warily.

"I don't understand—she's normally a very friendly little cat," I tried to assure them. Then my eyes fell on Mei-Mei, standing next to me, and I said, "Oh! You know what? I think she was being protective! She thought you were attacking the little girl and—"

The boys didn't seem interested in my theories. Mumbling amongst themselves, they hurried off down the street, throwing wary looks over their shoulders. I shrugged and gave up. The scratches had been superficial, anyway, and I was sure they would heal quickly. Perhaps next time, the boy would think twice before playing pranks on younger children. Still, the incident had made me nervous as I suddenly realised the responsibility I had, bringing the child out into the street without her parents' permission.

"Come on, Mei-Mei. We'd better get back."

This time, we took the lift up to our floor and I braced myself as we stepped out, half expecting to see Mrs Chow standing there, waiting for us. But the landing was empty and the door to the Chows' suite was slightly ajar, just as when we'd left. I breathed a silent sigh of relief and gave Mei-Mei a gentle push towards her room.

"I'll see you tomorrow, okay? Good night."

The little girl hesitated, then crouched down suddenly and pulled Muesli into a hug.

"I love you, Muesli," she whispered, dropping a kiss on the little tabby's head.

I felt a lump come to my throat and blinked hastily as Mei-Mei straightened again. Then she gave me that adorable gap-toothed smile, turned, and disappeared into her suite.

CHAPTER EIGHTEEN

The first thing I thought of, when I woke up the next morning, was my rash promise to Mei-Mei to take her to see the Lipizzaner stallions. Now in the cold light of day, I was beginning to have severe doubts that Mrs Chow would ever allow her daughter to waste one morning going to watch "dirty animals" perform. Still, I couldn't let the little girl down. I turned over in bed, tucking the pillow under my cheek, and frowned. What was the best way to approach Mrs Chow? *I'll find a moment over breakfast*, I thought. It would be less threatening if I brought the excursion up in the course of conversation, and since the Morning Exercises didn't start until ten o'clock, I had plenty of time. I would just have to play it by ear and pick my moment...

The anticipation made me restless and I decided to dress and go down early. Leaving Muesli curled up on my pillow, I wrote the Old Biddies a note and let myself quietly out of the suite. Downstairs, I found Stefan and a maid setting up the breakfast room, which felt unusually chilly.

"Ah, Frau Rose... I am afraid that breakfast is not quite ready yet," said Stefan.

"Oh, that's all right. I wasn't expecting to eat—I just happened to wake up early and thought I'd come down..." I shivered and rubbed my arms against the cold. Stefan saw me and made an apologetic face.

"I am so sorry! We have had a problem with the heating on this level—for some reason, it went off during the night. There is a man coming to fix it now, but I am afraid breakfast this morning might be a bit colder than normal." He glanced at the fireplace on one side of the room. "It is a shame that is fake, otherwise I could build a big fire to heat the room."

"Oh, is that a fake fireplace?" I said in surprise, turning to look at it.

"Yes, many of the fireplaces in this building are just for ornamental purposes. I think there *were* chimneys in the building originally but by the time we bought the property, the previous owners had already sealed them off and installed gas heating. However, for some reason, they decided to add fake ornamental fireplaces in several of the rooms. There is one in this room and one in the music room—"

"In the music room?" I stared at him. "The fireplace in there is fake?"

"Yes, that is right."

"Does Sofia know that it's fake?"

He laughed. "But of course. She personally went over the structural plans for the house."

A memory flashed in my mind: on the day Wagner had been murdered, I had gone back to the music room to retrieve Glenda's handbag, and when I'd walked in, I had found Sofia on her hands and knees in front of the fireplace. She had sprung up and claimed that she was thinking about making a fire to warm the room for the police... but she must have been lying because she had known all along that the fireplace was fake and making a fire was impossible. So why had she lied?

Stefan looked at me quizzically. "Is something the matter?"

"Oh... er... no, I was just surprised... the fireplace in there looked so real," I said. "I... um... can't believe it's just for decoration."

Stefan smirked. "Ah, well, actually the fireplace in the music room is more than just decorative—it conceals a secret chute that leads down to the wine cellar."

"A what?" I stared at him disbelievingly.

"Yes, you see, the businessman who owned this house during the Second World War was part of the Resistance movement against the Nazis. He and his family were very courageous people and helped to hide persecuted Jews in a concealed room in the wine cellar, at great risk to themselves. Many Jews, especially children, were hidden here for several weeks, even months, and then smuggled out to safety when the time was right."

"Wow... I can't believe it. I mean, you think you only see those kinds of things in movies."

"Oh no, it is not a unique story. The movies are based on real life, after all. There were many brave people during the war who risked their lives for others. And it is not uncommon in old houses such as these to have concealed passages between rooms or escape routes leading down to the basement and out into the street. Sofia and I have been thinking of turning *our* 'secret room' into an exhibit, perhaps. It is always nice when a house has a special history attached to it and many tourists are fascinated by stories about the war."

He grinned and added, "It is said that late at night, after the curtains had been drawn and it was considered safe, the family would give a special signal to the Jews hidden downstairs and the fugitives would climb up a ladder in the chute and come out of the fireplace in the music room. Then they could enjoy some freedom and socialising in more comfortable surroundings. And if there was any sign of danger, they could simply go straight down the chute to the safety of the cellar room again, without the risk of being seen in the hallway or other parts of the house by Nazi officers."

"Is the chute still there?"

"Yes... would you like to see it?" asked Stefan with a smile. He led me into the music room and crouched down in front of the fireplace. "Here you are... you see, there is a spring lever on the side of the mantlepiece, here... and you see how the bottom of the hearth is made of wood? This would all have been covered up during the war, of course, with a mat of fake ashes and burnt logs. Now, if you slide your finger into this knot in the wood and pull... there!"

I watched in wonder as he slowly lifted a trapdoor at the back of the hearth, revealing a gaping square hole that disappeared down into darkness. It was just big enough to fit a man—as long as it wasn't a large man—and I could see the top of a sturdy ladder attached to the side of the opening.

"This chute goes behind a false wall on the ground level and down into the original wine cellar of the house," Stefan explained.

My mind was racing. Suddenly, I saw a way Wagner's killer could have come into the music room and left again, unnoticed by the rest of the guests.

I asked: "So I could go down this ladder and come out in the wine cellar and then walk back up into the ground floor of the building?"

"Yes, in theory... although you cannot do it at

the moment," said Stefan. "The wine cellar is locked. It has fallen into disrepair and we are not using it at present, although we do have plans to restore it at some point. But for now, we keep it closed as we are worried about someone hurting themselves if they should go down there."

"And... does anyone else know about this chute?"

"Well, the people who rent the ground floor offices from us know about it, of course, as the entrance to the cellars is accessed via a door at the back of their office."

"No, I mean... one of the other guests."

"Ah... well, you are the first person I have mentioned it to. Of course, Sofia may have told one of the other guests, if they asked."

"Where's the key to the cellar door kept?"

Stefan looked surprised by my question but answered readily enough: "It is on a keyring, with the other house keys, in a safe in the manager's office."

"Oh." I felt a stab of disappointment. Any theories I had had of the killer helping himself to the key and sneaking down to the wine cellar were knocked on the head. If the key was locked in the safe, then none of the guests would have been able to get it.

Unless the murderer is Sofia Fritzl, who would have easy access to the safe.

I wanted to push the thought away but now that

it had popped into my head, I couldn't ignore it. Sofia would have been perfectly placed to use the secret chute to sneak into the music room and push Wagner off the balcony, then leave again, unseen. And when I had seen her groping in the fireplace, she could have been checking the trapdoor to make sure that it was properly closed and wouldn't give away her secret route.

I racked my brains, trying to remember where she had been yesterday evening when Glenda had discovered the body. I didn't remember seeing her in the lobby—she seemed to have just appeared out of nowhere when people rushed out after the scream. Of course, there could have been a logical reason for that—she might have been in the manager's office or even the private wing, which connected to the lobby via a door by the lifts, and so she would have been out of sight but close by. Still, I wondered if anyone was with her and could confirm her alibi...

"Frau Rose? Are you all right?"

I started and realised that I had been staring into space with a frown. Stefan was looking at me in concern. I gave him a wan smile.

"Sorry... my mind wandered for a moment. Um... thanks for showing me the trapdoor and telling me the history of the house. It's really fascinating."

"It is my pleasure. Perhaps when you visit Vienna again, we will have restored the cellar and then you will be able to see the secret room in its former glory."

The chat with Stefan left me feeling very uneasy. I didn't want to accept that Sofia could be a murderer—and the memory of my mother's reprimand from the night before added to my feelings of guilt—but I couldn't deny that there were so many things that fit. Aside from her furtive behaviour in the music room and the obvious way she was exploiting the publicity from Wagner's death, I remembered the conversation I had overheard the night I had been out with Muesli. Sofia was obsessed with making the hotel a success—the question was: would she be willing to commit murder to achieve that?

I was still pondering this when the Old Biddies came down for breakfast and I remained quiet and preoccupied as we helped ourselves from the buffet and sat down at the long table to eat. I didn't have much appetite and I was astounded to see the Old Biddies' heaped plates. I thought little old ladies were supposed to "eat like a bird"? These four ate more like rabid vultures!

Mabel glanced at me as she buttered a piece of *Schwarzbrot* and said: "Are you still stewing over your tiff with that young man of yours?"

I looked up. "Hmm? Oh no... no, not at all. Devlin and I have sort of made up."

"Then what's bothering you, dear?"

I hesitated. A part of me wanted to confide in the Old Biddies and tell them my worries about Sofia, but with their single-minded enthusiasm for finding the murderer, I was nervous about what they might do if they thought Sofia was a suspect. The last thing I needed was for them to ask her suggestive questions or break into her private apartment to "look for clues".

I pinned a smile to my face. "Er... nothing's bothering me. I was just planning our day and wondering what we should do after we see the Lipizzaners—"

"Oh yes, about that, dear..." Mabel exchanged a look with the other Old Biddies. "We don't think we will come with you to see the horses after all."

"You won't?" I said, astonished. "Why not?"

"Oh... we have other plans for this morning," said Mabel with a mysterious smile.

I eyed them suspiciously. "Would these 'other plans' involve snooping in places you shouldn't?"

"We never snoop!" said Mabel with great dignity. "We simply... reconnoitre. And I might remind you, young lady, that our efforts in the past have helped the Oxford police solve many a baffling murder mystery."

"I don't know if the police would see it like that," I muttered. Then remembering Devlin's warning, I added, "And speaking of which, this isn't Oxford— it's not even England. You mustn't do anything that will get you in trouble with the Austrian police."

"Oh tosh!" said Mabel, waving a hand.

I started to say something else but, at that

moment, the Chows entered the dining room and I remembered my earlier plan to speak to Mei-Mei's mother. As I watched, the Chinese girl and her father made a beeline for a table in the corner, whilst Mrs Chow wandered across to the buffet. Excusing myself, I hurried over to join her, casually picking up a plate and taking a position next to her at the sideboard.

"Good morning," I said brightly. "Did you sleep well?"

Mrs Chow looked surprised at my warm greeting but her face softened as she said, "Yes, thank you. Hotel bed very comfortable."

"Mei-Mei told me that your husband will be attending a conference this morning?"

She drew herself up proudly. "My husband is speaker for big international conference. He is top scientist in research for biochemistry. This is why we come to Vienna—also holiday for Mei-Mei to study Europe history and culture, to improve her brain."

Some holiday, I thought. But I kept my thoughts to myself and said aloud, "You must be so proud of your husband. You know, I was thinking... if you and he are busy with conference activities, maybe I can look after Mei-Mei for a while, take her out around Vienna with me?" I gave her a guileless smile. "Like Mei-Mei, I'm an only child too. I've always wanted a little sister. Mei-Mei is such a lovely girl. It would be great fun to go sightseeing together."

Mrs Chow looked surprised but pleased by my suggestion. She eyed me speculatively. "Thank you. Yes, very good for Mei-Mei to spend time with Oxford graduate. Maybe you teach her how study hard to enter top university in the world?"

"Oh... er... sure," I stammered. "Um... I could teach her a lot just showing her around the various museums and galleries... and you know, visiting places like the Spanish Riding School which has so much history—"

Mrs Chow stiffened. "No, no waste time for horse show," she said, glowering. "Mei-Mei already too much thinking about animal. She must learn about history and political and economy of Europe. Very important."

"Oh... um... yes, of course," I said, my heart sinking at the woman's unyielding attitude.

"You take Mei-Mei this morning?" Mrs Chow asked. "I can go see conference with husband, if Mei-Mei go with you. You take her to Art History Museum? This very good education place. We don't go yet."

"I..." I stared at her, my thoughts churning. Then, before I realised what I was doing, I was smiling and saying: "Yes, of course—I'd be happy to take Mei-Mei to the Art History Museum this morning."

"Ah! Good!" Mrs Chow beamed. "Thank you. Very appreciate."

Oh hell, I thought as I watched the Chinese woman walk off to join her husband and daughter. *What have I done?* I started to follow her, to tell her the truth—that I was also planning to take her daughter to "waste time" watching some horses prance around—but at that moment, I saw her reach her table and bend down to speak to Mei-Mei. The little girl turned a shining face in my direction. I faltered to a stop. I knew that if I went and confessed to Mrs Chow now, it would shatter Mei-Mei's dreams. I just couldn't do it.

What you don't know can't hurt you, I reminded myself. Mrs Chow didn't have to find out about this morning's additional excursion. And I hadn't really lied—I *would* take Mei-Mei to the Art History Museum. We were just going to stop off to see the Lipizzaners first.

CHAPTER NINETEEN

I was still feeling sick with guilt, though, when I met Mei-Mei and her mother in the hotel lobby an hour later, and the Chinese woman's profuse thanks only made me feel worse. Twice I opened my mouth to tell her the truth and twice I shut it again. I was glad when we finally said goodbye and started our walk towards Michaelerplatz. Mei-Mei skipped beside me, her hand in mine and her face wreathed in smiles as she chattered excitedly about the Lipizzaners. I was relieved that she hadn't asked me how I had managed to get her mother to agree—she had obviously assumed that her mother knew where we were going and had given permission. The last thing I wanted was to teach the little girl to lie to her parents.

We arrived at the Spanish Riding School to find

it just as busy as the other day, with large groups of tourists milling about outside and a familiar queue of people desperately trying to buy tickets for a performance. I managed to get a refund for the Old Biddies' unwanted tickets to the morning session and then we went through into the Winter Riding School, the enclosed arena where the Lipizzaners trained and performed.

Mei-Mei gasped as we stepped into the magnificent Baroque hall and I found myself staring in wonder as well. Sunlight flooded in through the enormous windows, lighting up the rich stucco relief on the walls and sparkling on the massive chandeliers which hung down from the ornate ceiling. The floor of the hall was covered in soft sand and it was easily half the size of a football field, overlooked by open galleries on two levels and lined with classical columns and stone balustrades. There were seats all around the hall, in both galleries, but the best seats were undoubtedly those in the Imperial Box at one end of the hall, where members of the royal Hapsburg family once sat and where a giant portrait of Emperor Charles VI, himself astride a white horse, still graced the wall.

Then I heard the thud of hooves and the sound of snorting, and I promptly forgot all about architecture as the Lipizzaner stallions entered the hall. I heard Mei-Mei give a squeal of excitement next to me and I found myself catching my breath too as I watched the majestic animals walk in, arching their necks and tossing their silken manes. After all the hype and celebrity, I was surprised to see that the Lipizzaners were not big horses. They were powerfully built, however, with the noble heads and majestic forms seen in paintings and sculptures of old war horses, and the muscular hindquarters that gave them the strength to perform the difficult dressage moves.

They came in single file and, at first glance, they looked like perfect replicas of each other, but as I looked closer, I noticed the unique markings and differences in each: the dappled grey on the hindquarters and legs of some, the fluffier manes and longer tails of others, and most of all, the distinct personalities and quirks that showed in the gleam of their dark intelligent eyes, which made them suddenly "real" horses rather than creatures of fairytale.

As the strains of Strauss's *Kaiser-Walzer*—the Emperor Waltz—started to fill the air, the stallions began going through their paces, skilfully directed by their riders. I was impressed to see that the latter were all in full uniform—the traditional Spanish Riding School regalia of brown tailcoat, white buckskin breeches, bicorne hat, black riding boots, and ivory deerskin gloves; for some reason, I had thought that they might be wearing more casual outfits like T-shirts and jeans during their informal training. Then I laughed to myself. No, certainly not in Vienna, where formal tradition was lovingly upheld!

Like many people, I had heard a lot about the Lipizzaners and their wonderful "ballet" and I had always been a bit sceptical. But now, as I watched the white stallions march, trot, canter, and pirouette below, I found myself entranced. It really did look like they were "dancing"—moving in beautiful harmony with the classical music that filled the air. One stallion side-stepped diagonally across the hall, the powerful muscles of his shoulders bunching as he maintained a perfect tempo, another stallion spun slowly in the centre, pivoting on his hind feet while circling with the front, and a third stallion moved past in a powerful trot, lifting his front hooves unusually high and striking out with every step. Everything looked effortless and yet I suspected it took great strength and skill to perform such precise, controlled movements with so much fire and grace.

I glanced at Mei-Mei and smiled. The little girl was hanging over the stone balustrade, her eyes shining and her mouth open in an "O" of delight, as she watched the horses and riders glide across the arena. The expression on her face was priceless and suddenly, I was very glad that I had gone against her mother's wishes and brought her.

As if echoing my thoughts, a voice spoke suddenly at my elbow: "Hey! You made it! And I see you brought the kid—good for you!"

I turned in surprise to see Randy McGrath

standing next to us, his white teeth gleaming in a big smile.

"Hello," I said, returning his smile. "I'm surprised to see you here—I would have thought you'd definitely have tickets for the proper performance."

He dropped down on the seat next to me. "Oh, I got tickets—but I never pass up any extra chance to see the Lipizzaners. Besides, for a horseman like myself, watching the basic training is just as interesting as watching the show."

"Yes, I noticed they don't seem to be doing any of the fancy steps I've seen in the videos, like those amazing jumps."

Randy chuckled. "They're not called 'jumps'— they're known as the 'airs above the ground'. They don't usually practise them in everyday training— it's too demanding for the stallions. But if you're *very* lucky, sometimes they might make an exception..."

"Can they really do that jump where they look like they're flying through the air or is that Photoshopped?" I asked.

"Ah, that's the *capriole*—when the horse leaps forward and kicks out with his hind legs straight behind him. Yeah, for a moment, when he's in the air, it does kinda look like he's flying," said Randy with a grin. "That's always the big crowd-pleaser during the performances. *My* personal favourite is the *courbette*—that's when the horse rears up and hops forward on his hind legs, and he never lets his front hooves touch the ground." He looked at me earnestly. "It's a really difficult move, especially for such a large animal, and only the best stallions can do it well. I've been trying to teach one of my boys to do this for years and he still hasn't quite mastered it."

I looked at the American with respect. "You know a lot about this—so you train your own Lipizzaners to perform like this too?"

He laughed. "Yeah, I train my guys to 'dance' and I think we're pretty good, but it's nothing like the performance here. Well, for one thing, I haven't got anything like this place..." He gestured to the chandeliers above our heads. "This setting is pretty cool, huh? It's not quite the same, dancing in a Florida ranch, as dancing in a Viennese ballroom. But it's also the way they train here. You know, a Lipizzaner stallion doesn't even start their training until they're about four—they spend the first couple of years of their lives up in the mountains."

"In the mountains?" I said, surprised.

He nodded. "When the foals are born, they stay with the herd of mares, running free in the hills, until the age of three or four. Isn't that awesome? And then only the best young males are brought to Vienna. They don't complete their training until they're about ten—man, they practise the basic stuff for *years*, before they even start learning the advanced '*haute école*' moves." He shrugged. "Well, I can't afford to do that. I don't have that many stallions and I need my horses to earn their keep. They gotta start working and performing and, you know, you just don't get time to refine things as much."

Mei-Mei turned excitedly to us and said, pointing, "Look! There is black one!"

"Actually, all Lipizzaners are born dark and get lighter as they get older," Randy explained to Mei-Mei. He leaned forwards and pointed. "You see those with the dappled grey markings? Those are the younger stallions. The fully mature ones are pure white. But Lipizzaners come in other colours too, like black and brown. It's just that the royal family preferred white, so that was the colour that was always bred for. But a dark one still pops up now and then—and they always keep a dark horse here at the School, even if he doesn't perform."

"Why?" asked Mei-Mei, hanging on his every word.

"It's kinda like a tradition—or a superstition, I guess. Legend says that as long as there's a dark horse in the stables, the Spanish Riding School will always endure... so I guess it's like a good luck charm, you know?"

"Good luck charm," repeated Mei-Mei dreamily, turning back to watch the horses.

Randy looked at her, then grinned at me. "She reminds me of when I was a kid. I was crazy about the Lipizzaners even then and I always knew I wanted to own a ranch someday."

"Oh—wasn't your family always involved with horses?" I asked casually.

"I didn't come from a family of ranch owners, if that's what you're thinking. But yeah, my father was into riding and stuff—I got my love of horses from him."

"And your mother?"

Randy's expression became guarded. "What about her?"

"Oh... I just wondered if she came from a rural background as well."

"No."

I waited but he wouldn't say any more. His sudden reticence after the recent chattiness seemed strange and he must have felt it too because he quickly changed the subject. Pointing down at the horses, he said:

"Hey—you might be in luck. Looks like one of the stallions might be trying a *capriole*."

Momentarily distracted, I watched with bated breath as one of the Lipizzaners snorted and rocked back and forth on the spot, shifting its weight between its front and back legs. Then suddenly, it exploded into the air with a mighty leap and kicked out its haunches. I felt my heart jerk with excitement and Mei-Mei gave a cry of delight next to me. For a split second, the white stallion was suspended in mid-air and you could almost believe there were wings around his shoulders—then he was on the ground again, arching his neck proudly and accepting a pat from his rider.

"It's awesome, isn't it?" said Randy, grinning. "I've seen it so many times and it still takes my breath away."

He stayed and chatted with us for a few minutes longer but although I tried several times, I could never get him back onto the subject of his family and background. After he'd left, I glanced idly at my watch, then gasped in dismay. It was nearly midday. The morning had flown by much faster than I'd expected and there was no time now to take Mei-Mei to the Art History Museum. I had to get her back to the hotel before her parents returned for lunch.

Pulling the girl reluctantly to her feet, I hustled her out of the arena, but as we passed through the Riding School foyer, the little girl lingered wistfully in front of a giant poster of a Lipizzaner stallion. On an impulse, I darted into the gift shop and returned a moment later with a package.

"Here... a little souvenir," I said with a smile, handing it to her.

She looked at me in surprise and carefully opened the paper bag. "Oh!" she cried. Then she was speechless for a moment as she stared at the sketchpad with the image of a rearing Lipizzaner stallion on the cover. She looked up at me, her face shining. "Thank you! Thank you!"

"You're welcome. But maybe you'd better... er... save this to use when you're alone," I said awkwardly. I could see from her expression that she understood immediately and a part of me felt uneasy again about what I was doing. It was wrong of me to encourage the girl to deceive her mother. On the other hand, I didn't want her to get in trouble or have the heart-breaking experience of losing her sketchpad again.

Shoving my misgivings away, I took her hand and said: "Come on, we'd better get going"—and began heading back towards the hotel.

CHAPTER TWENTY

The *Hotel das Herzchen* seemed curiously empty when we returned, with nobody in the guest lounge or lobby; there was no sign of the Old Biddies anywhere and I wondered uneasily what they were up to. I picked up the spare key to the Chows' room from Stefan at the reception and took Mei-Mei up to her suite. I'd planned to stay with her until her parents came back but Mr and Mrs Chow arrived barely five minutes later. Declining their invitation to join them for lunch, I went back downstairs in search of the Old Biddies.

"Ah... the old ladies?" said Stefan, looking up from his laptop. "Are they not in the guest lounge? I saw them in there having a conversation with Frau Bauer."

"Oh, is she still here?" I said in surprise. "I would

have thought that she would have gone home, now that Mr Wagner is... er... no longer here."

Stefan made a grimace. "She has not said as much to me but I think Frau Bauer does not wish to return to her own home, where she would be alone. Here at the hotel, she is surrounded by other people and there is always company to distract her from her thoughts."

"Oh, right..." I felt slightly sorry for the woman. If she hadn't played a role in Wagner's death, then her grief was genuine and she must have been suffering terribly. I wondered nervously what sort of conversation the Old Biddies had been having with Ana Bauer. "Um... there's nobody in the guest lounge now."

"Oh? In that case, I am not sure—"

"Are you looking for Mrs Cooke and the others?" asked Sofia, stepping out of the manager's office. "I saw them a few minutes ago—they were just leaving the hotel. I believe they are going to the sauna at the Vienna International Hotel around the corner."

The Old Biddies going to a sauna? I blinked.

"Perhaps you'd like to join them?" suggested Sofia with a smile. "It is a wonderful place—the only one of its kind in Vienna—which gives you the taste of a *therme*, a traditional Austrian spa such as you would find in the mountains."

As I hurried around the street corner, I was just in time to see Mabel, Glenda, Ethel, and Florence on the pedestrian crossing in the distance, heading for the other side of the road. I rushed after them, but the lights changed just as I reached the curb. I sighed in frustration. This was a bigger, busier road than the street that Sofia's hotel was situated on, and the distance to the other side was too large to risk jaywalking across the multiple lanes of traffic.

As I waited impatiently for the signal to change again, I watched the Old Biddies trot along the opposite pavement and disappear into a door on the side of a large neo-classical building. From the grand entrance farther along, marked by several flags, I guessed that it must be the Vienna International Hotel, and my hunch was proven correct when I finally made it to the other side and saw the hotel's name inscribed above the entrance.

I paused in front of the door that the Old Biddies had disappeared into and saw that it was a separate entry for the hotel spa. Inside, I found a bright, airy reception decorated in classic Scandinavian style, all pinewood and white upholstery, and a pretty blonde receptionist who nodded in answer to my query.

"*Ja...* yes, the old ladies have gone into the *therme.* Would you like to join them?"

"Oh... er... I don't have anything to wear. I mean, I didn't really come prepared, so I don't have a swimsuit or anything—"

The girl looked surprised. "*Ah,* that is no problem. You will not need a swimsuit." She reached below the counter and produced a key.

"You will find a towel in the locker."

Five minutes later, I adjusted the towel nervously around me as I stepped through a door of frosted glass into the inner spa. There were trickling water features, pots of lush ferns, and pinewood walls everywhere. The air was heavily fragranced and everything seemed pervaded by a calm, peaceful atmosphere. I felt myself relax as I inhaled the scent of *ylang-ylang* and lavender, and wandered slowly down the wide hallway, smiling to myself. Maybe the Old Biddies had had the right idea after all. There were worse ways to spend an afternoon on holiday than at a luxury spa—

I nearly yelped in surprise as a middle-aged woman came around the corner, smiling in a friendly fashion as she saw me. She was absolutely stark naked. She was followed a moment later by another nude woman. And then a bearded man. Yes, a man. Also naked as the day he was born.

"*Hallo!*" he said, smiling and nodding pleasantly as he walked past me.

"Er... hello..." I mumbled, hastily averting my eyes.

Blushing like a virgin, I fled down the corridor and into the first door I could see. It was a swinging pine door and as I stepped into the hot, dry interior, I realised that I had walked into the sauna room. I looked around in mute horror.

There were naked people everywhere.

Lounging on the pinewood benches, sitting,

talking, and laughing, pouring water on the hot stones... there was not one person wearing a stitch of clothing.

Oh God. I remembered now how comfortable Europeans were with nudity, especially in countries like Austria where saunas were mixed gender and nobody batted an eyelid at all the exposed flesh on show. If anything, *I* was the one who looked strange, with my towel clutched protectively around me. I knew I should enter into the spirit of the moment and "do as the Romans do..." (or the Austrians in this case). After all, I'd lived and worked overseas, I was young and open-minded, and I'd prided myself on being cool and cosmopolitan... It was embarrassing to discover that I was still very much a "British prude".

I whirled around to leave but there were two naked couples coming in right behind me, blocking my way. Hastily, I turned back into the room and scurried over to one of the lower benches. I sat down awkwardly, then realised my new problem. *Oh help. Where do I look?* There was almost nowhere to turn my gaze without a naked body part coming into view. I stared intently at the wall next to me, suddenly finding the patterns in the wood fascinating.

Then I made a choked sound as four little old ladies walked into the sauna. Oh my God, it was the Old Biddies. And they were stark naked too. They marched cheerfully to a bench across from me—

knobbly knees, sagging skin, varicose veins and all—and sat down with no trace of self-consciousness. So much for British prudishness.

"Gemma!" squeaked Ethel in delight as she saw me. "Fancy seeing you here!"

"You're a bit over-dressed, aren't you, dear?" said Glenda, looking me up and down.

"Aren't these seats wonderfully warm?" said Florence with a contented sigh as she settled her plump bottom more comfortably on the folded towel which she had placed on the bench.

"Come and sit with us, dear," Mabel directed, patting the empty seat next to her.

I hesitated, but just then, two naked men got off an upper bench and paused to stand next to me, still busily talking. I gulped. Prude or not, I wasn't going to sit here staring at a view of two bare buttocks right in front of my face. Getting up, I bolted across the room and joined the Old Biddies.

"What are you doing here?" I hissed, wiping sweat off my face.

Mabel's chest swelled importantly. "We're shadowing a suspect."

"Ana Bauer," said Florence, waggling her eyebrows.

"We overheard a conversation that Ana was having on her phone," Glenda explained. "She was very secretive about it, lowering her voice and covering her mouth with a hand."

"But I heard what she said," said Ethel proudly.

She leaned towards me and said in a dramatic whisper: "Ana mentioned 'the recent extermination'—"

"Which must refer to Wagner's murder!" finished Florence.

"It's obvious she was talking in code," said Mabel. "Ana Bauer must be a Cold War spy!"

"Er... the Cold War finished years ago," I pointed out.

Mabel waved a dismissive hand. "It's a Lukewarm War now."

I groaned. "That still doesn't explain why you're here."

"We followed her here," Florence explained. "After her phone call, Ana got up very quickly and left the hotel."

"She's coming here to meet someone, there's no doubt about it," said Mabel, nodding emphatically. "Perhaps they're exchanging information—"

"Or passing her a concealed weapon!" said Glenda excitedly.

I wanted to roll my eyes. Oh yes, that made perfect sense. If you were going to pass a concealed weapon to someone, you'd definitely pick a sauna where everybody was naked and the only place you could hide something was under a fold of skin. Great plan.

"That's the most ridiculous thing I've ever heard!" I said in exasperation. I glanced around. "And anyway, I haven't seen Ana—"

"She's just gone into one of the treatment rooms," said Glenda. "We heard the therapist say it would take half an hour."

"And Mabel's guidebook says that when one visits Austria, one *must* try a sauna," said Florence enthusiastically. "We've never been in one before... so we decided to come in here to wait."

"Sweating is marvellous for your immune system and your skin," declared Mabel.

"Yes, I'm sure I can feel all the toxins *oozing* out of my pores," said Glenda, daintily wiping sweat from her brow. "I never realised saunas were so beneficial."

"Or so educational," Ethel piped up, adjusting her spectacles and peering around. "I've never seen so many penises in my life—"

"Uh, right! Um... I think I've had enough now," I said, hastily standing up. "I'll see you back at the hotel."

Mabel glanced at her watch. "Ah! Ana Bauer must be coming out now."

The Old Biddies followed me out of the sauna, and as I stood panting in the cool air of the corridor outside, one of the doors near us opened and a woman in a bathrobe stepped out, her face in a clay mask and her hair wrapped in a towel. She turned away from us and walked down the corridor, disappearing around a corner.

Mabel clutched my arm. "That's her!" she hissed. "That's Ana Bauer!"

Before I could say anything, the Old Biddies shuffled after the woman, disappearing around the corner in their turn. I hesitated, then sighed and followed them. The corridor turned and opened out into a lounge area. As I walked in, I saw Ana Bauer draping a towel on one of the lounge chairs in the corner, while the Old Biddies hovered nearby, pretending to look at some magazines on a rack. Then Ana dumped her book, phone, and keys on the table next to the lounge chair and wandered off to the toilet on the other side of the room. As soon as the door closed behind her, the Old Biddies were on the lounge chair in a flash and I watched horrified as they picked up Ana's mobile phone from the table. I rushed across to them.

Mabel was holding the phone at arm's length and peering at the screen. "Can you make out what it says, Glenda? I haven't got my glasses."

Glenda peered through her spectacles. "I'm not sure... can you hold it farther...?"

"Oh, for goodness' sake," I snapped, snatching the phone from them. "It says 'T-Mobile'. It's the Austrian mobile network. Anyway, what are you doing with Ana's phone?"

"We were just having a little look," said Mabel with a sniff. "In case there was a message from her informant."

I blew a sigh of exasperation and was about to reply when someone tapped me on the shoulder. I turned around to find myself facing a huge, naked

Austrian man.

"What are you doing with my wife's phone?" he demanded.

"Y-your wife...?" I stammered.

At that moment, the woman came back out of the toilet and approached us. As she got closer, I realised with horror that it was not Ana Bauer at all. Yes, there was a vague resemblance, and the face mask and hair towel had confused things even further, but this woman was definitely not Wagner's ex-mistress. No, this was a total stranger and I had been caught snooping on her phone by her very irate husband.

"Um..." I looked at the Old Biddies for help but, to my dismay, there was no one behind me. Then I caught sight of them skulking away on the other side of the room. *Grrrr! I don't believe it!*

I turned back to the man, who was still glowering at me, and groped frantically for a reason why I'd be holding his wife's phone. I gave him a bright smile. "I was... uh... I'm thinking of upgrading to the new iPhone! Yes, and your wife's phone looked great so I thought... um... I thought I'd pick it up just to see how heavy it was—"

"That is a Samsung."

I glanced down. "Oh! Oh, right... so it is! Um, well... I'm thinking of switching to Samsung too. Great to see what it feels like in your hand. Anyway... er... here you go. Thanks for the help. Goodbye!"

I thrust the phone at him and bolted from the room. Back down the corridor, I found the Old Biddies huddled together, busily talking.

"I can't believe you just left me!" I fumed. "You were the ones who took the phone—and that wasn't even Ana Bauer!"

"It was an honest mistake," said Mabel indignantly. "I didn't see that she came out of the wrong door and she looked just like her from the back."

"That still doesn't—"

I broke off as the door next to us suddenly opened and the real Ana Bauer stepped out. She was wearing a bathrobe and had her hair tied back. The skin on her face was fresh and glowing.

"Hello..." she said as she recognised us. She gave us a tentative smile. "You are from the hotel, no?"

The Old Biddies looked taken aback by her friendly demeanour. They gave each other shifty looks, obviously at a loss over how to deal with a non-Cold-War-spy version of Ana.

The silence stretched uncomfortably so I felt obliged to step in and answer, "Er... yes, that's right. We... um... heard that there is a traditional Austrian sauna here and thought we'd come to try it."

"*Ah*, yes, the sauna is very relaxing," said Ana in her soft German accent. "The spa is extremely good also. I would recommend if you would like to have some treatment. I always come for regular exfoliation—it is wonderful for the skin."

"Oooh!" Glenda turned excitedly to Ethel. "It was 'exfoliation' that you heard, dear, not 'extermination'!"

I groaned inwardly. We had come here on a complete wild goose chase! Giving the Old Biddies dirty looks, I said to Ana:

"Thanks, I'll remember that. And now we'd better leave you to relax—"

"So do you come to this spa often, Miss Bauer?" Mabel interrupted, obviously not willing to give up the opportunity to find out more about the woman.

"Yes, whenever I have the time," said Ana. "The therapists are extremely good and it is very convenient—it is not far from my art gallery, so I can come at the end of the day."

It was strange to see her being so cordial, although I reflected that perhaps I'd had an unfair impression of her so far: the first time I'd met Ana, she had been caught up in a fight with Wagner, and every time since, she had either been hysterical with grief or numb and dazed. I felt like I was seeing the real Ana Bauer for the first time.

She gave me and the Old Biddies a friendly smile and said: "If you have the time, you would be most welcome to visit my gallery. It is a short walk from here."

"What sort of art do you specialise in?" I asked.

"Oh, I promote a variety of artists—but my personal interest is in Abstract Expressionism.

There is one of my gallery's paintings, in fact, hanging in the hotel lobby."

"Oh, the canvas with the big black squares," I said, remembering the first day we'd arrived at the hotel and how incongruous that painting had seemed, in the midst of the classical Baroque interior décor of the rest of the lobby.

"Yes, that is right. That is by a young Austrian painter—a protégé of mine—whose work I have been promoting since last year. He has not yet made a name for himself but he is extremely talented and I believe it is a matter of time. In fact, it was because of him that Moritz and I met..." There was an awkward pause, then Ana cleared her throat and continued, "In the meantime, clients like Sofia who invest in a piece from a young artist now may find that they make a huge profit on their investment in years to come." She fixed me suddenly with a shrewd gaze. "Perhaps you would be interested in purchasing a piece too?"

"Me? Oh, no... um... I don't have the funds at present," I stammered, not wanting to confess that even if I *had* been interested in buying a painting, I certainly wouldn't be buying one depicting random black squares! When it came to art, I was unashamedly conservative—I liked boring pastoral scenes and oil paintings done in the classical style. Klimt was about as modern as my taste in art went, and at least I could recognise what he was painting—well, most of the time.

"Oh, well, if you change your mind..." Ana fished in her bathrobe pocket and pulled out a card holder, from which she extracted a gold-embossed name card. "Here are the details of my gallery... and we can ship overseas with no problems," she said smoothly.

"Uh... thank you," I said, taking the card and thinking that here was a side of Ana Bauer that I had not seen before either: the coolly poised businesswoman, knowledgeable and persuasive, with a keen nose for a sale. She may have been prostrate with grief over Wagner's death two days ago, but that obviously wasn't stopping her from fishing for business at any opportunity.

And there was nothing wrong with that, I reminded myself. After all, her gallery was her livelihood—it was only natural that she should always be on the lookout for new clientele. Still, I couldn't help remembering Mabel's comment that Ana's hysterics on the day of Wagner's murder were simply an act. Could the Old Biddies have been right in their suspicions after all?

CHAPTER TWENTY-ONE

After the fiasco at the spa and sauna, I was relieved to pass an uneventful afternoon and evening doing nothing more exciting than taking a horse-drawn carriage ride around Vienna. It might have been a bit of a cheesy tourist trap, but I enjoyed it immensely. There was just something about the timeless romance of sitting in an elegant *Fiaker*—the traditional Viennese hackney coach—with its coachman in his dark jacket and bowler hat, and the rhythmic *clip-clop* of hooves echoing in your wake as you trundled through the narrow, cobbled lanes of Old Vienna...

When the carriage set us back down, we headed towards the sweeping pedestrianised boulevard that was famous for being the heart of Vienna's best shopping. We ogled designer shops boasting chic

European brands and grand old Viennese cafés with their delectable cakes and pastries on display, and jostled with the rest of the tourists milling down the wide avenue, taking selfies with the huge spire of St Stephen's Cathedral and admiring the street musicians playing a jaunty rendition of *The Blue Danube*... There was a wonderful, almost carnival-like atmosphere, despite the grey autumn weather, and for the first time, I really felt like I was "on holiday".

We had an early dinner in a local restaurant famous for its *Tafelspitz*, a traditional Viennese dish of beef boiled in broth with root vegetables and aromatic spices. It was known as the favourite dish of Emperor Franz Joseph I, although I had to admit, the initial description didn't really appeal to me. But when the dish was finally served, I was pleasantly surprised. The beef was mouth-wateringly tender and the accompanying crisp roast potatoes, tangy minced apples, and creamy horseradish provided the perfect mix of flavours. We finally returned, tired and sated, to the *Hotel das Herzchen*, and I was surprised to realise that the Old Biddies hadn't even mentioned Wagner's murder once in the last few hours.

My feet were aching, and I longed to put them up, but Muesli's insistent meowing reminded me that she hadn't had an outing yet that day. With a weary sigh, I picked her up and carried her downstairs to the music room. It was the lazy option, I knew, but I was just too tired to take her outside for a stroll on the street. Not that Muesli seemed to mind—she gave a happy chirrup as I set her down on the floor of the music room and immediately trotted off to rub her chin on various pieces of furniture. Then she gave another happy chirrup as she pounced on something in the corner, tucked behind the heavy curtains. A second later, she was zooming across the room, batting the thing with her paws and chasing it excitedly as it bounced wildly around. I laughed as I watched her, amazed at how cats could always make a toy out of anything... in this case, what looked like a crumpled piece of paper. As Muesli batted it near me, I bent down to pick it up... then I froze.

There was writing on the paper—writing that looked familiar.

Hastily, I smoothed out the crumpled folds and stared at the barely legible scrawl that covered the sheet of hotel stationery. My heart started pounding in my chest. It was Wagner's handwriting. I was sure of it. In fact, the bottom left corner was torn from the paper and I was sure that *that* was the corner which had been found and assumed to be the "suicide note". Now, as I read the words on this page, the strange tone of Wagner's "final message" began to make sense. Of course it had sounded odd and disjointed... it was only part of the original text!

What Wagner had been writing was not a suicide note but a review. He had obviously been working on a draft review of the hotel: various lines were crossed out and rewritten, words inserted and sentences edited, and even a few doodles drawn along the margins. There were two paragraphs, one in German and then one in English below, where Wagner had obviously been translating his original text for an English-language publication. It was this second paragraph that was partly missing. Now, I realised that the complete sentences read:

I had planned to stay the full five days, but I decided I couldn't take it anymore. I had suffered enough and I had to leave. I might be forgiven for calling this hotel an utter disgrace if you take into consideration the mediocre service, bland food, and appalling décor I was forced to endure...

I grimaced as I scanned the rest of the review. Wagner had obviously derived great pleasure from putting people down and making others squirm. I was sure that he would have argued that he had a duty to *entertain* as well as inform his readers; still, the review was filled with taunts and sarcastic criticism which—though not completely unfair—was unnecessarily cruel. I felt my dislike of the murdered man increase: Wagner had obviously relished his power over the poor businesses that had been his targets.

This was the kind of review that was every hotel owner's nightmare—the kind that they would do anything to prevent the general public from seeing. A part of me almost couldn't blame Sofia for hating Wagner and wanting to prevent him from sharing his opinions... the question was, how far had she gone to silence him? Could she have gone as far as murder?

It would certainly make sense. And it would explain what she had been doing at the fireplace that day: she had been searching for this note. For some reason, it had been crumpled up and tossed into the fireplace—and Sofia had been trying to retrieve it. I frowned. But why hadn't she found it? Admittedly, I had interrupted her when I walked in, and then the police had arrived—but she would have had time later to return to the room and search for it, maybe late at night, after all the guests had gone to sleep. So why hadn't she?

As if conjured by my thoughts, the door to the music room opened and Sofia Fritzl stepped in. I stiffened, then realised that she couldn't see me, crouched down by the curtains in the far corner, hidden from view by the back of one of the armchairs. In any case, she barely gave the rest of the room a glance as she made a beeline for the fireplace and dropped to her knees in front of it. I watched with interest as she leaned into the hearth and started groping around, muttering under her breath. Then she sat back on her heels and exhaled loudly in frustration. I fingered the piece of paper in my hands then, on an impulse, I stood up and stepped out from behind the armchair.

"Hello, Sofia," I said.

She jumped and twisted around. "Gemma! Er... how... how was the sauna?"

"What are you searching for?"

She licked her lips. "What do you mean?"

"Well, you can't be lighting a fire..." I looked her straight in the eye. "Because Stefan told me that the fireplace is fake."

Sofia flinched and looked at a loss over what to say.

I held up the note. "Is this what you're looking for?"

She gasped. "Where did you find that?" She reached out and tried to snatch it from my fingers, but I stepped back, keeping the note out of reach.

"Wagner wrote this, didn't he? And you didn't want him to publish it—which is why you murdered him."

"No!" Sofia gasped, putting both hands up to her cheeks. "I never murdered Wagner! How could you think that?"

"It would be understandable if you wanted to," I said gently. "I read the review. It's pretty scathing. No hotel owner would want that getting out into the public—"

"Yes, but I would not murder anyone for it!" said Sofia, aghast. She took a deep breath. "I admit—I did remove the note. I was the first in here after your friend, Miss Bailey, found the body, and I saw

209

the note lying there on the table, next to the armchair. I barely had time to read it and then everybody else rushed in. I... I just panicked. I crumpled it up and tossed it into the fireplace, so that no one else would see it." She made a rueful face. "I did not realise that part of the note had been wedged under Wagner's coffee cup and so when I snatched it up, a corner tore off and got left behind. When the police said they'd found a suicide note, I realised what must have happened—but I did not dare come forward and correct them, because then I would have had to admit that I tampered with the scene and I would have risked the note becoming public." She frowned. "In any case, I could not find it! I came back here as soon as I could, to retrieve it from the fireplace, but you interrupted me... and then the police arrived. By the time I was free to come back to search for it, it was past midnight. I thought it would be fine—not many people go in the music room anyway and no one would be fiddling with the fireplace—but I could not find it!"

My eyes fell on Muesli, who was lying on a faded rug in front of the fireplace, and I snapped my fingers. "That's because Muesli found it first," I said. "I brought her here that night, while you were still busy with the police, and she ran around, letting off steam, for several minutes. I saw her playing in the fireplace and pouncing on something, but I didn't really realise the significance of it until just now... Muesli must have found the crumpled note and batted it out of the fireplace. She chased it around and knocked it behind the curtains. That's why you couldn't find it."

Sofia sighed and sank down on one of the armchairs. She looked suddenly old and defeated. "It was wrong of me, I know, to remove that note. But... I just could not bear the thought of anyone reading Wagner's review. Oh, it was horrible—horrible—the things he said. I am sorry he is dead, but I am not going to pretend that I liked him. Moritz Wagner was a sadistic pig." She looked at me and raised her chin. "But I did not murder him. I was in the kitchen, making apple strudel for tomorrow's tea, when I heard the scream. I was not anywhere near the music room."

I knew I only had her word for it and yet... Maybe I was hearing what I wanted to hear, since I really didn't want to accept that this kindly woman, my mother's oldest friend, could be a murderer, but I did feel a sincerity in her words.

"I believe you," I said at last.

Sofia relaxed, then she asked tentatively: "Are you... are you going to tell the police about this?"

I hesitated, then gave her a regretful look. "Sofia, I have to. It changes everything about the case. I'd suspected that the death was suspicious before, but now this proves it. If Wagner didn't leave a suicide note, then that means he didn't kill himself... which means that he was murdered. The police need to know, so they can conduct a proper investigation."

She nodded silently, her shoulders slumping. I felt a surge of sympathy for her.

"I'll... I'll try to speak to Inspektor Gruber and convince him to investigate further, without mentioning this note, if I can," I said.

Sofia gave me a grateful look. "Thank you, Gemma."

I picked up Muesli and turned to leave, then paused as something struck me. "Sofia... Stefan showed me the secret trapdoor in the hearth and the ladder leading down to the wine cellar. Do you know who else might have known about that? It would be a way the murderer could have got in and out of this room unobserved."

Sofia frowned. "I may have mentioned it to some of the other guests... Ana Bauer, I think—she was asking me about the renovations the other day. But in any case, it would not have been possible for anyone to use that route since the door to the wine cellar is locked," she said, echoing what Stefan had told me.

"Are you sure about that?"

She gave a humourless laugh. "Yes, the door to the wine cellar is very heavy and the lock very solid. So unless they can walk through walls or locked doors, the murderer could not have come up the secret chute into the music room."

CHAPTER TWENTY-TWO

The confrontation with Sofia left me feeling troubled and confused. I was glad, of course, that she wasn't involved in Wagner's death, but her being innocent meant that the real murderer was still out there. He or she *had* to be one of the other guests. But who? The Chows were out of the question. And Jane Hillingdon and her mother were definitely out too, as well as Johann Müller and Stefan Dreschner, since they all provided alibis for each other: Mrs Hillingdon and Müller were together in the lounge, Stefan and Jane were in view of each other in the lobby.

So that left Ana Bauer and Randy McGrath. Somehow, I just didn't share the Old Biddies' belief that this was a "crime of passion" by a bitter, angry woman who wanted revenge on the man who had hurt her pride and feelings. However, after seeing Ana Bauer this afternoon at the sauna, I was beginning to think that it could be a "crime of gain" by a cool businesswoman who wasn't afraid of seizing opportunities.

But how could Ana have done it? Didn't she have an alibi too? No, in actual fact, she didn't really have an alibi since there was no one to vouch that she had been upstairs the entire time. Yes, I had seen her come out of the lift with the Old Biddies, but that didn't mean that she couldn't have killed Wagner, then escaped upstairs via another route to establish her alibi. In fact... I suddenly remembered the back stairs which Mei-Mei and I had used last night. They were accessed through the emergency exit at the end of the hallway, right next to the music room door. So in actual fact, Ana Bauer *could* have run down the back stairs, slipped into the music room, pushed Wagner off the balcony, and then run back up again.

I frowned. She would have to have been awfully fast, though, and it seemed like an elaborate, convoluted way to murder someone. If she was sharing a room with Wagner, there would have been ample opportunities to kill him without resorting to this—why not just push him off their own balcony? Or slip poison into his drink?

So maybe it wasn't Ana Bauer. I turned my thoughts to the other suspect: Randy McGrath. The handsome young American had certainly been acting strangely too. Why had he sneaked into the manager's office yesterday? What had he been looking for amongst the police files? Not that snooping by itself made you guilty, of course—after all, I had been creeping around in the office myself. And the Old Biddies would have been prime suspects every time if sticking your nose where you shouldn't was a sign of murderous intentions... Still, I had a strong hunch that Randy's furtive behaviour was somehow tied to the murder. The only problem was, I couldn't figure out *why* he would have wanted to kill Wagner.

I wondered suddenly if Devlin had managed to find out anything about Randy or Ana. It was barely twenty-four hours since I'd spoken to him so it was probably too soon. But then, patience was never my strong suit...

"Gemma, you know we only spoke about this yesterday?" said Devlin in exasperation.

"Yes, I know, I know... but have you got anything?" I wheedled.

"Well, for once you're in luck," said Devlin. "I was planning to call you when I got home. My contact at Interpol had a quiet moment earlier today and did some digging for me. He didn't find much about your Austrian lady—oh, other than a small thing."

"What?"

"The art gallery she used to work for, before she opened her own place, was involved in a scandal. They were accused of selling forged paintings and sued by a client, but the case was dropped due to insufficient evidence."

"Really? And was Ana involved?"

"No, that's the thing. She was questioned during the investigation, of course, but she was cleared of any possible criminal involvement. She left that gallery not long after the scandal broke out."

"Hmm..."

"I've got something about your American friend too," Devlin continued. "Seems like he was telling you the truth—he does own a ranch in Florida and breeds Lipizzaners, and trains and performs with them. Apparently, he's made a bit of a name for himself in the States as an expert on the breed."

"Has he owned the ranch for a long time?"

"For a fair while. He took out a massive loan to buy it five years ago but seems to be struggling to make his mortgage repayments now."

"Oh? Is he having financial difficulties?"

"Looks like it. Of course, I haven't got access to his detailed financial records."

"What about family?" I asked.

"He's single, an only child—no brothers or sisters. In fact, no living relatives: his father died of a stroke several years ago and his mother died of cancer last year."

"Do you know anything else about his mother? I tried to ask Randy about her earlier today and he clammed up."

"Hmm... well, she must have had him fairly late.

She was sixty-eight when she died—and Randy is thirty—so that means she had him just before forty. That might explain why he doesn't have any siblings."

"Did she get married late too?"

"No, let's see... no, in fact, she seems to have got married very young. Left Austria when she was just seventeen and followed her husband to the States. He was Irish. A jockey. And then he got work with a big stud farm in Wyoming."

"Wait... are you saying Randy's mother was Austrian?" I asked excitedly.

"Yes, born in Vienna, it seems. Her name was Birgit Wagner."

"*What?*" I sat bolt upright. "Her maiden name was Wagner?"

"Yes, why—? Oh, of course, your victim's name was Wagner," said Devlin, sounding annoyed with himself that he hadn't noticed. "I wasn't really paying attention when I got these notes. I just skimmed them."

"It's all right—you've got your own case on your mind," I said. "You can't be expected to remember all the details of something that has nothing to do with you. Anyway, this is brilliant! It could explain Randy's motive! I mean, supposing he's related to Wagner—who was a confirmed bachelor—well, then Randy could be his closest relative and the heir to Wagner's entire estate! You said he was having financial difficulties—"

"Gemma," said Devlin in a warning tone. "You've got to be careful of jumping to conclusions. Wagner is a very common name in Austria; in fact, I think it's the fourth most common surname—or something like that—in the whole country. Just because Randy's mother had the same surname may not mean anything."

"I'm sure it can't be a coincidence," I said stubbornly.

"And even if they *are* related, you don't know anything about the details of the family. There could be other siblings or Wagner himself may have fathered children outside of marriage. I know what you're thinking: that Randy could have murdered Wagner in order to inherit his estate, but it's not a given that he would be the one to benefit. You don't even know the details of Wagner's will. For all we know, he could have willed all his money to a cat rescue society!"

"All right, all right," I said, slightly sulky. "Keep raining on my parade."

"I'm sorry," said Devlin with a laugh in his voice. "I'm not trying to put a damper on things but it's important that you don't make assumptions based on little or no evidence."

"You're beginning to sound like a police college lecturer," I grumbled. "Fine! Can you get me some evidence, then? Find out if Brigit Wagner is related to Moritz Wagner and what other members of the family there are? Oh, and Wagner's will."

"That's a tall order, Gemma. I'll do my best—but I can't promise anything. And I'm *not* going to have an answer by tomorrow, no matter how much you hassle me," he added with mock sternness.

"O-kay," I said, grinning.

"That doesn't mean you can't call me just to hear my voice, though," said Devlin teasingly.

I smiled. "I just might take you up on that."

CHAPTER TWENTY-THREE

I left the hotel before breakfast the next morning and made my way to the local police station, where I asked to speak to Inspektor Gruber. The Austrian police officer was polite but aloof when he saw me and he listened to my theories about Wagner's murder with thinly veiled scepticism and impatience.

"It is a sad business, *Meine Dame*," he said at last. "However, it is not something that you need concern yourself with. I regret that your visit to Vienna has been marred by such an incident. I hope you can put this behind you and continue with your sightseeing."

"But..." I looked at him incredulously. "But don't you understand? This is now a murder inquiry! Wagner didn't commit suicide—he was killed! You have to come back to the hotel and question everybody and investigate properly!" I saw his expression harden at my tone and hastily softened my words. "I mean, it's important to find out the truth about Wagner's death, don't you think?"

"As I said, *Meine Dame,* this is not something that you need to worry about. I will review the case and see what needs to be done."

He refused to discuss things further and I left the station a few minutes later, feeling thwarted and frustrated. For the first time, I appreciated the benefit of having Devlin and his CID connections back in Oxford. Here, I felt like I was just being treated as a silly tourist with an overactive imagination... *Perhaps it would be different if Sofia speaks to him,* I thought. After all, she was a Vienna resident and a respected local business owner. The only problem was convincing her to do it, because any police investigation would not only disrupt the hotel but also reveal the truth behind Wagner's "suicide note" and show the damning review to the public. It would have been different if Sofia had liked Wagner and genuinely mourned his death, but given how much she had hated him, I couldn't see her making a great effort to have his killer brought to justice. I was so engrossed in my thoughts that I wasn't paying much attention to where I was walking and bumped into a man coming in the opposite direction.

"Oh! Excuse me—"

"*Ah! Verzeihung...* it is you, Frau Rose!"

I looked up to see Johann Müller regarding me with a pleased smile. The museum owner was looking very dapper, in a woollen *loden* jacket and hat, and a maroon scarf around his neck.

"You are out very early this morning," he said, eyeing me curiously.

"Yes, I've just been to the police station," I said, nodding in the direction I'd come from.

"To the police station?" He looked startled. "But why?"

I hesitated. "Because I think Moritz Wagner's death wasn't suicide. I think he was murdered."

"*Heiliger Strohsack!* Moritz murdered?" He stared at me in bewilderment. "But how? Why?"

"I don't know why, although I have some theories..." I saw him looking at me oddly and said quickly, "This isn't the first time I've been involved in a murder. I'm not a complete amateur. I mean—I *am*—I'm not a professional detective, but back home, I... I've helped the police solve some cases..." I trailed off, flushing, as I saw him look even more uncertain. *Oh God, I sound like some kind of sad Nancy Drew wannabe.* I took a deep breath. "Look, the point is, I think there is something suspicious about Wagner's death. He didn't jump off the balcony to commit suicide—he was pushed."

Müller looked stunned.

"You were a good friend of Wagner's. Would you mind telling me a bit about him? Did he have any enemies?" Then I caught myself and gave him an apologetic look. "Oh, sorry—were you on your way to something?"

"No, no, in fact, I was just going to Café Central for a coffee. Have you been to visit?"

"No, actually, I haven't—"

"No? Then we must go!" cried the little man. "Come, we shall go together now. Café Central is perhaps the most famous of Vienna's traditional coffeehouses, and it is something you should not miss as a visitor to the city. We can talk about Moritz over cake and coffee."

A few minutes later, he led me up to the Palais Ferstel, a magnificent building, built in the Venetian style, which was once intended for the stock exchange, but which was now better known for housing the legendary coffeehouse where great poets, leaders, and philosophers, such as Leon Trotsky and Sigmund Freud, used to meet. There was a long queue outside and a stern-looking doorman in a bowler hat guarding the entrance, but somehow we managed to get a table fairly quickly. I wondered if Johann Müller's "strudel addiction" had made him enough of a regular visitor as to get some special treatment!

I paused in awe as we stepped inside. The place seemed vast, with high, vaulted ceilings reminiscent of a cathedral, held up by Renaissance columns, and lit by the pale autumn sunshine pouring in through the tall windows. Huge portraits of Emperor Franz Joseph I and his queen, the

Empress Elizabeth—affectionately known as Sisi— dominated one wall, and Art Nouveau chandeliers marked out cosy spots between the various booths and tables. I knew Viennese coffeehouses were famous for their beauty and charm, but somehow I hadn't been prepared for such grandeur.

We were led to our table by a typical Viennese waiter—impeccably dressed in tie, black waistcoat, and white long apron—and I had to restrain myself from stopping to ogle the glass display case by the front door, in which a vast array of mouth-watering sweet treats were arranged in neat rows. Raspberries and chocolate mousse, salted caramel and peanut brittle, fluffy puff pastry and custard cream... I hadn't had breakfast yet and suddenly I was starving.

"Now, what will you have?" asked Müller, handing me the menu as we sat down. "They make wonderful cakes and pastries in the in-house patisserie here, and they also serve a selection of classic Viennese dishes, like *Wiener Schnitzel* and goulash soup and dumplings, although perhaps it is too early for those—"

"I think I'm just going to have cake," I blurted, thinking of that heavenly display by the front door.

Müller laughed. "Well, you *are* on holiday."

Our order came quickly, along with our coffees, each served on a little silver tray with a glass of water and a teaspoon.

"Why do they always serve the coffee like this?" I

asked, pointing to the tray.

"Ah, the glass of water is to help you cleanse your palate. And the spoon is always placed face-down, to show that the glass has been freshly filled. It is a form of etiquette from the Hapsburg times—and as you know, we Viennese love our traditions," he said with a smile. Then he sobered. "It is sad to think that Moritz and I will never come to Café Central together again. We used to make this our regular meeting place."

"I understand that you'd known him for a long time?"

He nodded. "Since he was a young man. It was I who first spotted the talent in him and hired him to work with me at my museum. Then I put him in touch with the right persons, to help further his career."

"He must have been very grateful."

Müller gave a wry laugh. "I would like to think that Moritz appreciated the help I gave him but... I am not naïve. I liked Moritz—he was clever, amusing, and very good company—but he was, above all, an egoist. He thought only of himself and his own pleasures."

"Like being cruel in his criticism of others, just to entertain people?" I said, thinking of the review I'd read.

Müller winced. "Moritz could be unkind sometimes—this I know. He had a very barbed tongue and he was not afraid to use it. In fact, I am sorry to say that he enjoyed using it on those less fortunate... but you see, he was also a very charming man, who had many admirers, despite his vices."

"Especially lady admirers?"

He gave me a rueful smile. "Yes, Moritz was never without female company, although he rarely committed to any one lady."

"I thought he and Ana Bauer were living together...?"

He looked surprised at my knowledge. "*Ah*, where did you hear that? Yes, it is true—Ana and Moritz had a very passionate affair, and she even moved into his apartment for a few months. I think she had hoped to be the one to change his mind about bachelorhood. But of course, it is not possible to change a man like Moritz." Müller shook his head. "Ana was very bitter when Moritz told her it was over. In fact, it put me in a very difficult position as she was also my friend. She owns an art gallery, you see, and I have also known her for many years. She wanted me to speak to Moritz, to ask him to 'give them another chance', as they say... When Stefan Dreschner invited me to come and stay at his new hotel, I suggested that he invite Moritz also. I thought that having Moritz leave the apartment for a few days would encourage Ana to pack her things and move back to her own place. But instead, she insisted on coming with him. And Moritz—he is not the type to fight and argue. He simply lets her come... and then ignores her completely."

Which probably made her even more furious, I thought. I leaned my elbows on the table and looked him in the eye. "Herr Müller... do you think Ana could have killed your friend?"

"Ana? No, no, surely not!"

"Oh, I don't mean in cold blood. Maybe they were arguing and she got angry—and pushed him off the balcony? Do you think she is capable of doing something like that?"

"Well..." He looked uncomfortable. "But Ana loved Moritz! She would not kill him!"

I nearly voiced the clichéd saying about the thin line between love and hate, but bit my tongue. Müller was distressed enough already.

"Well, if it's not Ana, then it has to be someone else in the hotel," I said. "I'm going to speak to Inspektor Gruber again and get him to recheck everyone's alibis on the day of the murder. I'm sure if the police just start asking questions, they'll find a clue somewhere which will lead them to the killer."

The conversation seemed to have put a damper on things and we finished the rest of our cakes and coffees in a slightly awkward silence. I was sorry to lose the earlier gaiety and, as I left the building, I vowed to return to Café Central with the Old Biddies, to enjoy its ambiance again—and to sample some more of its delicious cakes and pastries!

CHAPTER TWENTY-FOUR

When I returned to the hotel, I found the Old Biddies sitting in the guest lounge with Jane Hillingdon and her mother. I almost backed out again but it was too late—they had seen me. In fact, the four little old ladies looked at me with the haunted expressions of trapped animals desperate for a saviour.

"Gemma! Where have you been all morning, dear?" called Mabel eagerly. "Do come in and join us."

Reluctantly, I joined them on the sofa. "I... um... I just popped to the police station to have a quick word with Inspektor Gruber—and then I met Johann Müller in the street and he invited me for coffee at Café Central. Oh, I must take you all back there; that place is amazing!" I added, hastily trying to change the subject, as I saw Jane Hillingdon perk her ears up at the mention of "police station".

"Oh, we've been to Café Central, haven't we, Mum?" said Jane, glancing at her mother, who as usual had her knitting on her knee. "Lovely place and they have ever so many cakes and pastries! But what's this about the police station—have you been talking to the inspector? It's about Mr Wagner, isn't it?" She gasped. "Oooh, is it murder after all? I told you it was murder, didn't I, the day we met at the Belvedere? I thought there was something fishy about his death all along... I'm very sensitive like that... you know, someone once told me I could be a psychic—they were offering this course called 'Awakening Your Inner Psychic': six classes for two hundred pounds... except he said he'd give me a discount seeing as he could sense such strong clairvoyant talent in me and he didn't want me to waste the potential... but there was a pair of boots I really liked in Russell & Bromley which were two hundred quid too—not long boots, short ankle ones, I always think they look so much nicer, dontcha think?—and I decided to get the boots instead, although they turned out really disappointing, I have to say... I mean they were so comfy in the shop but once I started wearing them, they gave me awful blisters—"

"I... I think I'm going up to the room to write some postcards," said Mabel, standing up hurriedly. The other Old Biddies quickly followed with murmurs of "Oh yes, me too!"

I hid a smile as they walked out. I never thought I'd see the day when someone could out-talk Mabel Cooke—but it seemed like even Meadowford's bossiest busybody had met her match in the loquacious Jane Hillingdon. Then my smile faded as I realised that the Old Biddies were abandoning me, as usual, to a dire fate.

I made as if to leave as well, but just as I was about to rise, something on the coffee table in front of Jane caught my eye. It was a large A4 brochure featuring various dinner concerts around Vienna, with pictures of grinning orchestra ensembles in glitzy Baroque halls. There were several pen marks where Jane had obviously been making notes about each of the options, but what had caught my eye was something in the margins of the paper. I leaned over to take a closer look.

Jane looked delighted at my interest. "Are you thinking of going to a dinner concert too? We could go together—in fact, there'd be enough of us to make up our own table, dontcha think? With me and Mum... and you and Mrs Cooke and the others... that's seven and I think the tables—"

"Did you draw those?" I interrupted, pointing to the doodles in the margins.

"Me? Oh no! I can't even draw stick men, me," said Jane, laughing. "That was that nice American chap, Randy. He was in here earlier and I asked him which concert he thought we ought to go to, and he was doodling these while he was talking to me. They're lovely, aren't they? I'd never be able to draw horses like that! Look at all those fancy poses, like they're jumping up in the air or something—"

"It's called the 'airs above the ground'. They're the special dressage moves performed by the Lipizzaner stallions," I said, almost mechanically, my eyes still riveted on the doodles.

I had seen drawings like these before—so alike that I was sure they were by the same person. They had been in the margins of the piece of paper Wagner had been writing his review on. I had assumed at the time that Wagner had drawn them, but now I realised that those horse doodles could only have been done by one man. The same man who had done these doodles on the brochure. My mind was spinning with the implications.

"Where's Randy now?" I asked suddenly.

"Oh... I think he said he was going back to his room? I'm not sure...I saw him in the hallway, chatting to that Chinese couple with the little girl... Such a sweet child, dontcha think? And her English is so good for someone who—"

"I'm sorry—please excuse me! I've... I've got to go and do something!" I said, whirling and running from the room, leaving an astonished Jane Hillingdon staring after me.

Pausing only long enough to ask Stefan for Randy's room number, I hurried upstairs and stopped at last in front of the American's room. I wondered for a fleeting moment if I should take my suspicions to the police—let *them* question Randy instead—but the memory of this morning's interview with Inspektor Gruber still rankled. No, I wanted answers now, not when the police finally decided to take Wagner's case seriously.

Raising my hand, I gave a sharp rap on the door and Randy opened it a moment later. His face lit up as he saw me and he gave me his trademark gleaming smile.

"Hey! How're you doing, Gemma?" He looked at me expectantly.

"Er..." I had rushed up here, galvanised by the excitement of my discovery, and hadn't really given any thought as to what I was going to say. Now, as I stared at Randy's smiling face, I felt stumped. You might suspect a man of foul play but it was still hard to point a finger and accuse him of murder when he was standing in front of you in such an affable manner. I needed some excuse to get him talking, to ease into it... but my mind seemed to have gone blank. Then, as I saw the picture of the white horse on the front of his sweatshirt, I gave myself a mental shake. *Duh!* There was one topic that this man was always happy to talk about.

"I... er... I had a couple of questions about the Lipizzaners and I thought you might know—"

"Oh sure! Come in! Come in!" said Randy, beaming and ushering me into the room.

I felt slightly guilty about using his pet love to

dupe him, but then I reminded myself sternly that this man could be a murderer. As I followed him in, I cast a covert look around, trying to see if I could gather any more information about him. *I'll bet the housekeeping love him*, I thought, eyeing the tidy room with hardly any personal items on the desk and bedside table, and the neatly folded piles of clothing in the small case on the luggage rack. I wondered if his stables back in Florida were also similarly neat and organised, with hay bales arranged in perfectly aligned stacks and riding tack hung in symmetrical rows.

"So what did you want to know?" asked Randy, throwing himself into the chair by the desk and gesturing me to the facing armchair.

"Oh... er..." I groped at random for a question. "Um... I was wondering why it's called the 'Spanish Riding School' when it's actually in Vienna?"

"Oh, people are always asking that," said Randy with a smile. "It's because the horses are descended from Spanish horses imported in the sixteenth century. See, the Hapsburg family controlled Spain at that time and there was this big revival in classical riding during the Renaissance. Everyone wanted to breed light, fast horses for riding, instead of the big, heavy draught horses. So they crossed Arabian stallions with Spanish mares, and bred them to Neapolitan horses too... and they ended up with this great horse that was beautiful and intelligent and strong but also calm and really docile and easy to work with—that's the Lipizzaner!"

"They sound great."

"Yeah, I just love 'em. They're real 'people horses'. My boys get super excited when I take them out to train—you know, they really wanna please you."

"It's fantastic that you can share your knowledge with horse lovers in America," I said, seeing my opportunity. "You must be so proud when people come and see your shows, knowing that you're educating so many people about this wonderful breed."

Randy's face clouded. "Well, to be honest, the numbers have been really down lately—people just aren't coming to the shows anymore. I blame stupid technology! You know, everyone's always 'plugged in' these days, on the internet or Netflix or Facebook or something... They're all sitting in front of a screen. Nobody wants to get out into the open and enjoy some good old-fashioned entertainment—like having a family day out to the local ranch to see some beautiful horses."

I made a sympathetic noise. "Yes, it's awful, the way technology has taken over our lives. It must be so tough for you. I mean, if the attendance numbers are down, does that mean you're affected financially?" I asked delicately.

He hesitated, then nodded. "Yeah, the shows pretty much keep the ranch afloat. It's expensive breeding horses, you know! And I won't sell my foals to just anyone—they only go to the best homes."

"If things keep getting tougher, do you think you might be forced to sell your ranch?"

He set his jaw. "There's no way I'm selling the ranch! I'll do anything I have to, to keep it going."

I took a deep breath. "Such as committing murder?"

"*What?*" His mouth dropped open.

"You're Wagner's closest living relative, aren't you?"

"I... how did you know that?" he spluttered. "But that doesn't mean I murdered him! No way!"

"But you *are* related to Wagner, aren't you?"

"I... so what if I am? That doesn't mean that I murdered him!"

"But you did lie to the police—you said you had nothing to do with Wagner when, in fact, you are related. I know your mother's maiden name was Wagner and she came from Vienna. What was the connection? She was probably too old to be his sister... was she a cousin?"

Randy looked torn, as if deciding what to reveal. Finally, he said, "No, *I'm* his cousin. My mom was his aunt. Yeah, I know it seems weird with the age difference, but Wagner's dad was a lot older than my mom. Like nearly fifteen years. And he had Wagner early and my mom had me late, so although there's like twenty-five years between us, me and Wagner were cousins."

"But... Wagner didn't seem to acknowledge or recognise you at all," I said, frowning.

"Yeah, he didn't know until I told him."

I looked at Randy in surprise. "You were first cousins—how come he didn't know about you?"

"Well, my mom was estranged from her own family, so they didn't know anything about me." He hesitated again, as if still trying to decide how much to tell me, then finally said in a rush, "See, they didn't want her marrying my dad—he was an Irish jockey with no money and she was from this big-shot family in Vienna—so my parents eloped. They ran off to America and my mother cut all ties with her family in Austria. It wasn't 'til she was dying last year that she told me the story."

"So that's the real reason you came to Vienna," I said, more to myself than as a question.

"Yeah," Randy admitted. "When things were getting tough recently, I started thinking about contacting my mother's side of the family and asking them for help. I did some research and found out that most of the family is dead now—except for Moritz Wagner, my cousin."

"And you also realised that you were the sole heir to the whole Wagner estate if Moritz Wagner was killed."

He looked uncomfortable. "Well, that's sorta true... but that doesn't mean I came to Vienna to murder him! That's a crazy thing to say!"

"But you did come to Vienna to see Wagner,

didn't you?"

He fiddled with a pen on the table. "Yeah, Wagner was pretty active on social media and he mentioned that he was coming to try out this new hotel. I thought it would be a great chance to speak to him—you know, get to know him in a social setting and pick a good moment, instead of arranging a formal meeting—so I booked a room too."

"But then... why did you lie about that to the police? I was there; I heard you say you didn't know Wagner, that you'd never even spoken to him."

Randy threw his hands up. "I just sort of panicked and said the first thing that came to my head, okay? I know it was stupid but I... I freaked out. I knew I was the one with probably the most to gain from Wagner's death—he doesn't have any other close living relatives—so I was scared that people would think I had some kind of motive. I... I thought it would be better if nobody knew about the connection between us." He paused and gave me a quizzical look. "Hang on a minute—how did *you* know about the connection?"

"It's a bit of a long story... but one reason I knew you'd lied about your relationship with Wagner was because of your horse doodles."

"My horse doodles?" He looked bewildered.

"Yes, you've got a habit of doodling horses in the margins of things, haven't you? I saw the ones you drew on that brochure in the guest lounge just now, when you were talking to Jane Hillingdon. And you drew some in the margins of the notepad in Wagner's room... which he then later used to write his 'suicide note' on."

Randy winced. "Yeah, I've been trying to find that piece of paper ever since."

I snapped my fingers. "That's why you were snooping in the manager's office!"

He stared at me in alarm. "How the hell did you know that?"

I ignored his question. "You thought the police had found the whole paper and you were worried they might see the doodles and make the connection to you, weren't you?"

"Yeah. But when I was in the office, I saw that they only had a piece torn off the original page... and they never questioned me again... so I figured that maybe I was safe." He looked at me in confusion. "But I still don't get it—how do you know about the doodles if the police don't?"

"First, you tell me why the doodles were on Wagner's notepad."

He shrugged. "I went to see Wagner in his room earlier that day and told him everything: about my mother, the ranch, my situation.... He was actually pretty sympathetic and said he'd be willing to invest some capital in my ranch, help tide me over for a bit. He also said he had a lotta connections in Viennese high society and might be able to swing something for me, like help me get some PR for my

Lipizzaner shows in the States. I guess I must have been doodling on the hotel notepad on his desk while we were talking. And then the morning after his body was found, I heard the police talking about a note found with him on 'hotel stationery' and I suddenly remembered the doodles. I didn't know if Wagner would have used the same sheet of paper—but it was the top sheet on the pad so there was a good chance—and I panicked, especially 'cos I'd told the police that I'd never spoken to the guy. If they found out that I'd drawn the doodles, it would have looked like I was lying to cover up something." He shook his head vehemently. "But I wasn't! It was just a bunch of bad coincidences. I mean, Wagner was gonna *help* me—why would I wanna kill him? He was more valuable to me alive than dead." He realised what he'd said and winced. "Sorry, that came out wrong. I didn't mean—"

"It's okay, I know what you meant," I said. "But you know, you could also argue that with Wagner alive, you'd only get a bit of help, whereas with Wagner dead, you'd get the whole estate."

"But you don't know that!" Randy pointed out. "You haven't seen Wagner's will, have you? Neither have I, and I don't know if he left all his money to family. Maybe he's giving it all away to charity! Or to a girlfriend! And anyway, it's gonna take ages with lawyers and stuff to get money from the estate; Wagner was gonna write me a cheque the next day. I'm telling you, there was no reason for me to murder him!"

I had to admit, he was convincing. If everything he said was true, then there really seemed to be no motive for Randy McGrath to commit murder. I sat back, feeling my previous excitement drain away. I thought I'd found the answers at last... but if Randy hadn't murdered Wagner, then who had?

CHAPTER TWENTY-FIVE

I walked slowly back to my room, mulling over everything that Randy had told me. I was so preoccupied that I didn't immediately notice there was someone else in our suite, until Glenda waylaid me as I stepped in and said in an undertone:

"There's someone to see you, dear."

I looked over her shoulder and saw the Chows sitting on the sofa, with Mei-Mei huddled next to them. My heart lurched as I saw the expression on Mrs Chow's face. *Oh no.* The Old Biddies had been sitting awkwardly with the Chows but now they got up hurriedly and disappeared into their rooms. I was left alone with the Chinese couple and Mei-Mei, who kept her head down, her hands twisted in her lap.

"Er... would you like a cup of tea?" I blurted,

taking refuge in the time-honoured British solution to any adversity and realising with slight horror that I was obviously more like my mother (and Mabel Cooke!) than I thought.

Mrs Chow gave me a furious look. "Why you lie?" she demanded. "Why you say take Mei-Mei to art museum but no true? We see Mr Randy—he say he see Mei-Mei in horse show with you!"

"I did mean to... I—"

"And Mei-Mei no tell me! You teaching her that? You are very bad heart, teaching children to lie to mother!"

"No, I—"

"I trust you!" she cried, standing up to face me and jabbing a finger towards me. "You telling me you will help Mei-Mei, teach her study and get good education for improve her brain—"

"Yes, but education doesn't just come from museums and textbooks!" I burst out. "It's not just about learning every name and theory and formula in history and politics and science! There are other things that are valuable too, like art and music and... and... and just having life experiences!"

Mrs Chow made a dismissive noise. "Can enjoy life later. Now young, must study, work hard— otherwise what happen when get old? No house, no money... no enjoy life!"

I took a deep breath. "I am very sorry that I took Mei-Mei to see the horses without your permission but you should have seen how happy she was, how much she enjoyed it!" I gave her a pleading look. "Mei-Mei is just a child. She needs to have the chance to dream and do things just for fun and see beautiful things..."

Mrs Chow hissed, "You not mother! You don't understand!"

"I don't need to be a mother to know that you're pushing her too hard and killing her spirit!" I snapped, losing my temper. "If you really loved your daughter—"

I stopped, horrified, as I realised what I'd said. Mrs Chow's face was like stone.

I swallowed. "I... I'm sorry. I didn't mean that..."

The Chinese woman was breathing hard, two bright spots of colour in her cheeks. Her husband darted a nervous look at her, then at me, then back at her again. Mei-Mei seemed to shrink even smaller in her seat, her thin shoulders trembling.

"Please... I'm sorry," I said again. "I... I didn't mean to be rude. And I'm sure you love your daughter and want what's best for her. But... but please, can't you just change the way you think a little bit? I mean, have you ever looked at Mei-Mei's drawings? They are incredible! She has an amazing talent... you should treasure it and nurture it... and it doesn't mean that she can't go to a great university. At Oxford University, for example, there's a degree in Fine Art, where she can study art history and theory, and the tutors would mentor her to develop her own style ... I mean, I'm not saying she should do an art degree—I know you want her to be a lawyer and that's a great career—but... but maybe it's important to think about what Mei-Mei wants too?"

"Mei-Mei too young, no understand," snapped Mrs Chow. "I know what important for her life. She need good job and house and saving money—"

The little girl gave a muffled sob, then sprang up and ran to the door of our suite. Flinging it open, she ran out and disappeared.

Her mother turned a furious face to me. "You see?" she shrieked. "You teaching Mei-Mei bad way! Always before she listen to me. Now, she run away! No respect!"

She stormed out of the suite with her husband scurrying after her. I stared wordlessly after them for a moment, then groaned and sank down onto the sofa, putting my face in my hands. *What a mess!* I felt a mixture of guilt, shame, anger, and frustration roiling inside me.

The Old Biddies poked their heads out of their rooms. "Are they gone, dear?"

"Yes," I said with a sigh. I gave them a rueful look as they joined me on the sofa. "I suppose you heard everything?"

"Well, you really shouldn't have taken the little girl without permission, you know," said Glenda.

"And you *could* have been a bit more tactful, dear," Florence said.

I shrank even smaller on the sofa.

"But we do agree with you," Ethel said, patting my arm. "The poor child needs to have a bit of fun, and her mother needs—"

"More fibre in her diet," Mabel declared. "That woman is a clear example of irritability produced by constipation and excessive gas. A large helping of bran each morning would do wonders for her temperament, as well as her constitution."

"I don't think all the bran in the world is going to change Mrs Chow's attitude," I said dourly.

"Well, no good moping about it here, dear," said Mabel briskly. "Come along! It's nearly five-thirty—we might as well go down and have some tea."

"Ooh yes, I fancy a piece of *Gugelhupf*," said Ethel.

"What's that again?" I asked.

"I can't remember now," said Ethel with a giggle. "I just fancied saying the name."

"It's a Bundt cake," said Florence, who loved her food and seemed to have learnt the name of every Viennese cake and pastry. "I had a slice yesterday. It's wonderful—the inside is marbled sponge, with cocoa and rum, and the outside is dusted with icing sugar. And Sofia serves it with fresh whipped cream."

Even I was beginning to be tempted and I dutifully followed the Old Biddies downstairs. A part of me cringed at the thought of meeting the Chows again but—perhaps not surprisingly—they were not in the dining room. Everyone else seemed to be there, though: Jane Hillingdon had cornered Stefan next to the large *Gugelhupf* in the centre of the buffet and was gabbling away while the concierge listened politely; old Mrs Hillingdon had helped herself to some chocolate torte and—with her knitting tucked under her arm—was wandering off in the direction of the guest lounge; Randy McGrath was sitting with Ana Bauer, their heads together as they discussed something earnestly; and Johann Müller was hovering by the large platter of apple strudel, obviously trying to decide which piece to help himself to. I hurried towards him, relieved to have an innocuous person to talk to, and he smiled as he saw me.

"Ah, Frau Rose... have you tasted the apple strudel yet?"

"No, I haven't actually," I confessed. "I think I'm still digesting the cakes from this morning at Café Central!"

"Then you must have a piece now!" said Müller, enthusiastically loading a large slice onto a plate. He presented it to me, then looked around, making a clucking sound with his tongue. "*Ah!* There is no napkin. Frau Fritzl must have forgot to lay them out—"

"Oh, don't worry, honestly..." I said, but Müller was obviously of the old school and had decided that bringing me a napkin was the mark of a proper gentleman.

"No, no, I will go and find one for you..." he said,

wandering off.

The plate was warm in my hands and as I looked down, I inhaled the wonderful scent of cinnamon and melted butter, overlaid with that gorgeous smell of fresh baking. *I'm not going to wait until Müller gets back*, I decided, grabbing a fork and digging into the strudel.

Mmm... The thin pastry on the outside was light and crispy, and yet stretchy and chewy at the same time, and the warm filling of sliced apples, raisins, and breadcrumbs, all caramelised with sugar, was absolutely delicious. I closed my eyes as I chewed, savouring the flavours. *Müller's right*, I thought. *In spite of all the other amazing cakes I've tasted, I think apple strudel is going to win the title of best dessert in Vienna.* I swallowed and was just about to fork another piece into my mouth when the air was suddenly rent by a series of choked screams.

"Aaaahhhh! Aaa-rrr-rrr-gghh! Aarrgghh!"

I dropped the plate in surprise and whirled in the direction of the sound. It seemed to be coming from across the hallway. I dashed out of the dining room, followed by several of the other guests, and ran into the guest lounge to find old Mrs Hillingdon collapsed on the floor. She was clutching her throat and gasping, her face an alarming red colour.

"*MUM!*" screeched Jane Hillingdon, dropping to her knees next to the old woman. "Oh my God, Mum, are you all right? What happened? *What happened?*"

The old woman made a rasping, choking sound but couldn't talk. However, she made some hand motions that left no one in doubt about what had happened. The evidence of a struggle was there in the tangle of knitting needles, yarn, and half-knitted scarf on the floor around the old woman. Someone had come up behind her and tried to strangle her to death.

CHAPTER TWENTY-SIX

Mabel pushed her way through the crowd. "Well, don't just stand there—call an ambulance!" she ordered.

I saw Stefan standing beside Randy and Müller, all three men gaping stupidly at the stricken woman on the floor, but at the sound of Mabel's voice, Stefan jumped and seemed to come to himself.

"*Ach...* yes, yes, of course..." he mumbled, turning and hurrying towards the reception desk.

Sofia brought a glass of water and crouched down on the other side of the old lady, holding the glass up to her lips. Her own face was pale as she watched Mrs Hillingdon slowly take a few sips. She glanced up and our eyes met. I realised she was thinking what I was thinking: was this the murderer striking again? I scanned the faces around me. Aside from Mei-Mei and the Chows, we were all here, and unless the attacker was a stranger who had come off the street, he or she was likely to be *one of us*. From the whispering and murmurs around the room, it was obvious that I wasn't the only one with this thought. In fact, I could see people start to look sideways and eye each other warily.

The police and the ambulance arrived soon after, and Mrs Hillingdon was fussed over by the paramedics. She had recovered slightly, although she still couldn't talk, and her throat was showing horrible red swelling and purple bruises. Still, the old lady was a fighter—in fact, she even balked at going to hospital when the paramedics insisted that she needed to be kept under observation overnight, in case the swelling got worse and interfered with her breathing.

"Mum, you have to go—it's really important!" said Jane, for once mercifully brief.

Maybe it was the shock of hearing her daughter being so succinct but Mrs Hillingdon finally consented and allowed the paramedics to help her onto the stretcher. As I watched Jane follow her mother and the paramedics out of the hotel, I noticed grimly that the bruises on her throat were in exactly the right place to match the fingers of someone trying to strangle the old woman. But why? Why would anyone want to kill old Mrs Hillingdon? And who could it be? The Old Biddies were obviously pondering the same thing because as soon as the police had finished questioning us and we were allowed to return to our suite, they began arguing about the identity of the old woman's attacker.

"I still think it's Ana Bauer," said Glenda stubbornly. "I've said she was the murderer all along. First she killed Moritz and then she tried to kill Mrs Hillingdon."

"But she was sitting with that American boy, Randy, wasn't she?" asked Ethel. "I'm sure I saw them talking together."

"Maybe Randy was helping her. I always thought *he* was likely to be the murderer," said Florence.

"Neither of them is the murderer," said Mabel bossily. "I think the murderer is Stefan Dreschner. I got a good look at his hands for the first time just now. Have you noticed how short his index fingers are?"

"What does *that* have to do with anything?" I asked.

Mabel gave me a knowing look. "Ah... I read a book on Palmistry which said that people with markedly short index fingers are likely to have criminal tendencies."

I rolled my eyes. "That's the most ridiculous thing I've ever heard! You can't take against Stefan Dreschner just because the poor man was born with shorter index fingers. And anyway, what would his motive be? Come to that, what would *any* of their motives be in killing Mrs Hillingdon?" I shook my head. "It just doesn't make sense! When we thought this case was about Wagner, it was logical to suspect those with some reason to want him dead—but if it's not just about Wagner anymore, then everything has to be thrown out of the window!"

"Yes, now we have to consider those who not only had a relationship with Wagner but also with Mrs Hillingdon," Florence agreed, nodding.

"That's just... that's just too complicated!" I said irritably. "There isn't any connection between the two of them. One is an Austrian art critic with many lovers and enemies, the other is a sweet old English woman on holiday in Vienna, with no enemies that we know of. Why are they both being targeted by the murderer?"

"Maybe you're looking at it the wrong way, dear," said Mabel. "There *is* no connection between them, the murderer *was* just after Wagner... but Mrs Hillingdon became an inconvenience."

I frowned. "What do you mean?"

"The murderer doesn't want to kill Mrs Hillingdon for herself—they just need to silence her because she's a danger to them."

"Yes, yes," said Ethel. "Just like in Agatha Christie's *A Murder is Announced*, the second and third victims were killed because they might have been able to recognise the murderer—"

"But Mrs Hillingdon doesn't know who the

murderer is, otherwise she would have said," I protested.

"Maybe she doesn't know that she knows," said Mabel.

"What?" I was hopelessly confused now.

"Well, maybe—"

We were interrupted by a petulant meow and I looked down to see Muesli at my feet with a reproachful expression on her little whiskered face.

"*Meorrw!*" she said again, headbutting my shins.

I glanced at the clock on the wall. "Oh cripes! It's past eight o'clock and Muesli hasn't even had her dinner!"

I got up and went to fetch the cat food while the Old Biddies began a new argument, this time over where to go for dinner. In the end, they settled on a recommendation from Mabel's trusty guidebook and we dutifully followed her to a rustic-looking café nearby. The menu was quite small, offering only a selection of traditional Viennese dishes, in particular the iconic *Wiener Schnitzel*. But this was cooked so well—a paper-thin cutlet of pork covered in crispy breadcrumbs and fried to golden perfection, served with parsley potatoes and a wedge of lemon—that you didn't really feel like you needed anything else. Well, except maybe some dessert. With all the amazing cakes and pastries on offer, who in their right mind would ever pass up dessert in Austria?

By the time we finally trooped back, it was late—

well past ten thirty—and the hotel was quiet. The lights were dimmed in the lobby and nobody was in the guest lounge, although Stefan was at his usual place behind his laptop on reception.

"*Grüss Gott!*" said Stefan, smiling and giving us the traditional local greeting. "Have you had a nice dinner?"

"Yes, delicious. Um... have you heard from the hospital?" I asked.

He sobered. "Yes, Frau Hillingdon is doing well. The swelling has gone down, she has been given some painkillers, and she is resting now. They say she was very lucky—there was not much damage to her throat."

"That's great news," I said with some relief. I liked Jane Hillingdon's quiet, long-suffering mother. "So she'll be staying at the hospital overnight?"

"Yes, they think it is best. Her daughter will also be staying with her."

"Has she said anything about her attacker yet?"

Stefan shook his head. "I do not know. The police will be visiting her in hospital tomorrow." He looked around the lobby. "I have been talking to Sofia. We are wondering if we need to increase the security on this level. It is too easy for any vagrant to wander into the hotel from the street and attack a guest. Of course, we did not think we would have to take such measures, since this is a good neighbourhood... but I suppose criminals are everywhere."

I murmured a polite reply, although I thought that they were simply deluding themselves and hiding from the truth. Sofia knew as well as I did that Mrs Hillingdon's attacker was unlikely to be a random "vagrant" who had wandered in off the street. Still, I could understand them wanting to downplay the possibility of a monster in our midst. It was creepy enough thinking it without them spelling it out and they certainly didn't want to cause a mass panic and walk-out.

"By the way, have you seen Mr and Mrs Chow and their little girl?" I asked.

"*Ah*, yes—they came to see me earlier. They have decided to check out early," said Stefan, his expression regretful. "They will be leaving tomorrow."

"Oh." I felt a stab of guilt, wondering if the decision had anything to do with the nasty confrontation earlier. I hoped I'd have a chance to see Mei-Mei before she left—I wanted to say goodbye to the little girl properly and not end our acquaintance with that horrible scene. "Do you know if they're leaving first thing?"

"No, I think they will stay until late morning."

"Oh, good. I... I was hoping to have a chance to say goodbye to the little girl."

"The little girl? I saw her earlier..." Stefan looked around the lobby. "Perhaps she is in the guest lounge?"

I hurried eagerly down the hallway and peeked

into the guest lounge but it seemed empty. Sighing, I returned to the reception and followed the Old Biddies up to our suite. We were all tired and decided to have an early night. As I undressed, I noticed a bruise on my arm. I must have knocked it against something without realising. The purple mark reminded me of the awful bruises on old Mrs Hillingdon's neck and I thought again of what Mabel had said earlier: *"Maybe she doesn't know that she knows."* Was it possible that the old lady held the key to the identity of the murderer? But how? Something she saw on the day?

On an impulse, I picked up my phone. Jane Hillingdon had insisted on exchanging phone numbers the day we'd met at the Belvedere Palace and although my heart had sunk at the time, now I was glad for a way to contact the woman. She answered on the second ring, sounding slightly less ebullient than usual but almost back to her normal talkative self.

"Gemma! No, no, it's not too late... it's only just gone eleven, hasn't it? We don't usually go to bed until twelve... How nice of you to ring... *it's Gemma, Mum, calling to ask after you—isn't she nice...* oh, Mum's fine... the doctors say there's nothing to worry about... well, I think that's what they were saying, they were mostly talking in German and none of the words were in my phrasebook... but this head doctor chap came to speak to me and said Mum will be fine... I had a real scare, I can tell you... but she's eating and drinking now—oh, just soft foods, jellies and stuff—and they said she can leave the hospital tomorrow..."

"Has she told you what happened to her? Did she see who attacked her?"

"No, I've been asking her that... came up from behind her, he did... well, I'm assuming it's a man but I suppose it could have just as likely been a woman... Mum says she was sitting on the sofa, counting stitches, when this person grabbed her neck from behind—oh my goodness, wouldn't you be terrified if it happened to you? *I* would—I think I'd be paralysed, but not Mum—she struggled and wriggled and tried to pull his hand off and—*what's that, Mum?* ...Oh, Mum says she thinks she got her attacker with one of her knitting needles—stabbed them good and proper. That's when they let go and ran away—"

"She was very brave," I said admiringly. Then quickly, before Jane could start up again, I said: "Listen—can you do me a favour? Can you ask your mother to think back to the day of Wagner's murder and go over everything she saw or heard that afternoon? From the moment she came down to tea to when she heard Glenda's scream. Was there anything odd that stood out to her?"

"Oh... okay..." said Jane. Her voice faded away and I could hear a conversation in the background, then after few minutes she came back. "Mum says she didn't notice anything in particular—not that she was really looking, of course, she just took her cake and her knitting and went into the guest lounge and she was sitting in there when she heard the scream... *What's that, Mum?* ...Oh, she says she couldn't see the hallway, anyway, because her back was to the door—all she could see was part of the library and Mr Müller's apple strudel on the table next to his armchair—so she definitely didn't see anyone creeping past to go to the music room... Oh, but she did notice Mr Wagner's girlfriend coming out of the music room earlier—"

"Wait—*what?* You're saying that your mother saw Ana Bauer coming out of the music room?"

"Yes, but this was much earlier, when we first came down for tea... Mr Wagner was still fine then—I saw him at tea myself and he was chatting to Mr Müller—so she couldn't have pushed him off—Ana Bauer, I mean... but Mum says that was the one odd thing she noticed, because it seemed strange that everyone was coming down for tea and Ana Bauer was going up, in the opposite direction. She was carrying a plate of apple strudel, though, so maybe she was going to eat it upstairs? Anyway, why are you asking all this? Do you think Mum saw something important on the day of the murder?" Jane gasped. "Do you think that's why she was attacked? Because the murderer wants to silence her?"

I had to admit, garrulous and eccentric as she was, Jane Hillingdon wasn't stupid. In fact, she was pretty quick to connect the dots. Unfortunately, she was also quick to over-react.

"Oh my goodness! Does this mean Mum's life is under threat? Will she have to go into one of them things you see on telly—you know, those Witness Protection Programmes?"

"Er... I doubt it's that serious," I said, beginning to wish that I'd never put the idea into Jane's head. "Look, forget I asked you. It was just a silly thought I had, okay? In fact, Sofia and Stefan think it's nothing to do with Wagner's death. They think it was some 'vagrant' who sneaked into the hotel to attack guests for money," I added, hoping to distract her.

"Really?" Jane squeaked. "Oh my goodness! I must tell Mum that... good thing she didn't have her handbag with her, dontcha think? Although she wouldn't have had much Euros on her—I've got most of the foreign currency with me—but I suppose they could have nicked her cards and the ring from Grandma which she always carries with her—it's broken, you see, so she can't wear it—I keep telling her to take it to a jeweller and get it fixed but Mum says there's no need and besides—"

"Uh... well, it's getting late so I'll let you go now," I cut in. "I'm sure you're knackered and want to rest. Please say hi to your mother for me and wish her better soon!"

I hung up before Jane could get a word in and flopped down on my bed. *Whew!* I was exhausted after that phone call. And I was doubtful if I'd really got anything useful. I frowned as I thought over the conversation again. There was something—something that Jane had said—which nagged at me, but I couldn't put my finger on it...

Unless it was the strange report of Ana being in the music room just before everyone came down for tea. And why didn't she just stay downstairs to eat her apple strudel with everyone else, instead of carrying it upstairs? Did that have any significance?

Then something else Jane Hillingdon had said came back to me. The day we had met at the Belvedere, she had talked of "fake art" and the fact that nearly fifty percent of the art sold in galleries could be forgeries... Devlin had mentioned forgeries too, in conjunction with the gallery that Ana Bauer had used to work at. Of course, Ana had been cleared of any connection with the scandal, but still... was it too much of a coincidence that she should be linked in some way?

I felt a tingle of excitement. It would all make sense! I'd always been sceptical of the "woman scorned" motive that the Old Biddies had suggested for Ana (and I wasn't even going to consider their ludicrous "Cold War spy" idea), but a motive for murder that stemmed from commercial greed and gain was something I could easily believe in. In fact, remembering the cool, astute businesswoman we'd met at the spa yesterday, I could easily see Ana Bauer committing murder to protect her business.

I thought back to that first morning when the Old Biddies and I had been sitting with Wagner and Müller at breakfast: Ana Bauer had joined the group and she had reacted very badly to Wagner talking about the Museum of Fake Art. Had it been genuine disgust—or a sense of guilt that had prompted her to be so sharp with him? Maybe there really *was* no smoke without fire. Maybe Ana *had* tried passing off fake art as genuine pieces at her old gallery. She had escaped detection that time and, emboldened by her success, she had started a similar con when she opened her own place. But Wagner had discovered her secret—whether through his own expertise as an art critic or because Ana lowered her guard during their affair— and he had started taunting her, maybe even blackmailing her...

Yes, it all fits perfectly! I thought excitedly. Then I frowned. There was still one big question: *How had Ana done it?* According to Mrs Hillingdon, she was seen going upstairs while everyone else was coming down for tea. So she wasn't hanging around the lobby level. Therefore, the only way she could have returned to the music room to push Wagner off the balcony was if she had somehow sneaked back down without anyone seeing. How? Using the back stairs and the emergency exit? Could she really have done that, and then rushed back up again to "pretend" to come down the lift with the Old Biddies?

CHAPTER TWENTY-SEVEN

I didn't realise how long I'd been sitting on the bed, puzzling over the case, until I felt something rubbing against my legs and looked down to see Muesli.

"*Meorrw! Meorrw!*" she said plaintively.

I realised with a familiar stab of guilt that my little tabby had been cooped up in the room for most of the day again. I was already in my pyjamas and didn't want to get dressed again to take her for a stroll outside. Besides, it was nearly midnight and, safe as the neighbourhood was, I didn't fancy a walk by myself in the darkened streets. Then I brightened: I could go for the lazy option of a quick play in the music room. Scooping the little cat up, I let myself out of the suite and headed downstairs.

The reception was abandoned now and I

wondered if Sofia and Stefan had retreated to the private wing of the hotel. With no one about, I decided it was safe enough to let Muesli loose and have the full run of the lobby area as well as the hallway and adjoining rooms. The little cat was delighted, scampering about, making happy chirruping sounds, and sniffing everything with great interest. I let her explore at her leisure, following her as she made her way slowly down the hallway. I thought she might go into the guest lounge but, to my surprise, she made a beeline down the hall and around the L-bend to the music room. Perhaps it had become a bit of a routine for her now—or perhaps it was simply the lure of the familiar. She trotted in confidently, pausing to rub her chin on various pieces of furniture, marking them with her scent.

I wandered over to the French doors leading out to the balcony. It was dark outside and I could barely make out the shapes of the various potted plants arranged beside the railing. Only the arching canes of the climbing rose growing along the balcony railing caught the light spilling out from the windows, and I could see the few remaining leaves, furled over with the edges turning brown, fluttering in the wind.

"*Meorrw... meorrw...*"

I turned back into the room to find Muesli in the fireplace, scrabbling at the back of the hearth with her front paws.

"Aww, Muesli, don't play in there…" I groaned, starting back across the room.

"*Meorrw!*" The little cat gave a defiant twitch of her tail and ignored me, continuing to paw the back wall of the hearth.

"Come on, get out of there—you're going to be filthy," I said irritably, bending down to scoop her up. "You can play on the other—"

I broke off as I realised suddenly what Muesli had been scratching at. There was a tiny gap in the wall at the back of the hearth. In fact, it wasn't a solid brick wall like I'd expected—it seemed to be made of wooden panels, painted black to merge into the rest of the fireplace. And one of the panels had warped slightly and shifted sideways, leaving a tiny gap in the wood. This was what Muesli had been pawing at. Curious, I reached out myself and prised the gap wider with my fingers. To my surprise, the entire section came off in my hands and I was left holding a long piece of wooden panelling and staring at a large rectangular hole in the wall.

"*Meorrw!*" said Muesli excitedly. Before I could stop her, she hopped through the hole and disappeared.

"Hey, Muesli!" I cried, dropping the panelling and lunging unsuccessfully to grab her.

I peered into the gap. It led into a small space which seemed to recede into darkness. Then I remembered that on the day Stefan had shown me the trapdoor and the chute beneath the fireplace, he had mentioned that many old houses had secret passageways between the rooms. In fact, it stood to reason that if there was a chute down to the wine cellar, there was also likely to be a network of other concealed passages in the house, as a way for the Jewish fugitives to escape quickly from other rooms, if the Nazis were to arrive suddenly.

"*Meorrw?*" Muesli's voice drifted out from the darkness.

"Muesli? Muesli, come back here!" I called.

There was no answer. I squinted and saw a pair of green eyes glowing back at me mischievously. The little minx was taunting me! She obviously thought this was a marvellous game and wanted me to climb in after her and chase her. *Grrr.* For a moment, I was tempted to just leave her and go up to bed. I was sure she'd come back out by herself eventually. But then I remembered the time Muesli had climbed into the vent at my parents' house back in Oxford and how she had ended up stuck in the wall space and needed the fire brigade to come and rescue her. I didn't fancy repeating that here in Vienna. I sighed. There was nothing for it—I would have to go after her.

Trying not to think of spiders and other creepy-crawlies, I clambered through the hole and stood in the space beyond. It was very narrow—barely wide enough to fit a large man—and with the ceiling so low that I had to hunch over. Now that I was in here, I could see that it wasn't very big. In fact, in the dim light spilling in from the music room, I could see the other end of the short passageway and the outline of a square on the other wall. From my memory of the layout of the hotel, I guessed that the passage led to the library. Muesli had trotted down to the other end and was sniffing something on the floor.

"Muesli! Come here!" I hissed.

She ignored me. Grumbling under my breath, I hunched over and crawled to her.

"Gotcha!" I said triumphantly, grabbing her around her middle.

"*Meeeeorrw!*" She squirmed in my grasp.

"Oh no you don't! No more games. We're going straight back to the room now and—" I broke off suddenly, staring at the thing on the floor that Muesli had been sniffing. Without realising what I was doing, I released her and slowly picked up the item. I held it up to look at it more closely.

It was a leaf, furling over with the edges slightly brown. It had a prickly surface that felt rough against my skin—in fact, there were tiny hooks on the underside of the stem that snagged against anything it touched. I caught my breath as I realised what it was. *A leaf from a rose.* And I knew which rose—the climbing rose on the balcony, the one I'd seen just now with its arching canes growing along the railing and its few remaining leaves fluttering in the wind. I looked closer. This was a relatively fresh leaf that had come off the rose some time in the last couple of days... My heart skipped a beat as I realised what this meant. Someone who had recently been through this passageway had also recently been on the balcony.

In my mind's eye, I saw myself on the day we arrived in Vienna... Sofia taking me on a tour of the hotel and showing me the balcony... the climbing rose growing in a pot beside the edge of the balcony, snagging me with its prickly canes...

I drew a sharp breath as I realised what must have happened. The murderer, in going up to the railing to push Wagner over, had got snagged by the rose just like me, and as they had pulled free, they'd also pulled off some of the prickly leaves... one of which had clung to their clothing... and then dropped off here in the passageway, as the murderer hurried through to make their getaway.

I had been on the right track the day I was talking to Stefan—I had thought that the murderer might have used the secret passageway, built for the Jews, as an alternative entry to the music room. The only thing was, I had focused on the *wrong* secret passageway. I'd only been thinking of the trapdoor in the floor of the fireplace and the chute which led down to the wine cellar—I hadn't considered that there might be another secret passage.

I frowned. But if Ana Bauer was the murderer, how did this fit? Could she have come this way instead of using the emergency exit and the back stairs? She would've had to leave the passage to enter the guest lounge library, and surely that wasn't possible? The only two people in there had been old Mrs Hillingdon and Johann Müller. Mrs Hillingdon had been adamant she hadn't seen anyone else...

Then it hit me. Of course! How could I have been so stupid? It wasn't about what Mrs Hillingdon saw—it was about what she *hadn't* seen! And what she hadn't seen was Müller in person!

The murderer wasn't Ana Bauer... it was Johann Müller.

I thought back to Jane's words on the phone just now: she had said that her mother "...*couldn't see the hallway, anyway, because her back was to the door—all she could see was part of the library and Mr Müller's apple strudel on the table next to his armchair...*"

When Mrs Hillingdon had first told the police that she was in the guest lounge with Müller, it had given him the perfect alibi. After all, he couldn't be murdering Wagner if he was with her the entire time. But now I realised that she hadn't actually *seen* Müller himself. In fact, I remembered on my first day, when Sofia was taking me on a tour of the hotel and we had walked into the library alcove, I had been startled to find Müller sitting in the armchair—I hadn't even realised that he was there. The high back of the chair, and the angle at which it was placed, had completely hidden him from view.

This meant that you could think the chair was empty when somebody was there or—conversely— think that somebody was sitting there when it was empty. Especially if viewed from the other side of the guest lounge, it was in a complete blind spot.

And Müller had known that and used it to his advantage. If he placed his apple strudel in full view of the rest of the lounge, then everyone would assume that he was sitting there. And that is exactly what had happened. Everyone knew how much Müller loved apple strudel—he had made sure to broadcast the fact everywhere—and so when Mrs Hillingdon had seen the apple strudel on the table next to the armchair, she had assumed that he was sitting at the other end of the room from her and had provided him with an alibi.

Of course, there was always a chance that someone could have walked over to the library alcove and seen the empty armchair—and the gaping hole in the library wall—but it was a calculated gamble that Müller had been willing to take. He knew that most of the other guests were unlikely to walk over there, just as they had got used to him claiming that corner as his.

The whole thing was still very risky though. In fact, when you thought about it like this, I couldn't believe that anyone would come up with such a convoluted plan to commit murder! There were so many things that could have gone wrong, so many ways in which Müller could have been caught. Only a desperate man would have tried something so crazy...

But of course, only a desperate man would have attacked an old woman in public, with other hotel guests nearby. I realised guiltily that I might have inadvertently provoked the assault. Müller had felt fairly secure after the police had ruled the death as suicide—that is, until he'd met me this morning, just outside the police station. I remembered his shock when I told him that his friend's death wasn't suicide but murder. I'd thought that it was simply the surprise of a naïve bystander but, in fact, Müller must have had a nasty scare when I told him that I intended to hassle the police to re-investigate the death. If Mrs Hillingdon was questioned again, she might have let slip that she hadn't actually seen him—only his apple strudel—and he couldn't afford to take that risk, so he had to silence her.

"*Meorrw!*"

Muesli's petulant cry roused me from my thoughts and I realised that I had been crouched for so long in the dark that my legs had gone to sleep. I winced as I wriggled my feet, feeling the pins and needles tingle unpleasantly.

"*Meorrw?*" Muesli scratched at the square in the wall facing us. I hesitated, then reached for it, deciding that it would be quicker to come out in the library than crawl back to the music room. I just wanted to get back to the suite now, as fast as I could, and tell the Old Biddies about my discovery.

The panelling in the library wall creaked slightly, then came off as easily as the one in the music room. I crawled through the hole and out of the passageway into the library alcove.

Slowly, I straightened, dusting myself off—and stood up to find myself facing Johann Müller.

CHAPTER TWENTY-EIGHT

"H... Herr Müller!" I stammered.

He said nothing, just stood there looking at me. I shifted from foot to foot, wanting to bolt but also scared of what he might do if I moved. Behind me, I heard Muesli jump out of the hole and felt her furry tail brush my legs as she walked past me to sniff Müller's feet. I wanted to yell at her to get away from him but I felt paralysed. In any case, he didn't seem to notice her and she soon wandered off to the other corner of the library. For a fleeting moment, I wished that Muesli was a dog who could be sent to get help... then I reminded myself that this wasn't a Disney movie and knowing my luck, even if Muesli had been a dog, she would probably just wander off to the kitchen in search of food.

No, I was on my own, facing a desperate man

who had already resorted to violence twice. I wondered if I dared scream. Would anyone hear me? Sofia and Stefan were probably in the private wing, behind soundproof doors, and the rest of the guests were in their rooms upstairs, also behind soundproof doors. It was past midnight. They were all probably in bed. Even the Old Biddies had turned off their room lights when I left our suite with Muesli.

Surreptitiously, I eyed the space around Müller, trying to judge if I could get past him and into the main lounge, and then out into the hallway. Because of the way the library alcove was tucked around a corner, it wasn't a straightforward run past him—I would have to dodge around him but then curve back to get around that corner, which meant slowing down and potentially being grabbed by him or tripping over furniture in the way. Still, it was my only chance—and anything was better than standing here under that creepy unspeaking gaze.

But just as I was gathering myself to run, he spoke:

"I had hoped that you would not find it, Frau Rose. I could see that you are an intelligent woman. I knew that if you saw this passage between the two rooms, you would quickly understand... and you would know that it was me."

I swallowed. I wasn't sure I wanted to stand here making small talk with a murderer. I wanted to get away, to put as many doors between me and Müller as possible. But somehow my curiosity got the better of me, and before I realised what I was doing, I burst out: "But I don't understand—why? Why did you murder Wagner?"

His face darkened. *"Dieser Bastard!* After everything I did for him..." He unclenched his hands with effort and gave a humourless laugh. "You asked the other day, *Meine Dame*, if Moritz was grateful for my help in his career. Yes, he was grateful—so grateful that he demanded I pay him money so that he would remain silent about my shameful secret."

"Wagner was blackmailing you?" I said in surprise. "But... what about? What 'shameful secret'?"

"The great lie that I have been embracing, Frau Rose; the hoax which has made my museum a success and which hundreds of people pay money every week to see."

I stared at him. *Hoax?* Then it hit me. Of course! I had been right that Wagner had been murdered because he knew too much about "fake art"—but I had been wrong about the person trying to hide it. It wasn't Ana Bauer selling forgeries at her gallery... it was Müller exhibiting fake art at his museum!

"The Klimt," I said suddenly. "The rare lost painting by Gustav Klimt that's in your museum. It was supposed to have been stolen by the Nazis for Hitler's private museum but you claimed to have 'discovered' it at a deceased estate sale... except that you didn't, did you? It was actually a clever forgery and Wagner knew! That's why he was blackmailing you!"

Müller nodded, a bitter look on his face. "Yes, Moritz Wagner knew. He helped me produce the provenance to support the painting's authenticity. It was when he was a young man, working at my museum. I took him into my confidence—and I expected him to honour that trust. And for many years, he did. But then he changed. He became famous, admired, drunk with his own power. He discovered a new pleasure: tormenting others and watching them suffer. He knew that many years ago, my family museum had been facing disaster; we were almost bankrupt, but the 'Klimt' saved it. And now, the museum has become a great success, a highlight of any visitor's itinerary in Vienna." His voice rose passionately. "How my Papa and Mama would have been happy to see it! They were good people, they worked hard—you know they were part of the Resistance movement against the Nazis? They risked their lives to rescue many Jews and help them find a safe escape out of Austria, some from this very house."

It dawned on me. "That's how you knew about the secret passage," I said.

Müller gave a faint smile. "Yes, my parents told me many stories when I was a child: how they came to the house at night and even joined the Jewish fugitives for a meal sometimes, here, in this lounge, or in the music room. The house was owned by an Austrian businessman, one who pretended to sympathise with the Nazis while keeping many Jews safe in his wine cellar. He risked his life too, just like my parents, because he believed in compassion and acceptance... and in the unique talents of different races, without which we would not have such wonderful things as music and art..." His voice faded away as he looked sadly at the floor.

I shifted my weight, wondering if he was distracted enough for me to attempt to escape. But then Müller looked up, his face contorted with anger again.

"They worked hard, my parents. They spent many years building their collection and looking after our family museum... Do you think they deserved to suffer so much heartache and disappointment? To watch their life's work be taken away from them? Do you?" he demanded, thrusting his face into mine.

"N-n-no," I said, taking a step back. "N-no, of course not."

Müller calmed down slightly. "No, they did not. They deserved to be proud of the museum they had built, to see visitors enjoying their collection. But there are so many museums in Vienna—a small private one like ours just cannot compete." He looked at me suddenly like a small boy who was proud of something he had achieved. "So I thought of an answer: a lure to entice people to come to the museum—a rare 'lost' painting by a master, combined with a romantic story." He smiled a soft, almost dreamy smile. "People love stories of that kind; they like to think that they are viewing a treasure rescued from the clutches of the Nazis. And once they were there, they were always delighted with the rest of our collection—so we were not really misleading them. We were simply helping them appreciate something that they might not otherwise have found—"

An excited meow from Muesli in the other corner of the library interrupted him. She sounded like she had come across a favourite toy or treat, and I felt a sense of ironic disbelief that my cat could be happily playing while I was standing here, facing a murderer.

Müller glanced over at the corner in a distracted fashion, then turned back to me. For a moment, I thought he was going to say: "Now... where was I?" —and I felt a crazy urge to laugh.

I must be getting hysterical, I thought. Who on earth could think of laughing at this moment?

Müller didn't say "Where was I?"—but he did look at me earnestly and say: "I want you to understand—I did not plan to murder Moritz. I was still hoping to reason with him, to ask him to respect the trust I had put in him."

"You mean... it *was* sort of an accident, after all?" I said hopefully. "Did you mean to speak to Wagner on the balcony but then things got out of hand?"

Müller shifted uncomfortably, not meeting my eyes. "No... it was not like that. But... but I did try to speak to Moritz first. I thought our time in the hotel would give me a chance to speak to him, but I quickly realised that Moritz was beyond reasoning. He had no heart! He betrayed my trust—and he enjoyed watching me beg." He looked up, his eyes suddenly burning with anger and humiliation. "He even enjoyed taunting me in public, such as that morning when he joked about the Museum of Art Fakes.

"And later that afternoon, while we were in the dining room for afternoon tea, Moritz had the arrogance to ask me for more money again," Müller spat. "More money... just to let him continue to taunt me! I could not accept it anymore. I sat in the library, trying to read, trying to enjoy my apple strudel, but all I could think of was the years stretching ahead of me, with Moritz taunting me and bleeding me of money..."

He stopped speaking for a moment, breathing hard, his eyes unfocused as he went back to that moment on the day of the murder.

"Then I saw him through the library window—standing there on the balcony, smoking, looking at the view, so confident, so complacent!" Müller clenched his fists again. "I thought of how easily it could all end if there was a push—just a little push—off that balcony. I knew I could get to the music room easily through the hidden passage. It would be a matter of minutes..."

"But... you must have known that people would ask questions?" I said. "No one was going to accept that Moritz Wagner had just jumped off the balcony for no reason!"

"I did not think about it at the time," said Müller with a sigh. "It was as if there was another person inside me... and then afterwards, when it was over and he was dead and I was sitting back in the library again, I realised what I had done. But ah... *zum Glück*...the luck was with me. There was a note—a note which the police took to be the sign of a melancholy mind and so believed Moritz to have taken his own life." He frowned slightly. "I am still confused about this note. When Inspektor Gruber questioned me about it, naturally I lied and told him that Moritz had been in poor spirits. I saw the chance that had been given to me and I seized it. But I knew in fact that Moritz would never have committed suicide... so why was the note there?"

By a lucky coincidence, I thought. Müller was right—Lady Luck *had* been smiling on him. If Wagner hadn't been working on his review—and Sofia hadn't seen it and snatched it up, leaving a fragment behind—the police would never have been misled into thinking that Wagner had committed suicide.

Aloud, I said: "The note was a misunderstanding... and the police are aware of that now. They will be re-opening the investigation into Wagner's death, especially now that Mrs Hillingdon has been attacked as well. You didn't manage to kill her—so she *will* be telling the police the truth about your so-called alibi. There is no escape, Herr Müller. You will be arrested. You are better to give yourself up and explain the whole story. Blackmail and extortion are illegal, and I'm sure that the judges will be lenient when they hear what Wagner was doing to you—"

"No!" shouted Müller, shaking his head vehemently. "No, I will not surrender! I did not do anything wrong! Wagner was the one who was evil—he was the one who caused pain and misery for others—not me! I will not—"

He broke off suddenly as we both heard a faint "'*Choo!*" from the other side of the library alcove. Müller jerked around and stared at the direction where the sound had come from. It was the far corner of the alcove, surrounded by bookshelves and furnished with several large beanbags, which formed a sort of low wall and gave the area the enclosed feel of a "reading corner" in a children's library. I saw the tip of Muesli's tail behind a beanbag and heard her meow excitedly again, but the sneeze hadn't sounded feline. It had sounded human.

Then it came again—muffled, as if someone was covering their mouth with their hands and trying to hide the sound. "'*Choo!*"

"Who is there?" cried Müller, lunging across the alcove.

Oh God. My heart gave a horrible lurch as he bent down and dragged a small figure out from behind the beanbag. It was Mei-Mei.

"What are you doing here?" Müller demanded.

The little girl stared at him, her face terrified.

He shook her violently. "Did you follow me? Are you spying on me?"

"N-n-no!" stuttered Mei-Mei. "No, I c-come first! I... I want to draw picture..."

I saw that she was clutching a pencil and the sketchpad that I'd bought her from the Spanish Riding School shop. She must have crept out of the Chows' suite and come down here so that she could draw without the risk of her mother catching her. Then, when Müller had arrived and I had crawled out of the hole in the wall, she had stayed hidden, too scared to reveal herself.

"Let her go," I pleaded. "She's just a child."

"Yes, but she heard me speak," said Müller, glaring at the girl. "She knows!"

I started to reply, then something behind Müller's head caught my eye. A little red box attached to the wall, with a glass pane in front and some words printed on the glass. I was too far away to read the words properly but I knew what they would say: "*Break Glass*". I felt a surge of hope. If I could somehow get across to that little red box...

I glanced down again to see Mei-Mei's almond

eyes meet mine; the little girl had seen what I'd seen and understood. She gave a tiny nod, then raised the hand clutching the pencil and drove the sharp point down into Müller's thigh.

"*AAAAHHH!*" yelled the Austrian, reeling back.

It wasn't a bad injury—the pencil had barely penetrated through his wool trousers—but it caused enough pain and surprise to distract him. I dived past Müller and smashed my hand onto the red box on the wall, pressing the glass pane frantically. A wailing alarm filled the air, echoing through the hotel. I heard thumping above my head and muffled shouts as people woke up and ran out of their rooms. Outside, in the hallway, came the sound of running feet as Sofia and Stefan rushed out of their private quarters and into the guest lounge.

"Herr Müller!" cried Sofia, her eyes widening in shock as she took in the scene. "Gemma! What is happening?"

Stefan started forwards but Müller snarled something at him in German which made him jerk back. I saw with a horrible jolt that Müller was still holding Mei-Mei—in fact, he had the little girl in a headlock with his arm around her neck and her body held in front of him like a shield. Then there was a commotion outside and, the next moment, a crowd of people rushed into the guest lounge. The first among them was Mrs Chow and she screamed when she saw her daughter.

"Mei-Mei! *Ayah*—"

"No! No, do not come any closer!" Müller snapped, whirling to face the crowd and yanking the girl around with him.

Mei-Mei cried out in pain and Mrs Chow screamed again while others in the crowd gasped and protested. I wanted to do something, to grab Mei-Mei and pull her to safety, but I felt paralysed by a terrible sense of helplessness. Everything seemed to be receding from me: I could see Müller holding Mei-Mei, I could see Mrs Chow sobbing, and the other guests waving their arms and moving their lips; I could hear the terrible wailing alarm, and a strange growling sound at my feet, and the rushing of blood in my ears... and yet it all seemed unreal, far away...

"Gemma!"

It was Mabel's booming voice and it snapped me out of my daze. I blinked and looked around. The Old Biddies came into focus, clad in their flannel nightgowns, with curlers in their hair. They were standing with the crowd, looking helpless and horrified. Müller was still there, his arms still clamped around Mei-Mei. He was yelling at Sofia now, telling her to turn off the fire alarm. His eyes were wild and staring—he looked like a man who had completely lost it.

"Herr Müller, please, release the child and then we can talk—" Sofia was saying

"*Nein!* No, you do as I say! Turn off the alarm! TURN OFF THE ALARM!" he shouted, waving his free hand wildly.

Randy made a sudden rush as if to tackle him but Müller jerked back, pulling the little girl with him and tightening his arm around her neck. The American faltered as Mei-Mei gasped and choked. Mrs Chow screamed again and I couldn't stop myself crying out as well. Then the strange growling which had been growing louder and louder turned suddenly into a blood-curdling yowl.

"*GRRROWWW-YOWWWWWWWLLL!*"

A ball of screeching, hissing fur exploded from the floor and hurled itself at Müller. The man yelped and lurched backwards, releasing Mei-Mei and throwing his arms up to protect his face. He flailed wildly, yelling for help, as Muesli snarled and spat, raking him with her claws.

Mei-Mei ran sobbing into her mother's arms, just as Müller staggered backwards, tripped on a beanbag, and toppled over, my little cat still on top of him. I felt a stab of pity for him at last and ran over to drag Muesli off the hapless man. She was still hissing and growling, her fur standing on end and her tail twitching angrily when I picked her up.

As I stepped back, the others helped Müller to his feet. Randy grabbed a curtain sash and tied Müller's arms behind his back. But it wasn't really necessary. The man's face and arms were covered in scratches and he looked completely cowed.

"*Meorrw!*" said Muesli.

I looked down at my little cat and I could have

sworn I saw a smile on her face as she looked at Müller and twitched her tail with satisfaction.

CHAPTER TWENTY-NINE

"Oh my goodness! Mr Müller was the murderer? And he was ever so nice too! He told me and Mum that he'd give us a private tour of his museum, you know... although I have to say—not that I wanted to be rude and all—but I wasn't feeling that keen, I mean, some of those Klimt paintings are just plain weird, dontcha think? But what's happening to him now? Mr Müller, I mean, not Klimt... I know Klimt is dead, of course, poor bugger..."

"Well, the police have arrested Müller and I suppose he'll be tried for Wagner's murder."

"Did he put up a fight?" Jane asked with relish. "Did he try to escape out of the window or climb down the fire escape, like you see in the movies? I can't believe we missed all the excitement! Mum wanted to come back to the hotel yesterday after we heard the news but the doctors thought she'd better stay one more day and I agreed with them, seeing as Mum isn't as young as she used to be... but my goodness, I wish I'd been there! Stefan told me there was a jolly big scene in the library—you were the one who figured out it was him, weren't you? Weren't you scared?"

"I..." I thought of that horrible scene in the library two nights ago. It was slightly surreal now, like a vivid nightmare which was fading in the bright light of morning. In fact, even by the time the police had arrived, Müller had already returned to his usual quiet self and it was hard to imagine him as the hysterical man holding a child hostage. "Yes, I guess I *was* scared... although it all happened so fast, I didn't have much time to think about it."

Jane shook her head "I just can't believe it... Mr Müller! I would never have thought... and he was the one who attacked Mum as well?"

"I think he felt quite remorseful about that," I said. "I don't think Müller is a *bad* man, really... He was just provoked beyond endurance and lashed out, then panicked after that and tried to cover his tracks."

"Well, he shouldn't have tried to con people with a fake painting in his museum, should he? That's what Mum says—that's where all the trouble started... once you start lying, you just can't stop— like eating chocolate bickies, you know, you've just got to have another... and another..." Jane regarded me brightly. "So are you heading back to England now?"

"Oh no, we're here for another few days. We're attending an awards ceremony tomorrow. You see, we actually came to Vienna because I won a baking contest—well, my tearoom did—"

"Oh, you run a tearoom?" cried Jane in delight. "We love tearooms, me and Mum—nothing like a plate of scones with jam and clotted cream, dontcha think? Whereabouts are you? We must come and visit you... I hope you're out in the country somewhere—that would be lovely... nothing like a drive out into the countryside on the weekend... not that traffic on the M4 isn't enough to give you hives and I suppose we could take the trains instead, but my best friend Claire says British Rail is the worst—oh, it's not called that anymore these days, is it? So hard to shake off the old names... Anyway, so whereabouts are you?"

Reluctantly, I said, "My tearoom is in Oxfordshire—in a little Cotswolds village called Meadowford-on-Smythe. It's just outside Oxford."

"Ooh, Oxford! That's right, you said you lived there, didn't you? I love Oxford! Used to work near there, did I tell you? Now, that's easy... we can come up on the motorway or take the train—when did you say you're heading back? We're leaving tomorrow, but you've got my number, anyway, haven't you, and I've got yours... I've got a long weekend coming up in a few weeks' time and I can bring Mum... She loves scones... I'll give you a ring, shall I?"

"Er... that sounds great," I said with some trepidation. "I'll... I'll look forward to it. Um... excuse me, I need to ask Sofia something..."

I escaped the dining room and walked to the reception desk in the lobby. Sofia was busily tapping on the laptop, humming a little tune to herself, and looking more relaxed than I'd ever seen her. Since Müller's arrest, she had seemed like a different person—I hadn't realised before how much the strain of Wagner's critical presence, followed by his murder and her guilt over concealing the note, had affected Sofia. But even aside from that, she seemed particularly happy today. In fact, she was positively glowing.

"You look like you've had some good news," I said with a smile. I glanced at her computer screen and saw that it was a popular travel review site. "Ah... a five-star review?"

"Oh, no," said Sofia. "Why do you say that?"

I laughed. "Well, you look so happy—it must be something to do with the hotel's success."

"No, actually..." Sofia gave me a slightly shame-faced smile. "I think perhaps... making the hotel a success... well, it does not compare to having someone to share the success with." She blushed, then added, "Stefan asked me to marry him this morning... and I said yes."

"Oh!" My smile widened. "Congratulations! That's

wonderful news! My mother will be so excited to hear that."

"Yes, I have arranged it so that the wedding will take place when your mother and father come to Vienna next year. And if you are free too, Gemma, you would be most welcome." She gave me a rueful look. "It would be nice for you to enjoy a visit to Vienna that has not been spoiled by a murder."

"Oh, but I've enjoyed my visit very much," I protested. "Honestly, I've had a wonderful time, in spite of everything that's happened. In fact, I don't think I've ever had a holiday as exciting!" I laughed.

Sofia pursed her lips. "Well, we will try to make your visit exciting in a different way next time. Anyway, was there something in particular you wanted to speak to me about?" She looked at me questioningly.

"Yes, I was just wondering if you'd be able to forward a message on to the Chows? With all the police questioning and other things, I didn't get a chance to see them yesterday before they left and I wanted to say goodbye properly—"

"Mr and Mrs Chow? But they are still here."

"Oh! I thought Stefan said they were checking out yesterday?"

Sofia smiled. "Yes, apparently they changed their minds. I confess, I was a little surprised, given what had happened to the little girl—although the doctors confirmed that she was not hurt, thank goodness, and she does seem to have recovered completely from the incident. The resilience of children is amazing, is it not?"

"Um... yes, it is. But... but I thought the Chows had decided to leave early, even before what happened with Muller?"

Sofia shrugged. "Perhaps so, but they seem happy to remain. Oh, there they are now..." She pointed over my shoulder.

I turned to see the lift doors opening and the Chinese couple step out, accompanied by Mei-Mei. I took a deep breath and hurried over to intercept them. They stopped and there was an awkward pause.

I cleared my throat. "Mrs Chow—I'm... er... I just wanted to apologise again. It... it was very wrong of me to take Mei-Mei to the Spanish Riding School without your permission... I did mean to take her to the Art History Museum afterwards but we ran out of time—but still, I know I shouldn't have... I... I hope you won't blame Mei-Mei... it was all my fault." I swallowed and added in a rush, "And I'm very sorry for what I said afterwards. It's not my place to judge how you choose to raise your daughter and I was unforgivably rude.... but... but I hope you might be able to forgive me."

There was a moment of silence, then Mrs Chow said: "I am sorry also."

I stared at her, stunned. This wasn't what I had expected.

She gave me a shy smile, suddenly looking much

more like her daughter than I'd ever realised. "Sometime when you love your children, you are worry about their life after you die and cannot look after them anymore. You want to give them best chance, you know? I don't want Mei-Mei working very hard in bad job and no money for medicine and no place to live..." She reached down and clasped her daughter's hand, then looked up at me again with a smile. "But maybe I forget also important to be happy."

I felt a sudden impulse to hug her but I restrained myself. Instead, I beamed at her and said, "Yes, it's very hard to find the balance sometimes. It's something I've struggled with too."

Then I noticed that Mei-Mei was clutching a map of Vienna. I smiled at the little girl and said, gesturing to the map, "Are you off sightseeing? Which museum are you seeing today?"

"We don't go museum," said Mrs Chow. "We go Imperial Butterfly House."

"To... to the butterfly house?" I said, astonished.

The Chinese woman inclined her head with a smile. "Mei-Mei say very beautiful. Nice to see."

"Yes, I'd heard that it's very special. It's in a beautiful Art Nouveau palm house and it's such a novelty to see tropical butterflies in the middle of Europe, but... er... you know there are *real* butterflies in there?"

A look of uncertainty flashed across Mrs Chow's face, but she straightened her shoulders and said with a nod, "Yes, Mei-Mei tell me. But she say butterfly very clean. No disease."

"Oh yes, I'm sure they're fine," I said hastily. Then I smiled at her, feeling a surge of admiration for her and the way she was making an effort to overcome her prejudices, despite her fear. "I'm sure you'll have a great time."

I stood and watched them leave. Mei-Mei skipped between her parents, her hands held by each, but just before they started down the main staircase that led to the street, she glanced over her shoulder and gave me a wave, accompanied by that sweet gap-toothed smile. I felt my heart swell with gladness.

Turning back towards the lift, I reached for the call button, but before I could press it, the doors opened and Randy stepped out, together with Ana Bauer. The two were deep in conversation but the American's handsome face broke into a smile when he saw me.

"Hey! Glad I caught you, Gemma. I'm checking out in a minute and I hoped I'd get a chance to say goodbye."

I felt slightly embarrassed by his friendly manner and said quickly, "I'm glad I caught you too. I... I wanted to say again that I'm really sorry to have suspected you—"

"Hey, no problem. No hard feelings," said Randy, waving a hand.

I looked at him in concern. "What will you do

about your ranch now? Do you know the details of Wagner's will yet?"

"No, it's gonna take the lawyers a while to sort things out. But don't you worry about me." He glanced at Ana Bauer, who had wandered down the hallway and joined the Old Biddies, standing outside the guest lounge door. "Ana and I have been talking a lot and she's really interested in my ideas. She's getting a bit tired of the art gallery scene and she's been looking for a new challenge, so she's decided to invest in my ranch and help me promote the Lipizzaners over in the States."

"That's wonderful!" I exclaimed. "I really wish you the best of luck. You deserve it."

Randy grinned at me. "Hey, don't forget—any time you're over in the States and wanna see a horse show..."

"Oh, if I'm ever on that side of the Atlantic, I wouldn't miss it for anything," I promised.

When I joined Ana and the Old Biddies a few minutes later, I found them discussing the relative merits of a sauna versus a steam room. Ana was almost back to her old glamorous self, although there were still shadows under her eyes and a general air of sorrow about her. It struck me forcibly that this woman had really loved Wagner and, for all his faults and the way he had treated her, she was genuinely mourning him. There really was no logic to love, was there?

"Well, I hope you will enjoy the rest of your stay

in Vienna," she said, looking around at us. "I will say goodbye now as I do not think I will see you again—I will be checking out this morning and returning home."

"Do you live nearby?" asked Florence.

"Not far. In fact..." She hesitated. "My own apartment is only a few streets away from here. But my things are still at Moritz's apartment, which is on the other side of the city." She glanced down the hallway towards the music room, then sighed softly. "It is difficult to believe that he is really gone. My life has revolved around Moritz for so long—he was that kind of man, you know—and now I do not know how I will continue..."

Mabel reached out and patted her hand. "You'll be fine, dear."

I was surprised at the overly familiar gesture and I thought Ana would be offended, but the Austrian woman seemed to appreciate Mabel's maternal manner. She gave us a wry look.

"You think I am foolish, no doubt... I know the reputation that Moritz had; he was a great lover of women and I was simply one of many..." She flashed a glance at Glenda, tinged with resentment. "I know he was not even thinking of me that day— he was taking another lady to dinner—and yet still, I mourn him..." She shook her head and gave us a sad smile. "Do you pity me?"

"No," said Glenda suddenly. She stepped forwards. "And you are wrong, Ana. Moritz *was* thinking of you that day. We chatted quite a bit, you know, and he seemed inclined to confide in me. Perhaps it was because of the difference in our ages. Did you know that his mother died when he was very young? He said that I reminded him of her." She smiled at the Austrian woman. "And do you know what he told me? That while he was determined to remain a bachelor, if he was ever going to marry... it would have been you."

Ana drew her breath in sharply. Then she clasped Glenda's hand and squeezed it, her eyes shining.

"Thank you... thank you for telling me that," she whispered.

As we watched Ana walk away, I sidled up to Glenda and asked, frowning: "Did Wagner really say that?"

Glenda looked at me complacently. "Of course not, dear."

I looked at her, aghast. "Then you just told Ana a complete lie!"

Glenda glanced at the Austrian woman who had paused by the reception desk and was chatting to Sofia. Her cheeks were flushed with colour and her whole demeanour was lighter, happier.

Glenda turned back to me with a smile. "My dear, when you get to my age, you'll realise that there are times when lies heal more than they harm."

EPILOGUE

I flopped down on the sofa in my sitting room and looked around with a happy sigh. It was good to be home.

Muesli gave a little chirrup, as if in agreement, and began trotting busily around the room, rubbing her chin on various pieces of furniture and re-marking things with her scent. It reminded me of when she had done the same thing in the music room in Vienna. The events of the past week flashed through my mind and I gave a wry smile. Maybe the next time a holiday got cancelled, I would just accept it and stay at home. I mean, between the murder and the Old Biddies and the scaffolding acrobatics and the secret passages—not to mention *that* visit to the sauna—I would have got more rest and relaxation if I'd stayed at work!

Still, it had certainly been a memorable trip... and I couldn't wait to tell Cassie all about it when I saw her tomorrow. Heaving myself up, I walked around my cottage, drawing back the curtains and opening the windows to let some fresh air in. Then I dragged my case up to my bedroom and began to unpack.

Muesli trotted after me and jumped on the bed, watching me with keen interest as I lifted items out of the suitcase. I dumped all my dirty laundry in a pile on the floor, then unwrapped a gleaming bronze trophy in the shape of a teacup. I smiled to myself as I held it up and the light from the windows caught the inscription on the base: "*Euro-Tearoom Baking Contest ~ Winner*". This would look great on the mantelpiece at the tearoom and I could already see the Old Biddies taking it in turns to show it off around the village.

I set the trophy on my bedside table, then reached into the case and pulled out several souvenirs I'd brought back: a book on Viennese art for Cassie, a Walter Weiss men's shaving kit for Devlin, a cookbook of traditional Austrian cuisine for Dora, a couple of bottles of Austrian wine for my parents, and—a gift from the Old Biddies—a fridge magnet featuring an image of Klimt's *The Kiss*, purchased from the Belvedere Palace museum shop.

There was one last item in the case. Carefully, I lifted it out and withdrew the single sheet of thick canvas paper from the folder. I glanced at Muesli, sitting on the foot of the bed, then back at the paper, where her likeness had been captured perfectly. It was a beautiful portrait, with the deft strokes of the pencil highlighting the softness of her fur, the svelte lines of her body, and even the mischievous gleam in her eyes. I smiled as I saw the childish scrawl at the bottom of the page:

"To Gemma ~ Love, Mei-Mei"

It might never compare with the paintings of the great masters, but there was no doubt in my mind that this drawing by a little eight-year-old girl was the best gift I'd brought back from Vienna.

FINIS

THE OXFORD TEAROOM MYSTERIES

A Scone To Die For (Book 1)

Tea with Milk and Murder (Book 2)

Two Down, Bun To Go (Book 3)

Till Death Do Us Tart (Book 4)

Muffins and Mourning Tea (Book 5)

Four Puddings and a Funeral (Book 6)

Another One Bites the Crust (Book 7)

Apple Strudel Alibi (Book 8)

The Dough Must Go On (Book 9)

The Mousse Wonderful Time of Year (Book 10)

All-Butter ShortDead (Prequel)

For other books by H.Y. Hanna,
please visit her website:
www.hyhanna.com

GLOSSARY OF BRITISH TERMS

Bickies – British slang for "biscuits" small, hard, baked product, either savoury or sweet (American: cookies. What is called a "biscuit" in the U.S. is more similar to the English scone)

Bloody – very common adjective used as an intensifier for both positive and negative qualities (e.g. "bloody awful" and "bloody wonderful"), often used to express shock or disbelief ("Bloody Hell!")

Bugger! – an exclamation of annoyance or dismay (also used to describe a person who is silly or annoying, or a person you feel sympathy for, depending on context)

Cripes – an exclamation of surprise or dismay

Cuppa – slang term for "a cup of tea"

Dishy – handsome, attractive (used for men) – "dishier": more handsome

Gabble – talk a lot, chatter

Knackered – very tired, exhausted

Lift – a compartment in a shaft which is used to

raise and lower people to different levels (America: elevator)

Put paid to (eg. your plans) – to stop abruptly, to destroy

(to) Ring – to call (someone on the phone)

Row – an argument

(to) Take against (something or someone) – to take a violent dislike to, to feel hostile towards, often without good reason

(to) Talk up (something or someone) - to praise and promote something

Telly – television

TRADITIONAL APPLE STRUDEL RECIPE

(with the kind permission of
Ursula Schersch – Li'l Vienna Blog

INGREDIENTS:

For the strudel dough* *(I recommend measuring the flour by weight in grams since it is more accurate than measuring by volume.)*

- 1/3 cup lukewarm water (80 ml / 80 g)
- 1 tablespoon + ½ teaspoon neutral tasting vegetable oil (15 g)
- ½ teaspoon vinegar (or lemon juice)
- 1/8 teaspoon table salt or fine sea salt
- 145 g bread flour (1 cup) (substitute with all purpose flour)
- ½ teaspoon vegetable oil for brushing the dough
- flour for dusting

For the filling

- 3 tablespoons unsalted butter (40 g)
- 2/3 cups fine bread crumbs (80 g)
- 5 tablespoons granulated sugar (65 g)
- ½ teaspoon ground cinnamon
- 4 tablespoons raisins (50 g)
- 3 tablespoons rum or lukewarm water for soaking the raisins
- 2 lbs sweet-tart apples (e.g. MacIntosh) (900 g)

- 1 tablespoon lemon juice
- 2 tablespoons melted butter for brushing the dough (divided)
- confectioner's sugar for dusting
- whipped cream for serving (optional)

INSTRUCTIONS:

To make the dough

1. Mix lukewarm water, oil, vinegar and salt in a big bowl. Acid like vinegar helps relax the gluten to make the dough easier to stretch.

2. Stir in about half the flour with a spoon until well combined, then gradually add the remaining flour until it comes together and you can work it with your hands.

3. Knead the dough until smooth for about 10 minutes, either in the bowl or on a working surface. The dough should be moist but not sticky. If it is too sticky to knead, add a little more flour (you shouldn't need more than 1 or 2 additional tablespoons). Slam the dough onto the worksurface a few times to enhance gluten development, yielding a very elastic dough.

4. Shape the dough into a smooth ball. Brush a clean bowl with oil, put the dough into the bowl and brush it with oil (you can do this with your fingers).

5. Cover the bowl with a lid or plastic wrap and let it sit for 1 hour at room temperature. (see note)

To make the filling

1. Melt the butter in a pan over medium heat and add the breadcrumbs. Toast them, stirring constantly, until they are golden. Remove from the heat and let cool.

2. Mix sugar and cinnamon together, then add it to the buttered breadcrumbs and stir well. Set aside.

3. Soak the raisins in rum (traditional) or lukewarm water for about 10 minutes to get them softened.

4. Peel the apples, quarter and core them. Chop every quarter into 1/8 to 1/4 inch thick slices and cover them with lemon juice to prevent the apples from getting brown. Add the soaked raisins (but not the remaining rum or water) and mix well.

Stretching and filling the dough

1. Roll out the dough with a rolling pin on a clean and lightly floured surface. Flour the surface and the dough every now and then while rolling.

2. When the dough gets about 13-15 inch in diameter, pick it up then use the back of your hands, particularly your knuckles, to stretch it (remove all sharp jewelry first). This way you can straighten the dough like a pizza.

3. When the dough gets bigger and thinner, and thus difficult to handle, put it down on a lightly floured tablecloth, straighten out the wrinkles in both the tablecloth and the dough. Continue stretching the dough on the tablecloth using your hands.

4. Gently stretch the dough paper-thin from the inside to the outside, working your way around the sheet of dough. Stretch it until it starts to look translucent. You should be able to read the titles of a newspaper placed under the

dough (don't do this though, the ink would probably come off).

5. In the end, the sheet of dough should be stretched into a rectangular shape, with the shorter edge fitting the baking sheet lengthwise. Thick edges should be cut off.

6. Brush half the dough with half the melted butter. Spread the breadcrumb-mixture over the other half of the dough and pat down evenly. One side is brushed with butter now, the other side is covered with breadcrumbs. Leave 1 to 1 ½ inch to the edge. Spread the apples over the breadcrumbs.

7. Fold in the side-ends of the dough. Using the towel, roll the dough, starting at the apple-topped end all the way. Then gently roll the strudel onto a sheet of parchment paper with the seam-side down.

8. Put the dough onto a baking sheet and brush it with the remaining melted butter.

Baking the strudel

1. Put the baking sheet in the middle (I use rack 2 of 4 from top) of the preheated oven and bake it for ½ hour at 375 °F.

2. When the crust turns golden, the Apple Strudel is ready. Take it out of the oven, let it cool slightly, cut it into pieces and serve dusted with confectioner's sugar.

Notes:

- You can also make the dough ahead and keep it in the fridge for up to 3 days. Temperate before using.

Enjoy!

ABOUT THE AUTHOR

USA Today bestselling author H.Y. Hanna writes British cosy mysteries filled with humour, quirky characters, intriguing whodunits—and cats with big personalities! Set in Oxford and the beautiful English Cotswolds, her books include the Oxford Tearoom Mysteries, the 'Bewitched by Chocolate' Mysteries and the English Cottage Garden Mysteries. After graduating from Oxford University, Hsin-Yi tried her hand at a variety of jobs: advertising exec, model, English teacher, dog trainer, marketing manager, educational book rep... before returning to her first love: writing. She worked as a freelance writer for several years and has won awards for her novels, poetry, short stories and journalism.

A globe-trotter all her life, Hsin-Yi has lived in a variety of cultures, from Dubai to Auckland, London to New Jersey, but is now happily settled in Perth, Western Australia, with her husband and a rescue kitty named Muesli. You can learn more about her and her books at: **www.hyhanna.com**

Sign up to her newsletter to be notified of new releases, exclusive giveaways and other book news! Go to: **www.hyhanna.com/newsletter**

ACKNOWLEDGMENTS

A very special thank you to Ursula Schersch *of Li'l Vienna Blog* who kindly allowed me to share her grandmother's recipe for a traditional Austrian apple strudel.

My thanks also to Claudia Dahinden for checking the German words and phrases in the story, and ensuring that they are accurate and authentic.

As ever, my continued gratitude to my beta readers: Connie Leap, Basma Alwesh, and Charles Winthrop whose feedback always helps me immensely. I'm also indebted to Heather Belleguelle for both her eagle eyes and her wise insights during the final proofread, and to my editor, Chandler Groover, who I don't thank enough. I feel incredibly lucky to have the support of such a fantastic team.

And last but not least, to my wonderful husband for his patient encouragement, tireless support, and for always believing in me—I couldn't do it without him.

Made in the USA
Middletown, DE
24 February 2021

34370609R00187